Mending Helen's Heart

Clare Bills

To

Helen for so generously sharing the details of her life.

And to Ken, the cheerleader of my life.

Acknowledgments

My thanks to Anne Fleck, of Novel Spirits Books, for her guidance in the development of *Mending Helen's Heart*.

Many thanks also to Cecelia Kirihara, my careful beta reader and final editor.

My eternal gratitude to Tugboat Designs for taking my vision of Helen and transforming words into a beautiful cover design. Deborah Bradseth and Kylie Sek, your talents are truly spectacular.

As always, I thank my hubby, Ken, along with our children, their spouses, and our grandchildren, for continuing to egg me on to get this book to the finish line.

I'm also grateful for the support of the seven incredible women who make up my own "sister act." Thank you for showing interest when I blab on and on about a story idea and for refraining from eye rolls

Chapter 1

Helen's metal bed squeaked and screeched as she shoved it across the scratched wood floor to the middle of the room. She covered her bed in old sheets, then straightened her plaid shirt, dusted off her cuffed jeans, and climbed two steps onto a small ladder to reach the drab curtain on the only window. She tossed the curtain and rod onto her bed. The tall, four-drawer pine dresser was more resistant to movement, but she finally wrestled it away from the wall, then pulled her red hair into a ponytail. Ready. She placed a soft cover on a paint roller and anticipated the fun she'd have.

"Helen!"

Oh boy, here we go! Helen climbed over her bed to reach the door.

"Helen Jane!"

She swung the door open and shouted down the stairs. "What is it, Grandma?"

"Helen Jane! What in tarnation's all that racket?"

"I'm getting ready to paint my bedroom."

"What? Whered ya git money fer paint?"

"From my wages. I told you."

"Ya never did! Ya aint got permission ta go and paint."

"Grandma! I told you about it. I hate these dingy walls, and I'm painting them this morning."

Grandma backed away from the stairwell, muttering. "Wasting all that money!"

"Sorry, Grandma. But this will raise the value of the house by improving it."

Helen shut the door, took a deep breath, and looked around. Life was going to improve, starting today.

Helen threw her energy into the task, watching the room spring to life with every pass of the roller, erasing the dirty grey walls, along with her dark and dingy childhood. She was no longer the shy, smelly child with ragged clothes and greasy hair.

Now that school was out for the summer, Helen had more time to work at the store and less time for Grandma Gertrude's demands. She hoped. The long break also meant she wouldn't see the heartthrob from school until fall unless he popped into the store again. Helen sighed at the recent memory of Joseph standing at the lunch counter asking for a chocolate soda. She loved seeing him outside of school, without prying eyes to watch and belittle everything she said, did, and wore.

No time for lollygagging today. Time to transform her bedroom, or at least make marginal improvements. Since moving to town, she'd longed for the opportunity to make her bedroom reflect the person she wanted to be, not the scared, unwanted, unwashed child from the farm with the tattered, out-of-date ill-fitting clothes. Footsteps interrupted her thoughts, and when the door creaked open, Emily peeked in, her blond ponytail bobbing.

"Hi, there! Your Grandpa let me in. Is this a bad time?"

"Hi, Em! Welcome to my room. Wanna help me paint?"

"Neat! I've never painted before, but I'll try."

"Why don't you work on the edges along the ceiling, and I'll finish the walls."

She handed Emily a paintbrush, a small cup of lavender paint, and a rag. "Don't get any on the ceiling, or Grandma will bust my chops!"

Emily's blue eyes danced as she put her foot on the stepstool. "Someone's seen too many picture shows!"

"Hardly. But I'm hoping I'll see a few this summer."

Emily stepped up another rung and carefully worked her brush along the wall next to the ceiling. "Certainly easier than when you lived out in the country."

"Yes, lots of changes the past few years."

"How's your mom like Springfield?"

"She's so crazy about her new husband I think she'd live in an igloo."

Emily stopped painting and turned to Helen. "Do you miss her?"

"Yes, but I'm glad I didn't have to change schools."

"Me too. I'll bet you miss the country. I mean, it'd be romantic to live on a farm and so peaceful with all those rolling hills."

"Don't forget about stinky pigs, squawking roosters, and smelly cows that need milking at dawn and dusk seven days a week."

Emily glanced at Helen, eyes wide. "Oh! I hadn't thought about that. But you must have loved all that room to roam."

Helen focused on the task at hand. "It also meant we were far from town, from friends, and I couldn't participate in after-school activities." She stopped and looked at Emily. "And then there were the outhouses!"

Emily scrunched her face. "You didn't have running water?"

"Nope. We filled pails of water at our well and lugged them into the house. Every. Single. Day."

"So… no baths?"

Helen's face was getting warm with the memory. She regretted bringing up the subject. "We warmed water on the cook-stove, then poured it into a metal trough that we dragged into the kitchen. How's that for romantic country living?"

Emily stared at her, mouth open. "Sorry, Helen, I had no idea."

Helen turned back to rolling paint on the walls. She failed to mention that they all bathed in the same water. And as the youngest, she was last in line in the tepid, dirty water. No wonder Bernice and Diane had called her "stinky" ever since kindergarten. She tried to ignore their taunts and to avoid being around them, but couldn't escape the damage to her confidence, as she slunk in her classroom chairs and ate lunch alone outside whenever possible. As a teen, Helen took over the laundry to make sure her clothes were clean. And to bathe more often, she brought in water and warmed it when others weren't around. Still, her confidence had taken a hit, and she never shook off the feeling of inferiority and the expectation that an insult was moments away.

"That's why I never invited you, or anyone, over, Emily." Helen didn't want pity, and she worried that she'd made Emily uncomfortable with too much information. She took a deep breath and blew the conversation in another direction. "But we survived. And now I have a tub in a bathroom - with a door. And I don't have to lug the water in or warm it."

"I see your point. Much more civilized."

They worked quietly for a few moments.

"Um, speaking of civilizations, I saw Joseph from World History going into the Five and Dime the other day. Were you working?"

Helen's eyes lit up. "Yes, I was. He came in to order an ice cream soda, and I waited on him."

"Maybe just an excuse to see you?"

"Hardly! But luckily, I was there. I think another sales clerk has her eyes on him."

"Did you tell her to keep her mitts off?"

Helen giggled. "You're the only one who knows about my crush on him. I don't like being teased. Besides, I'm sure he barely knows I'm alive."

"Not true. I saw him flirting with you after class."

"He was just being nice."

The girls chatted about school, teachers, and boys as they finished transforming Helen's room. When they finally finished, they stood back to admire their work.

Helen took a deep breath. "Ah, the smell of fresh paint. I feel like I'm living inside a lilac bush, and I love it." It was a first step in erasing her past and focusing on her future. "But I'm afraid I need to get to work."

Emily said good-by, and Helen changed into a white blouse and a green cotton skirt and combed out her red curls carefully so they wouldn't poof out into a giant mushroom. She tied a white grosgrain ribbon in her hair to keep it out of her eyes and dashed down the stairs.

Grandma Gertrude stood, hands planted on wide hips in the living room. "Where ya goin 'in such a hurry?"

"Work. As soon as I grab a peanut butter sandwich."

"Did ya finish paintin'?"

"Yes, room's all done. I'll put the furniture back tonight."

Helen finished making her sandwich and planned to eat it on the walk to work.

"Sit and eat your lunch."

"I've got to go, Grandma, new store manager, and I need to be on time."

Grandma's eyebrows raised, and Helen noticed a slight tug at the corners of her mouth. "New manager, you say?"

Helen frowned at her. "Yes, why?'

"Nothin. 'Just curious. Why'd she leave?"

"Her baby's due, so she's not coming back. Bye Grandma!" Helen raced out the door and quickly walked the six or so blocks to downtown Greenberg where the Five and Dime store sat proudly in the middle of the town square. The store sold everything from fabric and notions to clothing, paint, hardware items, and canned food items. A prominent section at the back boasted a long lunch counter that served breakfast, lunch, or ice cream treats. Red fake-leather stools that pivoted around in circles sat on the other side of the counter, and a half dozen booths nearby were perfect for cozy meals for two or four.

Helen's mind festered on her grandmother's questions while she straightened clothing racks and sorted sewing notions. She needed to be vigilant to stay a step ahead of her grandmother. The chime above the door brought her back to reality, and she looked over to see the latest customer. *Joseph.* Heading for the lunch counter. The haze cleared, and thoughts of Grandma vanished. She took a deep breath and shyly approached him.

"Hi Joseph, can I get you something?"

"Hi, Helen of Troy! Strawberry malt today, please." His smile brought out his deep dimples and accentuated the prominent cleft in his chin. Secretly grinning at his nickname for her, she scooped ice cream, strawberries, and malt powder into a silver container and attached it to the malt machine to work its' magic. Then poured a hefty portion of the luscious liquid into a tall, curved glass and set both the glass and the silver container with the remaining malt in front of Joseph.

She looked over her shoulder and didn't see her manager—a chance to chat.

"Delicious! And the color of your hair."

Helen blushed. "Thanks, I think."

"I like your red hair. Don't you?"

"Not exactly. People always make comments about it."

"Like I just did. Sorry."

"No, not you. I didn't mean you."

Helen wiped the counter around Joseph, wanting to keep a conversation going. "Think we'll move into modern history next semester?"

He took a long sip of his malt. "Mmm. Tired of Greek mythology?"

"I'm eager to learn about things that actually happened."

"Practical minded."

"I suppose. I'd better stay busy if I want to keep this job." She felt breathless in his presence but nervous that her new supervisor would scold her for dillydallying.

"Time for a quick question?"

She stopped and turned toward him. *Anything, seriously!* "Sh...Sure."

"A few of us are going bowling Saturday night. Want to come along? "

"I've never been bowling. Is it hard? I'm not coordinated..." *Dang, why did I say that?*

"I'll teach you if you'd like. It's not difficult."

"Well, OK, then yes, I, I, I'll try not to drop the ball on my foot, or yours, or...." *Stop talking!*

Joseph's eyes crinkled as he grinned at her. "Thanks for the warning."

Her manager loomed near, so Helen moved to straighten the new shipment of dresses. A few minutes later, Joseph finished his malt and sought Helen.

"I'll pick you up at seven tomorrow night," he whispered and winked at her as he headed for the door. And he was gone.

Her face flushed as she dashed to another counter to assist a customer. *A date with Joseph! What should she wear? What should she tell Grandma?* Her heart was beating in her eardrums, but she didn't have long to float on the excitement building in her when the door chimed again, and she spied Grandma Gertrude entering the store. Helen ducked behind the rack of dresses and watched to see what trouble her grandmother was planning.

Helen peeked through the dresses as Grandma buttonholed Mr. Whitmer, the new manager, and handed him a piece of paper. Whitmer looked thoughtful but took the note, and after a brief discussion, Grandma left the store with a sly smile on her lips.

Helen was furious! Not again. Now, since Cora had recently moved to Springfield, Iowa, to live with her new husband, Warren, Helen was left to fight her own battles. Grandpa John was sympathetic to Helen but rarely stood up to the domineering Gertrude.

Helen took a deep breath and approached Mr. Whitmer, smiling to appear more confident.

"Excuse me, sir, I saw my grandmother here a few minutes ago, and I wondered if you could tell me what she wanted?"

"Well, Helen, she reminded me that you're a minor and said I'm to send your paychecks to her each week so she can help you manage your money."

Helen's cheeks flamed as the anger built inside of her. She took a breath to calm herself and stood as tall as her 5-foot-1-inch frame would allow. "Mr. Whitmer, my grandmother is trying to cheat me out of my pay.

She did this to me last year and took all my money and spent it. My mother, Cora Frantz, has spoken to her about this, but she's not here now."

"I see. So, you live with your grandparents?"

"Yes. My mother pays for my room and board, and she's my legal guardian."

Mr. Whitmer smiled. "Obviously, this is a family matter. Have your mother call me since she's your guardian, and I'll follow her wishes."

Helen nodded. She hoped her mother would be on her side and would take care of this once again. Why did everything have to be a fight with Grandma Gertrude?

Helen phoned her mother that evening when Grandma was out of earshot working in her garden.

"Mama? I need your help."

Chapter 2

"Helen, dear, what's wrong?"

"Grandma's up to her old tricks again. She came into the store and told the new manager to send all my paychecks to her." Helen's hand gripped the black wall phone in the kitchen.

"Here we go again!"

"Yes, but she told the manager that since I don't live with you, she is now my guardian and should control my money since I'm a minor. Is this true?"

"Absolutely not. I'm still your guardian, and I pay your expenses. I'm sorry you're dealing with this."

"Me too! And the manager says he doesn't want to get involved in a family issue. Will you please call him and get this straightened out."

"Of course, and where is your grandmother now?"

"Working in the garden, I think."

"I'll speak with her Sunday then, when we come for dinner."

"Thanks, Mama."

"Is there anything else?"

"Well, I'm embarrassed with …my clothes. Most are old and frayed. Now that I'm earning my own money, I want to spend some on clothes without it being a fight every time Grandma sees something new."

"You won't be able to spend much because of the war rationing, but of course, you can buy the things you need. I'll support you if Grandma gives you an argument."

"Thanks, Mama. I'll see you Sunday."

Helen breathed a sigh of relief that Mama would be in her corner. Now all she had to do was find something passable to wear bowling with Joseph. Every time she thought of it, her stomach felt like fireflies were tickling her insides.

Before her date, she twisted her hair into rags to help smooth her curls and selected a powder blue pleated skirt from her limited wardrobe. She usually kept it for Sundays, but this was a special occasion. *Wasn't it? My first date.* She hoped so. A white cotton blouse with fraying edges would have to do.

Grandpa John stopped eating his pork chop and looked across the Formica table at Helen. "You ain't eatin 'much Ole Bean."

"I guess I'm not hungry. I've never gone bowling, and I don't know what to expect."

Grandpa shook his head. "Afraid I cain't help ya none. Never been myself."

Grandma cackled. "I think them bowling balls are pretty heavy. Make sure ya don't drop one on yer feet."

Helen nodded and cleared her dishes, eager to get ready for her date. *DATE?* Yes, a date with Joseph. Another batch of fireflies took flight inside her stomach.

She rushed upstairs to get dressed and fuss with her hair until she heard the doorbell. *He's here.* Like a racehorse at the starting gate, she charged downstairs and dragged open the heavy wood door.

She was breathless while at the same time trying not to show her nervousness. "Hi there, um, Joseph! Want to, ah, to come in for a minute?" He nodded and stepped through the open door into their living room. Grandpa and Grandma came out of the parlor to meet him, Grandma still in her apron, and Grandpa in his faded blue overalls still chewing on a toothpick.

"Grandma and Grandpa, this is Joseph Donovan, from school."

Grandma Gertrude, hands on her hips, wearing her faded brown mid-calf house dress, her feet planted in sturdy shoes, she stood ready for the interrogation. "Hello, Joseph Donovan. Now, where do you folks live?"

"The edge of town. On Washington Avenue."

Grandma fired another round. "What's yer father do for a livin'?"

Joseph smiled easily and stood more erect. "He's a bookkeeper at the mill."

Helen looked at him and wondered how she hadn't realized how tall he was.

"What's yer mother do?"

His eyes danced as he tossed back answers."She's a homemaker."

Helen cut in. "We'd better be going."

"Don't be late. Curfews at 10 pm, young lady."

"Yes, Grandma. Goodnight, Grandpa." Helen reached for the front door, and Joseph swung it open so they could make their getaway, scrambling down the porch stairs into the warm night perfumed with lilac bushes and peonies.

Joseph held the door of his father's dark blue 1937 Packard for Helen, then went around to the driver's side and slipped behind the steering wheel. He gave her a quick smile, and they were off. *Why is he so calm?* Her palms were sweating.

"We need to get Emily and Jacob. They're coming too!"

"Oh, good! Emily's my friend."

She couldn't think of anything to chat about, but Joseph kept a stream of conversation going, asking questions and her opinion on everything in their path. Helen was relieved a few minutes later when their friends settled in the back seat so she wouldn't have to be the only one to answer Joseph's questions.

Emily tapped her on the shoulder. "Helen! I didn't know you were joining us. How fun!"

Joseph laughed. "I corralled her yesterday while she was working."

The conversation was light. Helen was mostly silent, unused to casual gatherings of her peers, and afraid she'd say the wrong thing. *What is it about Joseph that makes me more tongue-tied than usual?*

They arrived at the Bowl O'Rama, and to her dismay, she had to tell them the size of her feet. *And now I have to put on the clunky shoes in front of everyone?* Not only did she have to admit to having child-sized feet, but she also risked exposing holes in her bobby socks. She turned away from the others to shield her feet and spotted Bernice and Diane coming toward them.

Diane flipped her long blond hair back as she approached. "Hi, Joseph! I was hoping you'd be here tonight. Want to bowl with us?"

Joseph stood and motioned to Helen, Emily, and Jacob. "No thanks, I'm bowling with these three."

Bernice sneered and wrinkled her nose as she spotted Helen. "Helen! What are you doing here?"

Joseph shot back. "She's my date!"

Bernice leaned to where Helen was putting on her bowling shoes and snickered. "By the way, you've got a hole in your sock."

Helen looked away as heat crept onto her cheeks, then quickly finished tying her shoes.

Joseph reached to give Helen a hand to stand, then turned to Bernice and Diane and flashed a fake smile. "See you round, ladies."

He whispered in Helen's ear. "Just ignore them."

"I try to, but it isn't always easy." His warm breath tickled her ears and caused a little shiver down her spine.

"Let's find you a bowling ball." Joseph held her hand and walked her over to the wall with racks of balls in different sizes and weights. With Joseph's hand in hers, she could hardly concentrate. *Why is he so nice to me? Does he just feel sorry for me?*

"How will I know when one's a good fit?" The holes felt awkward to her fingers, and the balls were impossibly heavy, so they searched for a lighter ball with holes for smaller fingers on the rack designated for children.

Joseph was a patient teacher. But the rules sounded like gobbledygook to Helen. "Strike" was a bad thing in baseball, yet the goal of bowling. What kind of a term was "spare?" Grandpa's car had a spare tire, but that didn't seem to apply here. She nodded as Joseph explained but turned to Emily and shrugged and made a silly face when he looked away.

Emily giggled and whispered back. "Don't worry. You'll get the hang of it."

Joseph picked up his ball and approached the bowling lane. "Next, let me show you the ropes."

He demonstrated how to thrust the ball down the lane to hit the pins standing like stalks of sweet corn before a hail storm. Seven fell.

Joseph threw again, and the last three gave way. "Spare!"

When Helen's turn arrived, her ball landed at the top of the lane with a thud and rolled into the gutter. She tried to make light of it, giggling as she turned to face her friends.

"I feel like such a goof!"

Joseph hopped up and walked with her and demonstrated how to walk and when to release the heavy ball. In her next throw, she knocked down two pins.

And so it went, each of the four taking turns. They all cheered when Helen threw a spare.

Joseph squeezed her shoulder. "Now you're cookin 'with gas!" Her heart did flip-flops at his touch.

When their scorecards were complete, they stopped for ice cream at the Bowl O'Rama's soda fountain. Helen felt tongue-tied again. She noted Emily's soft pink blouse with the V-neck and padded shoulders. Her stylish navy blue skirt fell just below her knee. Helen's mid-calf pleated skirt felt out-of-date along with her once-white blouse. Joseph didn't seem to notice. The way he smiled at her made her feel as if she was important, as if her ideas were interesting. *What does he see in me?*

Even if she didn't understand Joseph's attention, she found it irresistible. But as they drove back to her home, her nervousness returned. *What if he expects me to kiss him?* They dropped Emily off first, and Jacob walked her to the door. Helen wanted to watch them to see if Emily kissed Jacob but didn't. Instead, she made small talk with Joseph. They dropped Jacob off next and finally drove to her home, and as Joseph walked her to the door, her head was spinning. *Should I let him kiss me? Is it too soon? Will he think I'm loose? What does my breath smell like?*

Just as they approached the door, the porch light came on right above them. Helen swallowed a laugh and put out her hand.

"Thank you, Joseph. I had a great time."

He took her hand in his and looked into her eyes, and held it for a moment. "Me too, Helen, me too."

Her knees almost buckled. She quickly went inside, and there stood Grandma Gertrude, making sure there was no hanky panky. "It's ten minutes past ten, child. If you think I'm about ta stay up late and wait for ya till all hours of the night…..."

"Good night, Grandma." She sailed up the stairs with a smile that even Grandma couldn't erase.

At work, Wednesday, Helen's manager, Mr. Whitmer, reassured her that she alone would be receiving her paychecks. While she was relieved, her heart was all atwitter at the thought of seeing Joseph again. *I wonder if he'll come into the store today? Maybe he'll be mad because I didn't kiss him. He's too good for me, anyway.*

Her stomach felt like a batch of chicks were pecking at her insides by afternoon. It was four long days since they went bowling, and she was sure Joseph must have either forgotten her or decided she was too backward for him.

And then he walked into the store, smiled at her, and winked. *Winked? What does that mean?* They exchanged small talk, and when he left a few moments later, her heart sank, as he must have decided she wasn't good enough for him. *But the wink was certainly friendly, so that meant something, didn't it?*

She shouldn't get her hopes up, but just in case anyone ever again asked her to go bowling again, she needed new socks. And a new blouse.

Helen saw little of Joseph the rest of that week and convinced herself that he didn't like her. *And I'm OK with that. Who needs men? I've always been alone, and I'll be fine alone for the rest of my life. Won't I?*

But when Joseph came into the Five and Dime the next week and sat at the soda counter, her heart sped, and a smile pulled at the corners of her mouth.

"Hi, Helen of Troy! What's buzzin 'cousin?"

"You are, apparently. Looks like you fell asleep on the beach, Joseph."

"Close! Got a job as a lifeguard at the lake. I know I look like a lobster from working long hours, but I'm making lots of lettuce."

"Lettuce?"

"Money."

"Joseph, you crack me up. Well, I've never seen a lobster, but you do resemble a radish."

"Same color as your hair."

Her eyebrows raised. "Oh, we're back to that, are we?"

"I might be a pain in the neck, but I don't mean to insult your beautiful curls. How 'bout a chocolate malt?"

She made the malt with extra chocolate, and after delivering it in a tall frosted glass with a tall spoon and a straw, she waited on other customers and pretended that his every word didn't make her heart soar. But it did.

Right before he left, he whispered, "Stick with me, kiddo. A new western's showing at the cinema. Want to go see it Saturday night?"

"Shh, sure," she stuttered. That was all she could manage. His whisper created an instant reaction in her tummy.

Helen had only been to the cinema a few times with a girlfriend and was unsure what to wear, but at least no one would be looking at her socks.

She'd saved her wages but doubted she had enough to purchase new fabric or the time to make anything, but before she left the store, she perused selections, limited due to the war rationing. No wools or silks, but there was a new fabric made from wood pulp –synthetic silk. So lightweight and soft to the touch but too pricey for her wallet. *Not enough lettuce*, she smiled at Joseph's memory.

As she walked home from work that warm June evening, past a second-hand clothing store, she remembered there were no wartime restrictions on the purchase of used clothing. The shop was closed for the day, but she tucked the thought away.

Saturday evening, she again pulled out her powder blue pleated skirt and dingy white blouse but took extra time with her hair and made sure she was ready long before Joseph was due so that Grandma wouldn't have time to grill him. She walked down the creaky wooden stairs and waited.

Grandpa was sitting in the living room, wearing his usual farmer overalls, reading the newspaper. He looked over the top of the newspaper and his bifocal glasses. "Make that boy come to the door. Ya don't want ta be an eager beaver."

Helen smiled and sat next to him on the sagging, brown sofa. "OK, Grandpa, I'll sit tight until he rings the bell."

In moments, she could hear Joseph bounding up the porch steps, landing at the door with his usual energy. Helen jumped up and pulled the door open.

"Hi-de-ho Helen! Ready to roll?" His grin was contagious.

With a quick nod to Grandpa, they were off to collect Emily and Jacob and headed to the picture show. Inside, the overwhelming smell of popcorn caught Helen off guard, and her eyes got misty.

Joseph teased her. "Someone step on your toes?"

"The smell of popcorn brought me back to a winter on the farm."

"You popped a lot of corn?"

"In a way. During the depression, the price of corn was so low that Grandpa used it for fuel instead of selling the crop. The air smelled like scorched popcorn whenever we went outside."

"I didn't realize you grew up on a farm," Joseph said.

"Yes, until recently."

"I'm so happy you're closer now," Emily said.

Helen was flushed from the attention. "Me too, and I can't wait to see this picture."

They found their seats and settled in. Joseph reached over and held her hand for part of it, causing her heart to race. She had to focus extra hard on the plot and not the emotions raging inside of her. Her face burned with embarrassment at a lengthy kissing scene, but she kept her eyes glued to the screen. *What would it feel like to kiss Joseph like that?*

After they went to a soda fountain for root beer floats, and the four of them crowded into a booth.

Emily gushed her enthusiasm. "That was so cool!"

Helen nodded. "How could she point the gun at him like that? My heart is still racing."

"Theatrics!" Joseph answered. "I didn't believe for a minute she'd shoot him."

Jacob chimed in. "I don't know, but the fight scenes were sure believable."

So, this is what it feels like to have friends, Helen thought. Despite all that was happening in the world, they enjoyed a summer evening together and let the movie transport them.

After Joseph dropped off Emily and Jacob, he pulled his car onto a quiet street to enjoy a few minutes together before her curfew. He turned off the engine, and Helen's heart jumped into her throat when he turned toward her. Would he want to kiss her?

"So, where was your farm?" Joseph asked.

"About twelve miles south of here."

"Just you and your Grandparents?" Joseph asked. *Oh, here it goes. Now he'll find out what a mess my life is and never want to see me again.* But she was determined to tell the truth. *He might as well find out now and dump me before I get any more attached to him.*

"No, my Mama lived with us until a few months ago. She got remarried."

"Your Pa's dead?"

She squirmed in her seat and blushed nearly as dark as the color of her hair. "No, he lives in Kentucky."

Joseph reached for her hand. "If you don't mind talking about it, why is your Pa in Kentucky?"

Helen looked at her faded skirt. "My Pa, well his name is Frank. He ran out on us when I was just a baby. And he took my sister, Ruby, who was two." She braced herself for his response. Would he ridicule her? Be repulsed? No response. She looked at him.

He was searching her face. "Did you ever meet him?"

"Just once, when I was ten. He was fairly nice but made a lot of promises he never kept, and I rarely hear from him. He likes me to call him Frank."

Joseph reached over and twirled a lock of Helen's hair between his fingers. "Great guy, huh?"

"Yeah, I think he's on his third wife. Must be difficult to live with."

Joseph traced an invisible line from her shoulder down to her elbow. "He was a fool to leave you. He has no idea what he's missing."

"Thank you." She was glad it was dark, and he couldn't see her flaming cheeks.

"I'd better get you home before your grandmother reads me the riot act."

"Yes, it's getting late." *This is the last time he'll ask me out, now that he knows my life's a train wreck.*

Chapter 3

Joseph pulled Helen toward him into a hug as they sat in his father's car. Her shoulders slumped a bit as she relaxed with the warmth of his chest, and then he looked into her eyes and kissed her lips gently. *Can he hear my heart pounding?*

He drove her home, and as they walked to the porch, he kissed her again lightly. She felt as if she were gliding through the front door, propelled by a force outside her body. *He kissed me!*

Helen and Joseph dated throughout the summer, and when school started again, Helen was determined to find a way to update her wardrobe from rags to glamorous - or at least not shabby. Taking inspiration from movie stars, she searched for a new look so that Joseph wouldn't be embarrassed and tire of her.

One warm September afternoon, Helen walked to Main Street, stepped into the second-hand clothing store, and spotted a used McCall's pattern that read, "New clothes from old." In it were directions on how to remake old clothing into new garments. Grandma taught her to sew by hand when she was a child, but now she could use the school's Singer Featherweight sewing machine during home economics class. Searching through racks of used clothes, she found a lightweight wool gaberdine coat and decided to make it into a skirt. It was emerald green with plenty of fabric and large decorative buttons. She quickly paid for it with her hard-earned money saved from working at the Five and Dime all summer.

Helen slipped into the house quietly with the coat hidden in a large bag, but not before Grandma Gertrude heard the door and came out of the kitchen. She was wearing an apron splashed with flour, and when she spied the package, Grandma glared at Helen over the top of her thick glasses.

"Whacha got there? You go wastin' money again?"

"It's a used coat."

"Ya don't need no new coat. This is why I wanted yer pay sent ta me. Money burns a hole in yer pockets!"

"I'm going to remake this into a skirt," Helen answered. "My home ec teacher said I could use the school's sewing machine after school if I wanted to."

"Humph. I s'pose you're tryin' ta impress that boy. Hope he's not jist usin' you."

"Joseph likes me, Grandma, for who I am." *Although sometimes even I wonder why.*

"We'll see. Supper's almost ready. Biscuits are in the oven. Maybe you could find time ta set the table if you're not too busy with yer sewin'?"

Helen let that roll off her back and forced a smile. "I'm sorry you're upset, Grandma. I only paid a dollar for the coat. If you like, I can make a new housedress for you after I finish this."

"I don't need the likes of you to make my clothes."

Helen turned away before she rolled her eyes. *Why does everything with Grandma have to be a fight?* She brought the coat to her room and hid it.

A cloudy sky and drizzle greeted Helen Monday as she bounded out of bed, excited for Home Ec, her first class of the day. She kept the coat in the large bag to protect it on the walk to school, eager to show it to her teacher.

Mrs. O'Leary held the coat up and looked it over, front and back. "Clever. With fabric hard to find, this is a great idea. There's plenty of usable fabric in the Reefer coat, and you can use these beautiful buttons for a decorative element. Perfect for one of your semester's projects."

Helen lowered her voice. "Neat! But I want to keep this a secret so Joseph won't see it. May I store it in a locker until it's finished?"

Mrs. O'Leary's bright blue eyes looked up, and she cocked her head to one side. "Joseph Donovan?"

"Yes, we started dating over the summer."

She nodded approvingly and handed the coat to Helen. "He's a handsome young man. You two make a cute couple."

"Yes, I feel lucky."

She smiled and looked into Helen's eyes. "It's not about luck, Helen. You're a lovely, intelligent girl with a lot of talent."

Helen's face flushed. She whispered, "Thank you." And then set about taking the coat apart at the seams. *This will be perfect if Joseph asks me to the winter dance as long as he doesn't tire of me by then.*

As Helen went to work ripping the seams of the coat, Diane walked over and hissed so Mrs. O'Leary wouldn't hear her. "Finally getting something else to wear? Although it's still used, isn't it?"

"It'll be new to me."

She sniffed and crinkled her nose. "I guess anything's better than the rags you usually wear. I can't believe Joseph's still dating you!"

Helen flashed her a fake smile. "I can't either. Must be about more than clothes."

Diane bent and cackled in Helen's ear. "At least you don't smell as bad as you used to." She straightened, flicked her hair, and returned to her work table.

Helen looked away so no one could see her embarrassment as she pursed her lips and focused on her project, but the insults still hit a soft spot inside her.

Growing up, Helen endured regular insults from Diane and Bernice about the way she smelled. The stench of the farm permeated her clothes, dried on an outside clothesline. Her weekly baths in the used water never left her feeling clean, but life was better now, and she desperately wanted to erase the memories of that sad little girl. If only they'd let her.

Helen had finished the skirt by the time the first snowflakes flew and was delighted to accept when Joseph asked her to be his date for the Winter dance. On a return trip to the used clothing store, she found an ivory blouse in her petite size and covered the collar in lace. A new tube of wine-colored lipstick would enhance her ivory skin.

The week before the dance, Helen went over to Emily's house for some pre-dance tips. The teens pushed back furniture in Emily's dining room because the hardwood floors would make slipping and sliding easier. Emily lifted the heavy cover of the Zenith phonograph and placed a 33 rpm long-playing record on the spoke, and set the needle in the first groove of a waltz.

Working in stocking feet, Emily took the lead and showed Helen the basic box step, how to keep her shoulders back, and the correct way to hold Joseph's hands.

"And forward, two, three, back, two, three. Just glide along in his arms for the waltz."

Helen tried to focus. "Ouch, two, three. Sorry, two, three."

Emily giggled. "OK, look at me, not at your feet."

Around and around they went until Helen learned the pattern and avoided stepping on Emily's toes.

"You're doing great, follow the rhythm of the music, which should be easy for you, the singer! Relax and melt into his arms."

"You're a romantic. I'm more worried that he'll see what a klutz I am and ditch me."

"He's crazy for you, Helen. Stop being such a worrywart. Glide and smile!"

When they stopped to catch their breath and grab a drink of water, Helen was elated. "This is a gas. Where did you learn to waltz?"

"My parents love to dance, and when I was little, they let me step on Daddy's feet as he danced. When I got to high school, I asked them to show me the proper moves to a few different dances so I'd be ready in case anyone asked me."

Helen nodded thoughtfully, and the two sat quietly for a few moments.

"What? Is something wrong?"

"Just imagining what it would be like to have a dad. Must be pretty great."

"Yes and no. He can also be pushy, nosey, and a pain. Sorry, I didn't mean to bring up, you know, a painful subject."

"It's fine. I like hearing what normal families do."

"I don't know what normal means, but we should practice the jitterbug next if you want to dance without bruising any toes. It's much faster, and you won't be as close."

Helen laughed. "Jitterbug, what a name!"

Emily was a fun teacher, and the two giggled and twirled their way through the afternoon.

The evening of the dance, Helen waited in her room until Joseph arrived to make an entrance and glide down the stairs. Despite her grandparent's presence, Joseph whistled when he saw her sashay toward him.

"You're a vision!" he gushed.

Helen blushed from his gaze.

Grandpa beamed at her. "All decked out, Ole Bean."

"Thanks, gentlemen."

Joseph helped Helen with her coat, and she took his arm as they walked out together. *How do I deserve him?*

"Don't be late!" Grandma barked as Grandpa shut the door behind them.

Once outside, Helen took a deep breath of the crisp air and then reached to kiss Joseph's cheek. "You smell yummy!"

"Old Spice aftershave. And, Helen, you look amazing. We're going to have a gas!"

She held tight to his arm as they descended the icy steps and into his father's Packard.

Emily was right. Once they started dancing, there was a perpetual grin on Helen's face. They laughed, spun, and swirled their way through the evening. Helen loved the way her new skirt swished around her legs. The jitterbug made her giggle, but her heart soared during a waltz as they danced face-to-face, and Joseph peered into her eyes and stole a quick kiss. She felt alive, accepted, and possibly loved. *Is this what it feels like to be loved?*

When they were alone in the car after the dance, Joseph pulled her into his arms. "I'm falling in like with you, Helen of Troy." His lips brushed the top of her head, and as she turned to face him, he kissed her forehead, nose, and lips. They melted into a long kiss, then after a moment, she pulled away and put her head on his chest and listened to the racing thump of his heart. Joseph wrapped his arms around her.

"I feel so at home with you. I don't want this to end."

"End? Are you planning to run out on me?" He teased.

She spoke quietly into his shirt. "It won't be me that does the running."

"Helen, why would you say that? You know I'm crazy about you."

"It's so hard for me to imagine this is real. That someone….cares for me."

He pulled back and grinned at her. "Because of your second head?"

She laughed. "It's like I was immersed in murky water, and I'm slowly being brought to the surface to see the world around me." He couldn't understand what life was like before she met him. She looked into his sparkling blue eyes, and he pulled her into another kiss.

Winter came roaring down on the hills of Southern Iowa, and the little town of Greenberg as her first Christmas with a boyfriend approached. She used one of her clothing ration coupons to purchase wool yarn to knit Joseph a scarf.

She and Emily holed up in Emily's bedroom wearing bulky sweaters and making Christmas gifts. Helen sat on Emily's bed, cross-legged in her stocking feet. "If Joseph breaks up with me, I can always give this scarf to Grandpa."

Wool felt, scissors, and glue covered Emily's desk, where she fashioned felt hats with flowers. "Practical! A gift suitable for an 18-year-old boyfriend or an old man! Glad to see you're thinking ahead. Expect disaster and have a plan for it!"

Emily held out several pieces of felt. "Do these colors work together? I'm thinking the black for the hat and then using the hunter green and yellow for the felt flower accents."

"Yes, Em. Maybe add some red for the flowers. But if I keep my expectations low, I won't be disappointed."

"Helen, if you hang onto low expectations, how will you know when you're happy?"

"I think I'm happy now – at least when I'm with Joseph."

"Thanks a lot! Not happy when you're with me?"

"Don't be silly. Of course, I'm happy when we hang out. But when Joseph and I are curled up on the couch after my grandparents are in bed, I think about whether he could be the ONE. But then, when he's not around, I wonder how long this will last."

"He'd be crazy to let you go! A girlfriend who is musical and artistic?"

"Great! Someone who can pick a paint color for the bathroom while singing in the shower! I'm not sure those are the qualities a guy's looking for in a wife."

"Wife? Aren't we too young for all that?"

"Maybe. But all my life, I've wanted a real family. Father, mother, kids. That's it! Don't you?"

"I guess, eventually. I've always assumed I'll get married and have kids, but I don't think much about it. We're young, Helen! We have plenty of time to dream about marriage."

"It's different for you. You grew up in a normal family."

"My little brother Tommy talks to squirrels, Dad shouts when he reads the newspaper, and Grandpa thinks there's a person inside the wireless. How's that for normal?"

Helen laughed. "I see your point. But at least you have a father and a brother. I'm stuck with a grandmother who's always spoiling for a fight. If someone isn't arguing when she walks in a room, they will be by the time she leaves."

"I've met your belligerent grandmother, but you've never experienced my Great Aunt Mertie! When she visited last summer, I woke in the night with her staring at me, holding a knife! Her eyes were like a vacant parking lot. I managed to wrestle the knife away without getting sliced and guided her back to the guest room in complete silence. Creepy!"

"Gives me the heebie-jeebies! But before we decide who has it worse, I better get to work. I'm creating a Christmas display for the store, and I want it to be spectacular."

Chapter 4

The Five and Dime manager asked Helen to design a window display for Christmas earlier in the week, and she delved into the project with gusto, creating an imaginative collection using items from every part of the store. She even made a series of wreaths using old grapevines. Paintbrushes from the home improvement department were tied to the vines and adorned with bright red velvet ribbons from the fabric area. Rolled-up socks were the basis for another wreath, decorated with spools of thread, and large unshelled walnuts and almonds were the focus of a third wreath. With a long shift on Saturday afternoon, she hoped to have time to pull it all together and install the items in the store windows.

Their shop joined the other Main Street stores in splashing red bows, garland, and glitter on every outside surface and lamp post. Store owners set a nativity scene on the town square next to the giant blue spruce tree decked in multi-colored lights. The United States entered World War II several years before, and citizens felt Christmas was a time to set aside worries in exchange for hope.

At school, students were doing their part by holding a holiday concert to entertain Greenberg residents. Helen was thrilled and terrified when her choir director asked her to sing a solo, but she practiced until she knew her song backward and forward and managed to deliver "O Holy Night" without throwing up. Mama and Warren came to hear her and sat with Helen's grandparents in one of the front rows. Even Grandma Gertrude told her, "she didn't disappoint."

Joseph invited Helen for Christmas dinner to meet his parents, Hazel and Henry Donovan. She was tickled to be asked but nervous they might disapprove of her, and she agonized about responding to their inevitable questions. Mama was having Christmas dinner with her new husband, Warren, and his children, so Helen accepted the Donovan's invitation. Grandma admonished her when Helen told Grandma Gertrude that she wouldn't be joining them for dinner on Christmas day.

"You better not be getting serious 'bout that boy. You two barely know each other."

"They invited me to dinner, and I want to meet them. I'm sorry you're disappointed, Grandma."

"Disappointed? Not me. We'll have an easy day, the two of us, without any fuss or bother. I just don't want ya goin' and gettin' ideas in that fool head a yers."

Helen, Mama, and Warren attended a Christmas Eve service with Grandma and Grandpa. Seeing her mother take Warren's arm and smile at him made her think of Joseph. But truthfully, everything reminded her of Joseph. *Oh boy! 'I 've got it bad, and that aint good '- just like the song.*

By the time Helen was ready to go to the Donovans, anxiety had swirled around her like gnats at a picnic. How to act? What to say? Had Joseph told his parents about her…background? Would they think she was good enough for their only child? She arranged decorated sugar cookies on her grandmother's platter and planned to sneak out of the house without Grandma Gertrude knowing she borrowed it. As she waited for Joseph to arrive, Helen looked in the mirror and saw black saucers dominating her light blue eyes, flushed cheeks, and dry lips. She rearranged the black velvet ribbon holding back her unruly hair, added a bit of lipstick to balance her flaming cheeks, and waited at the door with the cookie tray hidden under her coat. She was already wearing her snow boots and carried her Mary Janes in a shoe bag. Finally, he was at the door, and she opened it before he had time to ring the doorbell.

"Merry Christmas, Helen. Are you ready for this?"

"I hope so. I hope your folks will like me." She handed Joseph the platter as she quickly donned her coat and gloves and then shouted good-bye to her grandparents and braced herself for the frigid air.

When they reached the Donovan's home, Joseph led Helen into the entry hallway and called out for his parents. Helen slid her boots off and slipped on her shoes while Joseph hung their coats in the hall closet. The scent of roasting chicken filled the air.

Mrs. Donovan was the picture of elegance as she glided into the living room wearing a red velvet dress with padded shoulders, a cinched waist, and a flared skirt. A single strand of pearls glistened inside the sweetheart neckline. Her eyes took in Helen's red hair and tiny frame when they shook hands.

"What a lovely wool skirt, Helen. Did you make it?"

"Yes, for a home economics school project."

She cocked her head. "Oh, your mother doesn't own a sewing machine?"

"Ah, no, you see, she doesn't sew, and…well, I don't actually live with her…anymore."

"Mother, remember, I told you Helen lives with her grandparents. And look at the beautiful sugar cookies she made for us."

Mrs. Donovan admired the delicately decorated confections as she set them on a table. "Too pretty to eat!"

Mr. Donovan walked into the living room with a tray of mulled cider and invited everyone to sit. Joseph reached for Helen's hand and led her to a cozy curved loveseat with wooden armrests and legs. The conversation was anything but comfortable as the Donovans took turns hurling questions Helen's way. Mr. Donovan served the first one.

"Tell us about your family, Helen. What does your father do for a living?"

"Oh! Well…he's a musician." She could feel the color rising in her cheeks.

"Is that right? Where does he perform? Around here?"

"No, he lives in… Kentucky."

Mrs. Donovan's hand flew to her chest. "Kentucky! Oh my! So your parents aren't …together?"

Helen's face was flaming now. This would undoubtedly be the last time the Donovans would let Joseph see her. "No, not together."

"And you don't live with either of them?" Mrs. Donovan asked.

"Well, I did, but, um, you see, Mama just remarried."

Mr. Donovan's forehead creased. "So, she sent you to your grandparents?"

"Ah, no, I've, or we've, actually lived with them since I was a baby."

It seemed everyone was suddenly thirsty at the same time. Helen sipped her glass and wished she could escape into it.

Mr. Donovan broke the silence. "Any brothers or sisters?"

Helen squirmed from the intense questions, which were getting more difficult to explain. "Yes, I have an older sister, Ruby."

Somehow this tidbit of news was welcome to Mrs. Donovan. "Oh! Joseph, you didn't tell us Helen had a sister. Have you met her?"

Joseph shifted his weight and squeezed Helen's hand. "No, Ruby lives in Kentucky, so I haven't met her. Maybe after dinner, we can sing carols. Helen was a soloist at the holiday concert." Helen nudged him, embarrassed at the mention of it.

"Oh yes, that was a wonderful concert," said Mrs. Donovan.

Finally, they could think of no more questions, so Mrs. Donovan said the words Helen longed to hear. "Well, shall we eat?" With that, the interrogation was over, and the conversation moved into safer territory.

She caught Joseph's eye and bit her lip.

He leaned toward her and whispered in her ear. "Sorry." They moved into the dining room to take their places around an elaborately set table with gleaming china and polished silver. A roast chicken sat on a platter surrounded by dishes of creamed corn, stewed spinach, cranberry-orange relish, dinner rolls, and mashed potatoes and gravy. There was light banter about the food as they passed the serving dishes around the table, which helped ease Helen's anxiety, along with Joseph's reassuring squeeze on her hand under the table.

After dinner, they rallied around the upright piano in the drawing-room to sing Christmas carols while Mrs. Donovan accompanied them on piano.

Helen added a descant part to Silent Night, and Mrs. Donovan turned and smiled. "Helen, you do have such a lovely soprano voice."

Helen wondered if she was just feeling sorry for her but was grateful for the compliment. "Thank you."

On the way home, Joseph pulled into the parking lot of a small park and kept the engine running to keep them warm. They looked at the stars under the crisp, clear sky through openings in the car's frosty windows, and Helen suddenly felt life seemed full of endless possibilities.

He reached for Helen and kissed her on the forehead and lips and nuzzled her neck. His breath was warm in her ear as he whispered, "I think that went well." Despite the warm feelings stirring inside her, Helen pulled back and looked into his eyes.

"I don't know. They can't be happy that you're seeing a girl from a broken home."

"You aren't responsible for your parent's problems. And what I think about you is what's important here. And I'm crazy about you!"

"I'm crazy about you too."

He reached in his pocket and pulled out a small box, and handed it to her. She untied the ribbon and inside found a heart-shaped locket on a silver chain with her initials engraved on its front in an elegant scroll. When she opened the locket and found a tiny picture of the two of them, her eyes misted over.

"It's beautiful! I love it. I'll always treasure it. Oh, and I made something for you. Of course, it's not nearly as nice as this, but I hope you like it."

She thrust the bulky package into his hands, and Joseph unwrapped the hand-knit scarf.

"Blue! My favorite color. That'll keep me warm when you're not heating me up."

"Joseph!" She giggled. They hugged, and he kissed her on the top of her head. *Is this happening to me? Is it wrong to be this happy?*

They enjoyed a few moments of snuggling together in the warmth of his car until Joseph straightened himself and took a deep breath, his eyes dark and serious. "I registered for the draft today, Helen. You know it's mandatory now, right?"

"Yes, but I don't know why they want to take boys who are only 18."

"They need everyone they can get. And I'm not a boy anymore. I'm a man!"

"Will you have to leave right after graduation?"

"I'm hoping I'll be able to work a year before joining the Air Corps."

"The thought of you going to war makes my knees weak. What if something happens to you?"

"Let's not talk about the war tonight, Helen. I want my last few months of high school to be fun and carefree. Including senior banquet and prom. You'll go with me, right?"

Chapter 5

Carefree was not an adjective that ever described Helen. But for his sake, she tried not to feel the weight of the uncertain future.

"Yes, of course. I'd love to go with you. But…"

"No buts. Let's just make happy memories." He stopped her with a possessive kiss.

That night in bed, Helen's mind turned cartwheels. What would she wear to prom? She had hardly used any of her allotted 66 clothing coupons, so perhaps she could buy a new dress. And new pumps. None of her shoes were fancy enough. She vowed to save as much as possible of her weekly checks over the next few months.

Helen rushed to the front door on a crisp April morning and thrust it open. "Emily! I'm all set. Let's go."

Grandma Gertrude stepped in from the kitchen with an apron around her shapeless floral housedress. "Jist where do ya think yer going? Isn't this yer day ta work at the store?"

"I've taken the day off so Emily and I can shop for prom dresses. I told you about this last week, Grandma."

"Prom dresses? You never said nothin 'bout that. How do ya think yer goin 'ta pay for a fancy dress?"

"I saved my wages – what's left of them."

"Left of them? What's that supposed to mean?"

"Grandma, I mean, after I give you a portion and put a portion in savings."

"Well, if you've got money left to waste on fancy clothes, you should be handing over more to us."

"Mama helps pay for my expenses, and I give you plenty. I have a right to spend the rest the way I want."

"Right, huh? You're a minor living under our roof. Ya don't have no rights."

Helen took a deep breath and decided another tactic would work better on her angry grandmother. She smiled and softened her voice. "I'm sorry, Grandma. You're right. I am living under your roof, and I am grateful that you raised me."

Grandma glared at her but said nothing.

Grandpa stepped into the hallway when he heard the arguing. "Now, Gertrude, Helen here's been living under our rules all her life. She saved a bit of money from working at the store, sos she can spend it the way she likes. Goodbye, Ole Bean. Drive safe."

With that, Emily and Helen bolted out the door, down the steps, and into Emily's car.   Helen's cheeks were bright red, and her breathing was ragged. "I hate her. I know it's not Christian to hate someone, but I hate my grandmother."

"You don't mean that. She is difficult, but there must be something lovable about her."

"She's like a brick wall - no feelings or emotions. She simply doesn't care about me."

Emily put a comforting hand on Helen's shoulder. "What about your mother? Can she reason with your grandmother?"

"Mama never stands up for me. She says Grandma and Grandpa took us in, and we should be grateful and all that. Grandma's a miserable old woman, and I can't wait to leave home."

"One more year, Helen. We'll be seniors next year, and then you can fly the coup."

"I keep telling myself that. And the minute I graduate, I'm leaving, no matter what!"

"Agreed. But for today, let's focus on finding the perfect Cinderella dresses that will bewitch our fellas."

Emily and Helen drove to Des Moines to improve their chances of finding gorgeous gowns rather than settling for the few selections available in Greenberg. Buying a dress so far away also meant Grandma Gertrude wouldn't return it and keep the money if she found it in Helen's room. Eventually, Helen found a light blue taffeta gown with a V neckline, nipped-in waist, short sleeves, and flowing skirt that ended mid-calf. Emily chose an evening gown with layers of pink chiffon with a voluminous skirt and a gathered bodice that featured cap sleeves and a sweetheart neckline. They splurged on new pumps and stockings and were giddy with excitement all the way back to Greenberg.

Helen hid her new prom dress and shoes when she returned from shopping. She took the Saturday of prom day off work to take extra care with her hair, nails, and makeup and waited upstairs until Joseph was at the door. Grandpa was there to greet Joseph, and this time, Grandpa was the one who whistled as Helen made her entrance. Grandma swatted him with her dishrag, and Helen giggled.

"Thanks, Grandpa!"

Joseph took her hand and twirled her around. "Sweet! You look beautiful."

The attention added color to Helen's cheeks which were already rosy from the anticipation and her long bath in warm water. "Thanks, Joseph."

She took his arm, and as Helen floated out into the fragrant spring air, her new dress swished gently against her stockings. She delivered a quick peck on his cheek as he held the car door open for her.

Prom was a magical night she would never forget, laughing and dancing with hardly a care in the world. Hardly.

Helen slept in the morning after the prom, but when her mother gently shook her awake, she threw her arms around her neck. "Mama, I didn't know you were here."

Cora sat on the edge of Helen's bed, wearing a casual dark blue skirt and white blouse. "I just popped over to hear about your big night and to bring some oatmeal muffins. I'm so sorry I wasn't there last night to see you. A patient needed extra care. How was the prom? Tell me everything."

"Like a dream! We danced all night. I've got a few blisters this morning from my new shoes."

"New shoes? What did you wear?"

"I didn't want to tell you before, but I saved my wages, and Emily and I went shopping for prom dresses, pumps, and even stockings! I used most of my clothing rations, but it was worth it. Joseph said I looked spectacular!"

Cora's forehead creased. "I'm surprised you didn't tell me this."

"Grandma said I was wasting money buying fancy clothes, but this was a special occasion. She thinks I need to give her more of my wages. I was afraid she'd take the clothes back and keep the money, so I hid them, and I didn't tell you in case you accidentally mentioned it to her."

"Oh! I'm so sorry, Helen. She's had a difficult life and constantly worries that there won't be enough to pay the bills. But you don't need to give her more from your wages."

"What made her so mean?"

Cora picked at some lint on Helen's blanket. "I wouldn't say she's mean all the time. She did spend many hours teaching you to sew, embroider, and quilt. And she cooked for all of us for many years."

"Then why isn't she ever happy? I never see her smile or hear her humming."

Cora nodded. "It's true. She does seem miserable. She never wanted to live on a farm, with the daily grind of taking care of animals, growing and cooking food, and even making soap. When we were young, it would take her an entire day just to do all the laundry, washing it on a board, running each piece through a wringer, and hanging them to dry. All she focused on was a steady stream of chores, week after week, and then year after year. Instead of seeing the blessings in her life, she focused on what was wrong."

Helen nodded and was thoughtful for a moment before she stated in a near whisper. "I still don't like her."

"I hope that you find love for her in your heart. I think Grandma envisioned a life with more beauty in it. She was always drawn to beautiful things and bright colors. Remember the wine-colored piano cover she had to have at the height of the depression? She traded chickens for it when we barely had enough to eat. I think it represented a contrast from her dreary existence."

"That explains the cookie jar with the Dutch girl on it."

Cora's eyes brightened. "Yes. I don't know why she sold that when we moved to town. Enough about this. Will you model your clothes for me?"

Helen hopped off her bed. "Happily. Hide your eyes until I'm ready." She quickly dressed. "Ready." She twirled around in the small room and took a few steps to show off her skill at walking in heels.

"My little girl's all grown up! You look beautiful, Helen." She reached out and smoothed her long red hair. The color inherited from her father.

"Thanks, Mama."

"I hope you don't rush into marriage like your sister. You've only been dating for ten months."

"And two weeks and three days. No proposals yet, Mom."

"And three days?" Mama smiled. "Young love is breathless. I do miss you."

"I miss you too. But one more year and I'm moving out of Grandma's house. I don't know where to, but I'm not staying once I graduate."

"Don't be hasty. You still have a year to figure it out."

Helen and Joseph were snuggled together in his car on a secluded road the week after prom. The air was chilly, and the moon was full as Helen filled him in on the latest antics of Warren's youngest grandchild. Joseph smiled, said nothing.

Helen pulled away and looked at him. "You worried about something?"

He took a deep breath. "I guess so. I need to tell you something."

Helen sat upright, afraid to breathe.

Joseph reached for a lock of her hair and twirled it around his finger. "I got a job in Des Moines, so I'll be leaving the first week in June."

"June? But that's so soon. I was hoping we'd have the summer together."

"I won't be too far away." He stroked her cheek. She held her breath, wondering if he was about to break up with her. "I'm hoping to work before I join the military. At least that's the plan, but I don't want to lose you."

"Why would you lose me?"

"Will you wait for me?"

A burst of air gushed out of Helen. "Of course, I will. How can you even ask that?"

"We've been going together less than a year."

"Ten and a half months."

He smiled despite his serious mood. "I know I love you, baby. You're beautiful, talented, and kind."

She whispered, "I love you too, Joseph. I can't imagine life without you."

He reached into his coat pocket, took out a small box, opened it, and produced a tiny diamond ring.

Helen gasped at the ring, and her eyes sparkled as she searched his face.

"Will you marry me, Helen? We can wait until after you graduate next year, but I want to spend the rest of my life with you. I know the rings not much, but I'll replace it when we can afford it after we're married."

She had never known love like this, and she was ready to give him her heart. "Yes, Joseph, I'd be thrilled to be your wife." They kissed passionately before he pulled back, looked at her, and grinned.

"Think what beautiful children we'll have."

"Whoa," she giggled. "Let's not rush into children. I want you all to myself for a while. But I do hope they get some height from you."

"And your curly red hair. I hope they inherit that, Helen. It's so pretty. When should we tell your Mama?"

"Are you going to ask her all nice and proper?"

"I was planning on it. Unless you think I should write to your father."

"Joseph, don't tease. He couldn't care less what I do. Mama's the one who raised me, so she's the one to ask."

"Sorry, Helen. Must be painful to know you have a father, but he doesn't want to be part of your life."

"When I was younger, it hurt more, but now, it doesn't seem to matter as much. Maybe I'm more accepting, or I've had more to distract me. Like you."

"I want to be such a good husband that it makes up for your not having a dad."

"Thank you. I want us to have a happy household with no fighting."

"I'm not sure it's possible never to fight, but let's promise that we'll make up right away if we do."

"It's a promise." Helen felt a warm glow thinking about the home they'd create together.

As she tried to fall asleep that night, his words whirled in her head. "I know I love you, Helen. You are beautiful, talented, and kind. I want to spend the rest of my life with you." She had never heard such tenderness. *I don't deserve him, but thank you, Lord, for putting him in my life.*

Chapter 6

The following Saturday, Joseph came bounding up the steps and rang the bell.

"Hi-de-ho Helen. Ready to go?"

She shook her head and smiled. "Starting to sound like a poet."

They drove to nearby Springfield, Iowa, to see Mama and Warren. As they walked to the brick and stucco Tudor-style home, Joseph stopped for a moment and took a deep breath before knocking on the heavy oak door. Mama's smiling face greeted them, and she pulled Helen into a hug before inviting them to sit on the couch next to the window. Joseph kept fidgeting with his keys, and Helen was eager to show Mama the ring she had hidden in a pocket of her skirt. Warren served tall glasses of iced tea with lemon, and the usual discussions about the war and the weather began until finally, in a pause in the conversation, Joseph found his moment.

He cleared his throat and sat a bit taller. His words came rushing out like steam from a tea kettle. "I'd like to change the subject. Helen and I've been dating less than a year, but I know we love each other, and we want to be together, so with your permission, we'd like to marry after Helen's graduation."

Helen nodded eagerly as she clutched his hand.

"Seems rather sudden, but I know you've made Helen happy this past year," Mama responded.

Warren knit his brow as he puffed on his pipe. "What are your plans for the future?"

"I've registered for the draft, but I'm hoping to work for a year first - I've already got a job in Des Moines so I can earn some money – and then join the Air Corps."

"Where will Helen live while you are in the military?" Again, Warren was in lawyer mode, issuing hardball questions.

"I figured we'd get a small apartment after we're married."

Mama looked from Warren to Helen. "What about your plans, dear? What will you do while Joseph is away in the service?"

Helen shrugged. "I've got another year to decide. Perhaps community college, or I'll work to save money."

"Don't forget about your talents, Helen. A woman needs to use her talents to find a way to earn a living."

Joseph sat straighter. "With all due respect, I'm hoping to support Helen and our family."

Cora smiled at him. "Life doesn't always go along as planned. Helen will want to find a way to use her talents to contribute to the household."

"Like you did, Mama."

"Yes, teaching and working as a nurse saved me in more ways than one. I'll gladly help you explore your options, dear."

"But do we have your permission to marry, Mama?"

"Yes, you have my permission, as long as you finish high school."

While Helen showed off her diamond Monday in the school cafeteria, Diane walked by, looked at it, and sniffed.

"Such a tiny diamond. But I guess you had to accept the first offer that came along."

"Joseph loves me, and that's what's important. Besides, he said he'd replace it with a bigger diamond in a few years."

"Well, good luck with that!" She tossed her hair and walked away, leaving Helen steaming mad.

Emily linked her arm through Helen's. "It's a beautiful ring, and I'm happy for you both. Diane's just jealous."

Poignant moments dotted the next few weeks. Helen attended Joseph's graduation and gleefully flaunted her engagement ring.

Then the time came to say goodbye when Joseph left for Des Moines. Helen hugged him and burrowed into his neck in a puddle of sobs.

"I'll come back every month to see you," Joseph assured her. "And I'll call each week. The time will go quickly. I need you to be Helen of Troy. Strong and fearless."

"It's so wonderful seeing you all the time. That's what made me strong."

"Nonsense Helen. You're one of the strongest gals I know. We'll get through this."

She nodded through a curtain of wet eyelashes.

"It isn't just that you're moving for a job, but I'm already dreading the time when you'll join the military. How will I get through that?"

"Helen, you're a world-class worrier. Let's meet one challenge at a time. This year will go quickly with your Senior activities and wedding plans. I want you to enjoy it all."

"Oh, the wedding! I haven't even begun-"

Joseph laughed. "Helen, there's time. We just want a simple wedding, right?"

"Simple and elegant, yes."

They kissed goodbye, and he drove off.

Helen worked full-time at the store all summer, trying to save as much money as possible. The store manager praised the window displays she created to match the changing seasons, and she enjoyed the creativity and the camaraderie with other employees.

Shortly after the start of her senior year, she and Mama were having lunch together after church. Warren was at his law office, so the two of them sat in Mama's kitchen enjoying grilled cheese sandwiches and tomato soup.

"I don't know why I have to finish school. With Joseph gone, I want to be done with school and to focus on the rest of my life."

"I understand why you feel restless, but life has a way of surprising us. You'll be glad you have a high school diploma, and I hope you consider college."

"Grandma says it's a waste of time."

"Since when do you listen to anything Grandma says? I had to battle it out with her to stay in school once I turned 13, and I'm so glad that I did. She thought I should leave school and get a job, so I had to convince her that education was vital to my life every single year."

"But you didn't go to college and still found a job after high school."

"Teaching at a poor mission school was the way for me to find independence and leave Ma. But with only high school education, I wasn't qualified to teach anywhere else."

"Why didn't you stay at the mission?"

"It's complicated. Some thugs burned down the cabin where we lived as part of my teaching contract. I barely escaped with you and your sister. Then the mission couldn't afford to rebuild the cabin, and I couldn't afford to rent another apartment on the paltry income."

"What about my dad? Didn't he earn anything?"

"Very little. So Grandma and Grandpa sent us money to come back to Iowa and help with their farm. But Frank hated it and left one night with Ruby. I was devastated."

"Sorry, Mama, I didn't mean to dredge up that nightmare."

"I've learned to face the pain. But my point was that after Frank left, I needed more education to secure a future and bring in income, so I went to college for three years to become a nurse-midwife. My only regret was that I didn't get more education when I was younger and single, so this is why I'm encouraging you to think about additional education."

"I could never do what you do. Nursing just doesn't interest me." Helen looked at the deep lines around her mother's eyes and wiry grey hairs springing around her face. "I know it was sometimes heartbreaking for you."

"You don't have to follow my path, Helen. God has given you your own talents and gifts. Figure out what they are, and you'll be happier in your work."

"But I don't have to worry about Joseph running out on me. I think my gift will be making him happy. Besides, how would I pay for college?"

"There are scholarships, loans, and grants. Have you looked into those?"

"No, I haven't. I assumed I couldn't go to college since money's always tight. And now, I just want to plan the wedding. All I want is to create a normal family with a father, mother and children." Helen could hardly focus on anything other than the burning love she felt for her fiancé. "But we hardly get to see each other because of the gas rationing."

"Does he still call?"

"Yes, of course. Every week. But it's not the same as seeing his beautiful blue eyes."

"So, what else can you focus on?"

"I'm enjoying my job at the store. And I do love music. My chorus director, Mrs. Finnegan, wants me to try out for the school solo contest."

"Helen! That's wonderful. When is it?"

"In November. I'm working on Schubert's Ave Maria. 'It's just for school, so hopefully, I won't be too nervous."

"I can't wait to hear all about it."

Helen's palms were sweating as she took the stage in the high school auditorium to perform her solo. No one could see her knees shaking under her wool plaid skirt, but she managed to keep her vocal cords under control. When they announced the winner, Helen felt heat rushing to her face and a pulse in her ears when they called her name. She couldn't wait to dash home and call Mama and Joseph.

"Mama, I won!"

"Congratulations! You're finding your gifts, Helen. I'm so pleased for you."

"Mrs. Finnegan is taking me to the county contest to face the other high school winners. I feel excited to represent my school, but nervous too."

Helen practiced and practiced her solo. She found a dress at the used clothing store and remade it into a wine-colored skirt for the event. A few weeks later, Helen faced a group of judges. And, again, she won.

"I can't believe I won the county solo event," she told Joseph that night when he called. "But I'm not sure I want to go on. It was so nerve-wracking. Each time, I was afraid I'd throw up on the stage. I'm not the competitive type."

"Give it a try, Helen. If you don't, you'll always wonder if you would have won the state title."

"Oh Joseph, there's no way that'll happen. With all the talent in the larger schools – and the students who take lessons – it's unlikely I'll even win one of the top ten spots."

"Do it for me, Helen of Troy."

"Any chance you can be there for me? I'd be calmer if you were there."

"Sorry, Helen. I can't get away. But I'll be thinking of you."

"I'll be thinking of you, too, Joseph. Do you miss me?"

"Of course I do."

"What do you do on your days off in Des Moines?"

"Oh, this and that. Sometimes I hang out with co-workers."

"Any of them girls?"

He sighed. "Are you jealous?"

"I just wish you'd find a way to come to Greenberg more often."

"You know it's the gas rationing keeping us apart. Now, go practice your solo and let me know how the competition goes."

She hung up but sat quietly for a while, thinking about their conversation. Was she driving him away with her questions and jealousy?

Chapter 7

Helen decided to phone her father in Kentucky to see if he'd come for the state competition. She still clung to the hope they could have a relationship. With music as the thread that connected them, certainly, he'd feel the same way, so she found a quiet time when her grandparents were grocery shopping and dialed.

"Hello, Frank? Um, this is Helen."

"Helen?"

She bit her lip as she wrapped her hand around the long cord. "You know, from Iowa."

Nothing.

"Your daughter?"

"Oh yeah, how you be, Helen?"

She breathed out a sigh of relief. "I'm good!"

"Cold up there?"

"Cold, yes, and snowy."

"Hopin 'ta get away from it?"

"Well, no, actually, I was wondering if, um, if you'd like to visit here."

"What? Why would I do that?"

"Well, um, I got, ah, first place in a singing competition."

"That's great, Helen."

"Yes, and I know you're a singer and all. And I thought, well, maybe, you'd like to hear me sing in the state competition."

"State competition, eh? When is it?"

"Beginning of December. It's in Ames."

"December? A freakin 'cold month! Uh, ah, unfortunately, I doubt I'll have enough gas rations to make it."

Helen slid down the wall, still clinging to the phone. "Oh, yes, the war. I didn't think about that."

"Sorry, kiddo. You sing pretty, okay?"

"Yeah, thanks, um, Frank."

They hung up, and she sat on the kitchen floor, defeated. What was she thinking?

But weeks later, Mrs. Finnegan drove her to Ames for the state competition. Helen thought about Joseph and all that he would have to face once he entered the military. Would he end up fighting in the war? She imagined his face as she sang and felt calmer as she took a breath and began.

"I did it, Joseph. I sang in the state competition, but I'm glad that's over. I was so nervous." Helen downplayed her words.

"And how did you do?"

"Not that great."

"Really?"

"The competition was fierce."

"But I'll bet you were amazing."

"Actually, I'm kidding. I won first place!" The words burst from her.

"First place in the solo contest?"

"Yes, first in the state of Iowa."

"Helen, I'm so proud of you! I would be even if you hadn't won, but wow, that is wonderful news! I can't believe you kept me thinking you lost."

"Well, I went through several rounds as they eliminated other students, and finally, there were just six of us on stage, and I nearly fainted when they told me I won. And now they want me to go on to the competition."

"Nationals! Where's it held?"

"St. Paul, Minnesota. I'm going to ask Mama to drive there with me."

"Congratulations, Helen! I knew you could do it."

"You did? I sure didn't. But I'm glad I went through with it and happy I didn't get sick on the stage."

Joseph spoke softly into the phone. "You're quite a gal. I don't know if I deserve you."

"Well, you're stuck with me."

A moment of awkwardness stretched across the phone line as she chewed on her bottom lip.

"Right? Aren't we stuck with each other, Joseph?'

"We sure are. Well, it's your nickel, Helen, so we'd better go."

She called her mother next. "Oh, Helen, I'm so thrilled for you. I'll check my ration coupons to see if I can scrape together enough gas."

A few days later, Mama called her back. "I don't have enough gas rationing coupons to get you to Minneapolis and back. I'm so sorry. With my work, I drive all over the county, and I use most of my allotment each month."

"It's okay, Mama. This war is causing much bigger problems for others than just missing a contest."

"That's so mature of you. Of course, winning was a bonus, but finding the courage to compete was a big step, Helen. You do know how proud I am that you competed, don't you?"

"I do. But it's still great to hear it."

"You must get your musical talent from your father."

"Thanks for saying that, Mama. I rarely hear anything nice about him."

"He sang in a band and played guitar. I heard him on the radio a few times, and he did have talent."

"I hope you're not mad, but I called him to see if he'd come to the state contest."

"You called Frank?"

"Don't be so shocked. I thought since he was a musician, he'd want to hear his daughter sing."

"What did he say?"

"He said he wouldn't have enough gas ration coupons."

"Were you okay with that?"

"Mama, I knew it was a long shot. I just thought I could have some sort of relationship with him. But it's okay."

Helen wasn't looking forward to Christmas with the same enthusiasm as she did the year before when she and Joseph saw each other every day. But she was excited that he'd be home for Christmas Day, and they planned to spend all of it together.

She daydreamed about what their life would be like in a few years. Happily married, and together every single day with no more separations. She longed for that time. Then she would be happy. No more getting reacquainted every time they saw each other.

When Christmas day arrived, Joseph arrived at her door to pick her up. She opened the door, and he stepped inside and gave her a quick peck on the cheek. "Hi there."

"Merry Christmas, Joseph."

He looked at the floor and shifted from foot to foot. "Yes, Merry Christmas, Helen. Shall we get going? My parents are expecting us for brunch."

"Sure. I made date pinwheels to bring along."

"Good. I'm sure they'll be delicious."

"And I have a gift for you."

"We can do gifts later."

She said goodbye to her grandparents, and they headed to his car. He opened her car door and went around and slid behind the wheel as usual, but instead of reaching for a hug and kiss, he started the engine and looked straight ahead.

"I've missed you, Joseph."

"Yes, you told me that on the phone."

"But don't you miss me?"

"Of course I do, Helen. It's nice to see you."

After brunch at the Donovan's, Joseph insisted on popping in to see her grandparents. They chatted about the war and the weather and little else. Finally, they headed to Cora and Warren's home for Christmas Dinner.

In the car on the way to Springfield, Helen said, "Let's stop for a few minutes so we can exchange our gifts."

"Good idea." Joseph pulled into the parking of a favorite park. Helen reached for him, and they hugged and kissed for a moment. Then she pulled back and looked into his eyes.

"You've changed. Is it your job?"

"I'm just tired, Helen. My job is grueling, the foreman's demanding, and the work isn't interesting. I feel like I'm a hundred years away from high school. Every week it's the same grind, waiting for the weekend."

"It's not much more fun here with school, work, and my grandmother."

"Yes, but you're still doing things you love, like singing and winning competitions. I feel like you're out of my league now."

"That's ridiculous! I'm the one from a broken family. The smelly little girl that grew up on the stinky farm. I've worked hard to overcome that, so I'm worthy of your love."

"You don't have to prove yourself to me, Helen. I, I've always, you know, cared for you. Well, loved you."

They looked at each other uncertainly, and Helen wondered why his words felt so strained. Finally, Joseph handed Helen a small box. "Merry Christmas, Helen. I hope you like it."

Helen unwrapped the plain, silver bracelet and put it on. "Thank you. It's charming. Here, I made you something." She handed him a bulky package.

"Another scarf?" he said, smiling.

"No, open it."

Inside was a tailored wool vest, lined with synthetic silk and finished with wood buttons and a belt buckle in the back.

"Helen, this is beautiful! Did you make it?"

"Yes, I used some wool from a garment at the used clothing store and then purchased the lining fabric with my ration coupons."

"You are incredibly talented. Thank you so much." He reached over and caressed her hair, then planted a quick kiss on her cheek. "We'd better not be late to your parent's."

After Christmas, the countryside froze solid and made travel even more difficult for Helen and Joseph. Their visits became more infrequent, and there was an unexplained chill between them during their weekly phone visits. Helen couldn't shake the feeling that something was wrong. Finally, on March 1, Joseph called Helen. She ran to the kitchen, where the only phone hung on the wall.

"Joseph? Hi! How are you?"

"I'm okay, Helen, but we need to talk."

"About the wedding? I know we still have a lot of planning to do."

"Yes, about the wedding. But no, not about the planning."

"Then what? What's going on?"

"I need you to take off the ring I gave you."

"Joseph, what are you talking about? Why?"

He took a deep breath then blew it out in a bundle of painful words. "I don't know how to tell you this, but I've found another gal, and we've been sort of seeing each other for a few months. I didn't think it was a big deal, so… I, I didn't tell you. But, um, it's gotten more … complicated, and I need to break our engagement. I…I'm so sorry, Helen."

The veins in Helen's head tightened. "What? I don't understand."

"I know this is difficult. I can't believe it myself. I met this gal, and she kept inviting me to have dinner with her. I was alone, and I didn't know anyone in Des Moines. I didn't think a few dinners would be a problem."

Her pulse pounded in her head. "But we were engaged!"

"Yes, I know. But it just happened."

"What happened?"

"I got…involved with her. With Lucy. Lucy's her name."

"I can't believe this. You said you wanted me to wait for you, and now this?"

Joseph let out a breath. "I'm not proud of myself, Helen. I'm confused, and I can't go ahead with our marriage."

"Are you marrying her?"

"I don't know what I'm going to do. I'm sorry, Helen. I need to go."

He hung up.

Helen fled upstairs to the privacy of her bedroom. She cried until her throat nearly swelled shut. For once, Grandma Gertrude showed compassion and the next day called a doctor to the house. The doctor diagnosed Helen with Quincy's throat, an infection in the back of the mouth. Helen would have to work to rebuild her lungs if she wanted to sing again. After the doctor left, Grandma imparted her tactless advice. "Men are like streetcars. There'll be another 'round the corner at any minute."

No, there is only one Joseph. I trusted him with my heart. And he stepped all over it.

Helen mailed the ring back to Joseph. Her head felt foggy at school the next few weeks, and she struggled to focus on her classes. When classmates asked how the wedding plans were going, she struggled to stay in control when she explained there would be no wedding.

And no Senior Prom. Without Joseph, she didn't want to attend.

Diane and Bernice laughed and pointed at her in the cafeteria, but she was numb to their insults.

Emily stepped in to cheer her and tried to help Helen focus on graduation and the future. Helen rebuilt her vocal cords' strength in time to sing a solo at the graduation ceremony.

Instead of calling him, she decided to write to Frank and invited him to attend the ceremony, and when he wrote a few weeks later, her excitement surprised her. She was elated when his letter arrived, saying he'd try to attend. After all these years! He said he'd try to borrow gas rations from a friend.

The last time she saw him was also the first time she met him. Helen and Mama took the train to Kentucky to see Frank and Ruby, Helen's sister when she was a little girl. Frank promised to stay in touch after the visit, but he rarely did. Despite that, Helen continued to hope for his support. Especially now. She imagined her father's face beaming with pride as she sang and looked forward to an affectionate hug. Perhaps now he'd see she inherited his musical gifts and want to stay in her life. Surely, they could rekindle the father-child bond.

As she prepped for finals, the phone rang downstairs in the kitchen a week before Helen's graduation. She raced down the stairs to get it and was shocked to hear her sister Ruby's voice since she rarely called. "Helen, are ya sittin'?" She could hear the tremor in Ruby's voice. Helen pulled a kitchen chair over near the phone and held onto it.

Chapter 8

"What's wrong, Ruby? Have you been in an accident?"

Ruby struggled to stammer out the news. "I'm fine, and my kids are okay. It… it's…Frank, er Pa. He's… he's dead."

Helen plopped on the creaky wooden chair. "Dead? What do you mean? How?"

Ruby sniffed and tried to keep control of her voice. "They don't know yet. He was eatin' breakfast when suddenly he started gaggin' and foamin' at the mouth."

"Ewweeh. Was he alone?"

"No, his new wife Mable just fixed him some eggs."

"Did she call an ambulance?"

"I guess so. Mable said he had hisself an attack of the heart and then fell on the floor, twitching all over. She said when he stopped twitchin', she called the ambliance."

"Mable was his fourth wife?"

"Yeah, but I think they were 'bout to split."

"Wow! How are you doing, Ruby?"

"I'm in shock, is all."

Helen stared into space. "Ruby, I'm so sorry. I didn't know him much, but I'm sorry for your loss."

Ruby was understandably upset but too nervous to talk long.

"Thanks, Sis. I have ta go. Can't ring up a big phone bill. I I'll write soon, Helen." And she was gone.

Another blow. *It feels as if the world is against me. God, where are you in all of this pain?*

She phoned her mother with the news. "Mama, Ruby just called to tell me some bad news."

"Ruby? Are the grandkids okay?"

"They're fine. It's Frank. He...he passed away."

"How did that happen?"

Helen repeated what Ruby told her about the gagging, twitching, and foaming at the mouth.

"That sounds more like poisoning than a heart attack."

"Poisoning? Ruby said she thought Frank and his current wife were about to split up. But do you think she'd poison him?"

"I don't want to speculate about who'd want to harm him. We'll let the sheriff in Kentucky do the investigation. I'm sorry Frank won't be able to hear you sing at graduation."

"Yeah, I think I was still hoping he'd want to be part of my life."

"I don't want to speak ill of the dead, Helen, but Frank was not a nice man. He thought only of himself. I was relieved he never reached out to you, considering his influence on Ruby. First, he kidnapped her and wouldn't let me see her or talk to her. He ripped her from my life! He threw away the letters and gifts I sent and told her lies about how I willingly gave her up. And then he let her marry a 23 year-old-man when she was only 13! Disgraceful! It took me years to let go of my anger."

"I didn't mean to stir it all up again, Mama."

"It's not your fault, Helen. But I'm relieved I won't ever have to see him again, and neither will you."

Helen hoped that having Frank and her mother at her graduation would make her feel like a complete family. And a little piece of her heart still wanted him to like and approve of her. Would he have liked her singing? That hope was dashed forever. She shivered when she thought about someone purposely poisoning him. What kind of a man was he? And who hated him enough to kill him?

Graduation day was finally here, and Helen was relieved her voice recovered enough to sing her solo at the ceremony. She poured emotion into her performance that came from deep within her. The heartache of losing Joseph – the one person who said he would love her forever. She was in too much sorrow to be nervous. The anguish of growing up fatherless without her sister, along with the daily torture from her cruel grandmother, weighed on her broken heart. And now her father's bizarre death.

When she finished singing, the applause startled her back to reality. She received a standing ovation and saw several friends with tears streaming down their faces. She was grateful for their applause, but she felt numb as if her heart was ripped out and frozen under a block of ice.

The horror of the past few months threatened to swallow Helen emotionally. But getting out of Grandma Gertrude's way would be a step toward the freedom she craved. She needed something to look forward to – and something to do, so she and Emily plotted their futures at Emily's home shortly after graduation.

"I know I could work full-time at the Five and Dime, but I need to get out of this town. Too many painful memories. I'm thinking of getting a job in Des Moines and working for a year or two."

"Des Moines? Are you planning to woo Joseph back into your arms?"

"Well, would it be so bad if I just happened to run into him?"

"I don't know, Helen. I'd hate to see you hurt again. From what he's told Jacob, he's still seeing that floozie."

"Don't tell me anymore. It's too painful to think about him with someone else."

Emily got the newspaper and opened it over the kitchen table. "I know, but let's not spoil today by thinking about him. The best thing we can do is to take charge of our lives. Maybe I could also find a job in Des Moines for the summer so we could hang out now and then."

"That would be great, but you're still going to college this fall, right?"

"Yes, and I'll need more moolah to help with college expenses."

"Moolah, is it? Well, let's get crackin'!"

They poured over the help wanted ads in the Des Moines Register.

"Here's one for a beautician," Emily said. "I've always loved fussing with hair." Emily's pencil was poised and ready to circle any possibility.

"You have to know more than just fussing, Em. Like actually cutting hair and doing perms."

"Okay, how about this one for a florist. I love flowers. How hard could it be? Wait, they want a year's experience? Where would I get that?"

"Apparently, you have to already have a job doing that. Hmmm. We can skip all these ads for nurses. I know that takes some college. Mama studied for three years for her degree."

"What exactly are we qualified for?" Emily looked exasperated.

"You could probably be a model with your heart-shaped face and widow's peak. I read those were two classic signs of beauty."

"Thanks, Helen, but what about you with your porcelain skin?"

She gestured with her pencil. "Ah, but my freckles aren't a beauty sign. Besides, I'm short, flat-chested, and have out-of-control red hair. Not exactly model material. Let's keep looking." She grinned and turned back to the papers in front of them, pencil poised.

"There are lots of factory jobs, Helen."

"It's too confining for me. I couldn't do the same thing over and over all day. The country girl in me would be miserable."

"Okay, country girl, how about horse trainer?"

"There's an ad for that?" Helen's heart quickened.

"No, silly. I'm just teasing."

Helen shook her head and exhaled. "Okay, here's something I know I can do…clean. This lady wants a maid. It's not glamorous, but it would get me out of Grandma Gertrude's."

"Maid? That doesn't sound like much fun."

"I only want to work for a year or two, and then I'll see where the road leads me. Hopefully, by then, the war will be over, and the world will come to its senses." Helen cut the ad out, took it home, and wrote them a letter.

Within a few weeks, Helen landed the position.

When Mama and Warren came for dinner Sunday night, she sprang the news on everyone while they were eating strawberry-rhubarb pie.

"I'll be moving out next week. I got a job as a maid."

"Maid? With all that education, you's just workin 'as a maid?"

"It's a start, Grandma. I'll be able to live with them, so you'll finally have the house to yourself."

Grandpa cracked a crooked little smile and winked at her when Grandma wasn't watching. "Be awful quiet around here, Ole Bean. Hope you visit often."

"I will, Grandpa. When I can."

Mama looked thoughtful. "Who're you working for, dear?"

"The owner of some car dealership in Des Moines, Bud Bennett. I'll be living there to help his wife, Lorraine."

Warren set down his fork. "Which dealership?"

"Not sure."

Mama nodded. "Well, they must have a beautiful home. Do they have any children?"

Helen bit her lip. "Um, five. But the ad didn't say anything about babysitting. Just that Mrs. Bennett needs help managing the household."

Mama's forehead creased. "You don't have much experience with children. Will they expect you to watch little ones while you clean?"

Helen shrugged her shoulders. "I'm not sure. Don't know how old they are. I guess I should have asked more questions. But my room and meals are included, I know that."

Mama's smile was apprehensive. "Well, you were looking for an adventure, and it sounds like you found one."

"I know it's not glamorous, but it'll be fun to live in Des Moines. And Emily found a job as a waitress in a downtown restaurant for the summer. We'll have each other."

Grandma Gertrude pointed her fork at Helen. "Des Moines! Ain't that where yer old beau is living? Ya ain't tryin ta cozy up ta him again, is ya?"

Helen let out a sigh. "No, Grandma! But there aren't many jobs in Greenberg. Des Moines is a big city, so I doubt I'll ever run into Joseph. But Emily and I are planning to meet every week."

"If Mrs. Bennett lets ya outta her sight," Grandma cackled.

Helen shook her head. "I'm supposed to have Sundays off."

Mama drove over to Greenberg to take Helen to the Bennett's when she was ready to start work. Helen hugged Grandpa John and waved to her grandmother on her way out the door. "I'll visit when I can."

They pulled up to the Bennetts, and Mama turned off the car, and the two of them took in the sight of the grand three-story colonial style home perched at the top of a grassy hill.

Mama's eyes widened. "Well, dear, this is what you'll be cleaning."

Helen's mouth drooped open as she gazed at the house on the hill. "Yikes!"

Mama smiled playfully. "Do you want to run? It's not too late."

"Sort of, but I won't give Grandma the satisfaction of quitting. Let's go in."

Chapter 9

Mrs. Bennett opened the large oak door. "Hello. Helen, is it?" She appraised Helen's tiny frame.

"Yes, Mrs. Bennett? Or should I call you Lorraine?"

"Mrs. Bennett will be just fine. Please come in."

Helen nodded. "Yes, Ma'am. And this is my mother, Cora."

"Charming. Helen, you're not what I expected. Your letter said you lived on a farm, so I was expecting someone bigger and, probably stronger."

"I'm stronger than I look."

Mrs. Bennett's eyes widened. "I see. Well, would you both like a tour?"

Cora and Helen nodded.

They stepped into a grand foyer with a chandelier that sent tiny rainbows of light in all directions. A curved staircase flowed from the second floor.

Mrs. Bennett looked at Helen's single cloth-sided suitcase. "My, you certainly travel light. Is that all of your things? I hope you're planning to stay with us awhile."

Cora and Helen followed like homeless puppies looking for shelter. Mrs. Bennett obviously enjoyed the role of tour guide as she sauntered through two lavishly furnished living rooms with fresh floral arrangements on marble stands. The extensive kitchen boasted the latest in cooking appliances and a sizeable Formica-clad table at one end. Dirty dishes were piled high on the counter and in the sink.

"The children eat here in the kitchen. Their dinner should be served promptly at 5:30 pm. Mr. Bennett and I dine at 6:30 pm in the dining room." She led them to a room with oak hardwood floors, flocked wallpaper, and a long shiny walnut table with an elaborate floral centerpiece. A matching walnut china cabinet filled with gold-edged dishes, crystal bowls, and silver serving platters glistened under a spotlight. Helen's shoes squeaked on the hardwood floors as she turned in all directions to take it all in.

"You'll be expected to clean these floors daily and beat the Oriental rugs in the hallways. There's an electric vacuum in the basement to take care of the living room carpets."

Helen nodded. *Not too bad so far.*

The second floor hosted six bedrooms with thick piled carpet, heavy drapes, and distinctive wallpaper. Each room was decorated to represent a different European country. Bathrooms sat at both ends of the lengthy hallway.

"Bathrooms must be cleaned daily, naturally, with so many children using them. The laundry room is in the basement, so there are clothes chutes in each bathroom. You'll need to keep up with the washing and ironing. There's less to do in the summer, but the children's uniforms need to be washed and pressed daily during the school year. Naturally, you'll also need to vacuum the carpets up here daily." Mrs. Bennett stopped her tour and peered at Helen. "Now, you do cook, and bake, don't you, Helen?"

"Ah, yes, a little. Nothing fancy, just the basics."

"Good! We expect you to make a hearty cooked breakfast and a nourishing supper for the family Monday through Saturday. And, of course, bake fresh cookies for snacks. You may eat in the kitchen with the children. Now, if you require a Sunday off, prepare extra food on Saturday. And, when school starts again, you'll need to pack lunches for the children. While they're at school, you may go to the market for groceries."

Helen's eyes widened, and her eyebrows raised as she listened to the litany of chores. She peeked at her mother, who mirrored Helen's concern

Mama stopped Mrs. Bennett. "Helen will have Sundays off, won't she? I mean, a person can't be expected to work seven days a week."

Mrs. Bennett shook her head and massaged her neck. "Oh, well, yes, if she wants a day off, I suppose that'll be fine. But she shouldn't be too tired. After all, it's just a bit of light house cleaning and a few meals. None of the children are in diapers anymore, so managing them is quite simple."

Helen's hand flew to her chest. "Managing the children? How old are they?"

"Timmy is six, Johnny's nine, MaryAnn's eleven, and Joannie's thirteen. Stephen will be helping at the dealership this summer, and then he'll be away at college in the fall.

Helen nearly gasped."But your ad didn't say anything about managing children or cooking meals."

"The ad said that I need help managing the household. Cooking and children are part of the household."

I wonder what she does all day.

"Where are the children?"

"Stephen's at work, but the others are with their grandparents today. They're helping out until you get settled."

They climbed a steep set of stairs in the back of the house to the third floor—no plush carpets here, only bare floors adjacent to rough plastered walls that slanted inward. A small bed was pushed against a wall in the last of three cramped rooms. It sported a single curtainless window.

Mrs. Bennett swooped her arm with a flourish. "Here's your room, dear. You should be quite cozy. This speaker on the wall connects to a buzzer in the kitchen in case we need to ring you after dinner. Sometimes Mr. Bennett craves a late-night snack. Oh! And please remember always to use the back stairs."

Seriously? Ring me at odd hours? Is this the 1800's in England?

But Helen kept her mouth shut and nodded as if she expected this. Instead of freedom, she was a household servant with mounting expectations.

Mrs. Bennett crinkled her mouth as if to smile, but no other part of her face participated in the phony gesture. "I'll leave you to get settled. When you've unpacked, you can get started on those dirty dishes and make meal plans for the week."

As soon as Mrs. Bennett was out of earshot, Helen turned to her mother. "Planning meals for the week? Mama, I thought I was being hired just to clean."

Mama shook her head. "You should have asked more questions."

"I was just so excited to find a way to leave Grandma's."

Mama put her hands on Helen's shoulders. "I didn't realize you were so miserable."

"The constant tension gets to me. You know how she's always arguing and controlling. Anyway, I'm here now, so I'll have to figure this out. Hopefully, the children will be okay."

Mama brushed her cheek affectionately. "You're young with lots of energy. Think of this as a learning experience."

Helen rolled her eyes and groaned. "Thanks, Mama, but some things I'm not interested in learning."

Mama laughed. "Call me in a few days, and let me know how you're getting on."

"Sure, if they'll let me use the phone."

"Hang on, dear," Mama whispered as she hugged Helen goodbye. "At least you'll make some money."

Despite what she told her family, Helen hoped she'd find a way to see Joseph. Maybe if he saw her again, he'd realize he was making a big mistake. She went to sleep the first night in Des Moines with her head spinning plots to seek him out.

Accustomed to hard work, Helen threw herself into the position, trying to fulfill the enormous expectations. She was awake before dawn, making breakfast, and starting laundry. Then, a few days into her employment, or interment as she thought of it, Stephen waltzed into the kitchen.

"Oatmeal again? I'm not eating that farm slop."

Helen's face reddened. "Would you like me to make fried eggs for you?"

"Is that all you know how to make?"

"I'm not a trained cook."

"Well, what are you trained for?"

"They hired me to clean."

"So, do you have any training or education?"

"Yes! I graduated from Greenberg High School."

He sniffed. "Tiny rural school. I suppose there wasn't much competition. And now you want to be a maid?"

"It's not that I wanted to be a maid. I just wasn't sure what I wanted, so I thought this would be a way to…."

"To live in our beautiful home?"

"No, just a way to make a little money until I figure out my next step."

"Next step. Sounds like a code for looking for a husband."

"That's the last thing I'm looking for."

"Well, good. If your cooking skills don't improve, no one will want to marry you."

Helen slammed the frying pan onto the stove to make Stephen's eggs.

So much for an adventure! She signed up for monotony, drudgery. Each day, once Bud and Stephen left for the dealership, she started wielding mops and rags. Mrs. Bennett was rarely pleased with anything she did, and at first, Helen washed the tiled kitchen floor three times to accomplish the expected shine. In her spare time, they expected her to find activities for the four younger children. She could hardly wait for Autumn when they would be in school most of the day.

She was supposed to have a day off, but they expected her to prepare meals and wash dishes, even on Sundays. The children were rude, the adults demanding. If she didn't get the floor shined to her standards, not only did she have to redo the floor, but Mrs. Bennett docked her pay. "For the wasted time." *This seems to fit the pattern of my life - misery heaped upon more misery.*

At night, Helen fell into bed, almost too exhausted to think about Joseph. Almost. She thought about going back to her grandparent's home but didn't want to see the smug look on Grandma Gertrude's face. *I'm trapped, alone, and miserable, just like always.*

Emily phoned her one day, and the two arranged to meet for a Sunday afternoon movie. Mrs. Bennett complained the family would have to have cold sandwiches for their evening meal. Helen didn't care. She needed to see a friendly face. After the movie, the two teens headed for a small restaurant with outdoor seating.

Emily munched on a crisp piece of fried chicken as she stared at her friend. "Helen, I mean this in the nicest way…you look horrible! What's going on over there?"

"Thanks!"

"I didn't mean to insult you. It's just that you're so pale, and there are dark circles under your eyes."

"I know I'm a mess. I'm exhausted! The family's sucking all my energy from the moment I get up until I drop in bed at night. Polishing, dusting, scrubbing. And she even expects me to keep her brats entertained with educational activities. Give me a break! While she attends her charity events and has her nails done."

"Sounds horrible. It's just that I miss you. I was hoping we'd see each other more this summer."

"I miss you too! I'm living a nightmare, and I can't make myself wake up." She took a swallow of her milk and stared at the clear summer evening. "At least we found a table outside. After we eat, let's take a quick walk in that park over there. I need to enjoy some daylight."

"I know what you mean. This waitressing is exhausting. But at least I get to go home at night. School starts in two months, so the time will go by quickly."

"Not for me. Every day seems to drag on. They're so demanding they even buzz me sometimes after I'm in bed to get them a snack."

"That's horrible! You've got to get out of there, Helen."

She pushed a curl behind her ear. "I will - as soon as I have the energy to look through the paper."

And then she spotted him. Joseph.

Helen's eyes got wide as she whispered. "Emily, there's Joseph. Should I hide?"

Emily craned her neck around. "Too late. He's looking right at us. Or at you."

"Should I wave or ignore him?"

"I say ignore him."

Too late. Joseph crossed the street and approached their table.

"Hi, Emily, Helen. How are you, Helen?"

Helen blushed and stammered. "I'm fine, I guess. Busy. Working. Fine."

Joseph stood awkwardly, staring at Helen. "Where? Where are you working?"

"Here in Des Moines… as a live-in maid."

"Maid? Must be hard work."

"Yup. Exhausting."

"Do you think we could meet for coffee sometime?"

"Why?"

"I just didn't like the way we left things."

"WE didn't leave things. YOU did.

"I'd like a chance to explain."

"Explain?"

"Why I broke it off."

"You still dating whatshername?"

"Lucy, yes."

"Then, I don't' think we have anything to talk about."

Joseph shifted from foot to foot, and Helen focused on pushing food around her plate while her pulse raced as she waited, hoping this nightmare would end. Where was her Joseph? The energetic, fun-loving guy who made everything seem possible.

Finally, Joseph said softly, "I didn't mean to hurt you, Helen," and he walked away.

Helen's whispered to Emily. "I was hoping to see him this summer, but not like this."

Emily reached for her hand and squeezed it. "I think he still cares for you."

"And yet, he stays with her. It's so humiliating and painful."

Summers typically flew by for Helen but not this year. She dragged herself out of bed each day and endured the complaints of the Bennetts. The food was too plain, the children were bored, the house was never clean enough. Even though Stephen was her age, he treated her as if she were an ignorant fool. She caught herself thinking, "Joseph would never be this rude to another person," Then pushed thoughts of him from her mind.

Just before Emily was ready to start college, the two friends spent one last dinner together.

"Are you searching the want ads for a better job?"

"Yes, but it's very frustrating. There isn't much available for someone without training."

"But you have talents, Helen! You're an incredible singer, and you can sew and do embroidery."

"Thanks, Emily, but sadly there are no want ads for a singing sewer. Unless you want to buy a Singer Sewing Machine!"

Emily laughed. "Well, are the Bennett brats treating you any better?"

"The oldest just left to get a jump on the college semester. The other four will be starting school soon, and I can hardly wait! Of course, Mrs. Bennett expects me to do a deep clean of the house and polish all the silver and clean every closet and cupboard."

"Makes me crazy to hear about all this."

"What about you? All packed for college?"

"I'm excited. I wish you were coming with me."

"Me too! Maybe after I save some money, I can go."

Emily nodded as they both enjoyed burgers and fries. And a moment of quiet between friends.

"How is Jacob? I assume you're still going together."

"Yes, but since we're going to different colleges, we agreed to date other people."

"That's so civilized of you."

"We're planning to stay in touch, naturally."

"I shouldn't ask, but has Jacob said anything about Joseph? Is he still going with that floozy?"

"I was planning to tell you. I just didn't want to ruin our day."

Chapter 10

"Tell me what? Is something wrong with him?"

Emily clasped her hand over Helen's. "Wrong in the head. He married Lucy in July and then left for the war."

Helen was speechless as a french fry stuck in her throat. She bit her lips to stop the tears forming in her eyes and looked away. *He married her. He's gone forever. Serving in the war!*

"Are you okay, Helen?"

Her voice shook. "No, but there's nothing I can do about it. I've lost him forever. It's as if he died."

"It's time you think about yourself, Helen. After all you've gone through, you need to find some joy and try to forget Joseph."

Helen nodded weakly. "You're a good friend, Emily. I'll keep looking for another job."

"Something better has got to be out there."

Sunday, the family was on a rare outing to an apple orchard, which gave Helen time to think.

Now that Joseph was married, she was even more motivated to find a new position. But doing what? She flopped across her bed while searching the Des Moines want ads. The pay was so dismal for anything she was qualified to do that she wouldn't be able to afford an apartment. At the Bennett's, her salary was also bleak, but she didn't have to shell out any earnings for rent, food, or utilities. And she certainly didn't need to spend any money on clothes. She looked at the frayed slacks and stained blouses she worked in and wondered what happened to the girl who loved to sew and dress up? Hair pulled into a ponytail, she schlepped around in the same rags day after day. No point dressing in nice clothes to scrub toilets, mop floors, and fry food.

Her confidence sunk to new lows. Could she live with Mama and Warren and work in Springfield? That was an idea. She tried to remember how many businesses lined Main Street in that tiny town. A small grocery store, a flower shop, a bar, and a coffee shop. No hope there. Running back to her grandparents was not an option. She'd rot here before giving Grandma Gertrude the satisfaction of seeing her beg for help.

At least she was saving money. That was the silver lining. And thank goodness the younger Bennett kids were in school all day now. When Mrs. Bennett left for social engagements, Helen managed to squeak in time to read again. An hour of peace here and there helped sustain her. Her third-floor bedroom reminded her of the attic alcove she escaped to as a child. To read, play with her dolls, and eventually, to sew. But that alcove was cozy, with fluffy pillows to sit against and her books and doll clothes. Not like the room she slept in here. Bare walls, simple chenille bedspread, a hard mattress. More like a holding cell.

On September 2, 1945, President Harry Truman declared that World War II was finally over. Cities and towns across the country held parades and celebrations, and Greenberg was no exception. Helen helped look after the youngest Bennett children at the town's parade, and although she was on duty, she began to feel lighter. Almost weightless. She hadn't realized how much the war affected her vision of the future, but now she felt untethered. All she had to do was find a way out of the Bennett household and into a new life. She didn't have to wait long for an opportunity.

In late October, the Bennett's oldest son, Stephen, was in a minor car accident after a fraternity party. He totaled his car but wasn't injured, so his parents decided to bring a new car to him. They needed someone to drive Stephen's car alongside theirs to Texas and back, and since Helen drove her grandparents' Model A Ford after she passed her driver's license, she was the logical choice. They asked her to take Stephen's car to Dallas while Mrs. Bennett's parents looked after the children in Des Moines.

Helen drove behind Bud Bennett's car, like a miniature parade. As she drove along the open roads, Helen opened the windows for air, and a scarf tied loosely around her neck was sucked out the window and into the air twirling high above her car. She gasped and then realized it was gone. Just like Joseph. Gone. There was nothing she could do about him other than to find a new path for her life. Joseph was married. She had to accept this so she could get over him. Before she learned he was married, she hoped he'd realize his mistake and come back to her. But that wasn't going to happen.

Her scarf was a sign that adventure beckoned. And along with the invitation came courage.

There's a big wide world out there, and I've never seen it, other than one trip to Kentucky. What am I doing? I'm wasting my life cleaning bathrooms and trying to please people who can't be pleased. I need to find my own life. And why not enjoy a warm winter in Texas instead of the ice and snow of Iowa. They don't own me, and they can't force me to stay with them.

She formed a plan as the miles flew by. Leave the pain behind and begin the rest of her life—no more pining away and feeling sorry for herself. The fresh air pushed the cobwebs out of her brain.

Once in Dallas, they drove to Stephen's fraternity. He introduced her as the "family maid" to his fraternity brothers. Their eyes were all over her, assessing her like an animal they might purchase.

After dinner, Bud said, "Hop in the backseat. We'd better see how far we can drive before we have to stop for the night."

Helen saw her break and took it. "Please drop me at the train station."

Bud studied her as he chewed on the end of a lit cigar. "You taking vacation time already? You've only worked for us a few months." His eyes narrowed, and smoke swirled around his head.

"I'm sorry, but I'm not going to work for you any longer."

Helen looked at Bud and stood a little taller. "I've never traveled, and I'm eager to see some new country. I've decided to take the train to Austin. I'll have my mother come for my things. Please give her my final check."

"Well, I'll be...." Bud was stunned.

Mrs. Bennet stomped around the car, hands on her hips. "You can't just leave us high and dry!"

"I'm not bound by a contract."

"What am I supposed to do?"

"Take care of your children and polish your own floors, I guess."

"What would your mother say about your abandoning us and sassing me?"

"Mama will be happy for me."

"But you haven't found anything else?"

"I will." She needed to step through her mind's cage and make a dash toward a new life.

They drove her to the train station, and Helen bolted from the car with only an overnight bag and her pride.

She was free. On her way to Austin - a city of adventure where new people and places were awaiting her.

On the train, Helen felt a new confidence surge through her. No more timid Helen. She would shed that skin and reinvent herself. Starting now. In the dining car, she smiled at a young woman in a brimmed black hat, introduced herself, and asked to share her table. The woman answered in a thick Southern drawl.

"Certainly, you can join me, Darlin.' Name's Louise." She thrust her manicured hand out, and Helen happily shook it. Louise's soft, graceful fingers ended in long nails painted in crimson that matched her sensual lips. Helen self-consciously hid her overworked hands and chipped nails under the table.

"Where y'all come from, Helen?"

"From Iowa. Hoping to find a job in Austin. Someplace warm."

"Well, darlin', I might be able to help you. I work at a clothing store in Austin called the Foxy Lady. I'll put in a good word for you." She took a long drag off her cigarette, and as she did, Helen noticed the beauty mark just below the right side of her lip.

Helen had never met anyone like her. "That would be swell, Louise. It sounds fancy."

"It is! The Foxy Lady's snazzy! We sell everything for the hot mama. Lacy panties, silk stockings, hats, cashmere sweaters, jewelry, and even fur coats." Smokey green eyes sparkled when she described the store.

Louise's coal-black lashes popped up and down like puppets to punctuate her words.

Helen could hardly focus on Louise's words as she took it all in. She tried not to gawk at her but admired a jeweled hair clasp holding a ponytail pulled to one side. Helen pictured herself wearing fancy dresses and bright red lipstick and couldn't believe her good fortune meeting someone who could teach her about the world.

As they rode along, they moved to benches opposite each other and continued to share a bit about their lives. Louise offered Helen a stick of gum, which she reluctantly accepted. Mama always told her ladies never chewed gum in public, but Mama wasn't here.

"Y'all have a fella?"

"Used to. I was engaged to a guy named Joseph."

"Engaged. My, my. Y'all look young to be engaged."

"We were going to marry when I graduated high school."

"You got cold feet?"

"No, someone lured him away, and he broke it off, and, well, he's already married." Her lips pursed tightly to avoid crying.

Louise was filing her long oval nails. With one leg crossed over the other, she swung her free foot and snapped her gum. "He's hitched! Well, hot damn! He didn't waste time."

Helen looked at her lap and sat on her rough hands. "No, I kept hoping he'd come to his senses."

Louise stopped and pointed her nail file at Helen. "Listen darlin', men are like fish in the sea. If one's not working out, throw him back. Plenty more where that one came from."

Helen pouted. "But I'm the one who got thrown back."

"You need to throw him back mentally, honey. Get over him! He isn't worth losin' sleep over. I'll introduce you to some dreamboats I know, and we'll show you how to party!"

"Well, okay…thank you! It would be great to meet some folks, er fellas." This was all working out. To think she almost endured that maid job through the winter. Instead, she was going to live it up in sunny Texas. Free of Grandma, free of snow, free of rules.

"Before I introduce y'all to my friends, want to go shoppin'? I'll bet you could use some party clothes."

Helen looked at her brown wool plaid skirt and sturdy leather shoes and was too embarrassed to admit the pathetic shape her wardrobe was in. Being in high school and working as a maid left few occasions to dress up. And little money for extravagances.

"That sounds great, but my budget is pretty tight, and first, I need to find a place to live."

"There's a boarding house near the store that rents by the week or the month. I know another gal who lives there." Louise had it all figured out.

"So, it's a house for girls?"

"No, for guys and gals. You're in Austin now. No girls' boarding houses here." Louise's smile was so confident. Things were definitely different in Texas.

Helen found the rooming house and rented a room just for a week, in case she didn't get work. But when she went to the store the next day to apply for a sales position, they hired her on the spot when she told them about her work at the Five and Dime and her ability to sew and alter clothes.

It's as if I've stepped through the looking glass, like Alice in Wonderland.

Helen twirled the phone cord of the public phone booth near the boarding house. "Mama, you should see where I'm working – it's the bee's knees! The Foxy Lady carries much fancier garments than the stores we have back home. Everything from hats to wedding dresses, fur wraps, and even silk stockings."

"How long have you worked there?"

"Nearly a month."

"A month! Why have you waited so long to call? I was worried sick."

Helen studied her newly polished nails. "Oh, Mama, I'm a grown woman now. You can stop worrying. Anyway, I met a gal on the train who helped me get the job."

"A gal on the train?"

"Yes, her name's Louise. We hit it off big time, and she also helped me find the boarding house where I'm living."

"Boarding house for girls?"

"Ah, no. There are guys and gals here. But I have a good lock on my door."

"So, who is this Louise?"

"She's a few years older than I am and so glamorous. She's helping me get my wardrobe in shape and plans to introduce me to a few of her friends!"

In truth, Louise hadn't invited Helen to meet her friends, but she held onto hope that it would happen soon.

Mama sounded worried. "I hope you're not spending all your paychecks on clothes."

"No, Mama, I still have to pay for rent and food. But I'm getting a few items with each paycheck. Can't look like a farm girl when I'm selling fur coats!"

"Just don't get carried away buying silk stockings."

"Couldn't even if I wanted to. Ladies have to put their names on a waiting list to purchase them. Some come in every few days to see if their name is near the top of the list."

"I don't think any of the shops here in Greenberg sell them, but even if they did, I doubt I'd put my name on a list to purchase any."

Helen's laugh took on an unfamiliar giggly quality. "Always the practical one, Mama. I can't afford any yet, so I put face makeup on my legs and use an eyebrow pencil to draw the seam up the back."

"What women will do to look fashionable."

"Yes, and because silk stockings are so expensive and hard to find, one of my jobs at the store is to mend holes in them. I have a tiny little hook, and I reknit them inch by inch. All that time doing needlecrafts with Grandma has come in handy."

"I'll tell her. Have you called your Grandma since you've been in Texas?"

"No, she was happy to get me out of her life."

"She does love you – in her own way."

"Well, it would be nice if she'd shown it now and then."

There was an awkward pause.

"Sorry, dear. Have you found a church yet?"

"Not yet, Mama. I haven't had time. I do laundry, errands and tidy my room on Sunday. "When her mother didn't respond, she raced on. "But I'm enjoying my job, and Louise is showing me the ropes." *Mama disapproves.* Helen waited for a response. "It's not that I don't want to go to church. I just haven't found time."

"You do sound like you're having fun. But don't forget about God because he hasn't forgotten about you."

"Sure, sure. Okay, Mama."

"Well, it's your nickel, so we should probably go."

Chapter 11

They hung up, and Helen felt a pang of homesickness but pushed it aside as she stepped out of the phone booth and let the sun wash over her. Mama was undoubtedly enjoying Sunday with Warren, and Helen was happy. Mama finally found someone to share her life after decades of being single. She deserved love and affection from an honorable man, but Helen wasn't ready to make that commitment again anytime soon. She enjoyed the other young clerks in the store and the occasional date. What Mama didn't know about her dates wouldn't hurt her. After the disaster with Joseph, she was guarding her heart. *Besides, this is the happiest I've ever been, so why do I need God?*

For once, Helen felt as if she was in control of her life and her destiny. No one told her what to do, where to go, or how to spend her time and money, nor did they suspect she was a farm girl from Iowa who was unloved and unlovable. When someone mentioned the difference in her accent, she claimed Des Moines, rather than the farm or Greenberg, as her hometown. Here in Texas, she was fashionable, fun, and unattached. And she intended to stay that way.

And yet…no harm against a bit of fun, was there? She couldn't help it if a dangerously handsome man – Dirk Betzini rented one of the rooms in her boarding house. Helen walked across the front porch to get to and from her room, and Dirk planted himself in the swing on the porch, smoking, just as she came home from work each day.

"Hey there, Kitten," Dirk tipped his cowboy hat as she walked onto the porch.

"Hello," she said and quickly stepped over his cowboy boots to get to her room.

This routine repeated itself several times until Dirk broke the cycle.

"You're a looker tonight." His voice reminded her of chocolate, dark and smooth. "Care to have a cup of joe with me?"

"Maybe. Where?"

"Coffee house 'round the corner."

"Okay, as long as it's not in your room."

Dirk stood, and his height and physique dwarfed Helen. He was easily a foot taller than she was, with broad shoulders and long legs. Her heart fluttered at the sight of him.

They walked to the coffee house and shared a few laughs. She made a point of closing the door quickly when they got back to her room. No kisses, just friends.

A few days later, he was again on the porch when she came home from work. "You're lookin' fine, Helen. How about lunch this Sunday?"

It sounded innocent enough, and she made sure it was. The conversation was flirty and light, revealing little about her background. Next, Dirk asked her to a movie on a Saturday night. She chose a sapphire blue dress with a full skirt and cinched waist and adorned her curls with a jaunty black hat. After the movie, he suggested they go for drinks at the Twisted Sister Tavern, and no one questioned her age.

As Dirk ushered Helen to a booth in a dark corner, his hand slid from her waist to her bottom, and she quickly brushed it away. She'd never been inside a bar and was a bit put off by the smell of stale beer and smoke. "Can I get you a drink?"

"Just a 7Up, please."

"7Up! Y'all a teetotaler?"

Helen laughed lightly. "No, I just fancy a soda."

Dirk shook his head but fetched their drinks and settled back into the booth. He lit a cigarette. "So, what did y'all do back in Des Moines, Helen?"

"This and that! After school, I wanted to travel, so I hopped a train to Texas."

He laughed as he blew smoke in her face. "Helen, you're quite the little lady. I have a feeling we'll have lots more adventures together."

"Don't get any ideas. I like my freedom."

"Oh sure, Kitten, I don't intend to cramp your style. But we can still have us some fun."

Dirk downed several beers before driving them home. When they got to Helen's door, he grasped Helen's shoulders and pulled her toward him as he leaned in for a kiss. Helen was surprised at how quickly she responded to his passion but gently pushed him away after one long kiss and reached for her door.

"Come on, Kitten. Let's keep this party going."

"Sorry, Dirk. I had a lovely time, though." She wiggled out of his arms and went inside her room, leaving a disappointed Dirk on the porch.

After several weeks of dating Dirk, Helen decided to confide in Louise while on a lunch break together at the Foxy Lady. "You're not going to believe this guy I'm dating. Movie star gorgeous with black hair and dark chocolate eyes."

"Mmm, he sounds delicious! Is he a good kisser?"

Helen's face reddened. "Yes, he is."

"And why haven't y'all told me about this hunk of mankind before? Keepin' him to yourself then?"

"I wasn't sure he liked me, but he keeps asking me out."

"Well, darlin', why don't we double date so I can feast my eyes on him?"

"That would be swell. I don't have any confidence in choosing men, and I'd love your opinion."

The following weekend Dirk suggested they go dancing, and Helen asked if they could meet Louise and her date, Jimmy, at the Fits and Starts Bar and Dance hall. Dirk reluctantly agreed. "Kitten, I just love having y'all to myself."

Helen donned a navy-blue dress with a white collar and a full skirt that ended below her knee. Cork pumps would be comfortable for dancing. She pulled her curls back and held them in place with a hair clasp. She was excited to go dancing, especially with Louise to guide her.

The four of them met at the Fits and Starts Bar and Dance Hall, which was decked out in Christmas splendor. Sparkling and blinking lights decorated every wall, inside and out. Helen remembered the Christmas displays she made for the store last year, but they faded in comparison with the all-out festivity of the Dance Hall.

And then, Louise walked in, capturing the attention of every man in the room and the disdain of every woman. She was a vision in a slinky black dress with a plunging neckline that revealed ample cleavage. The skirt ended above her knee, and to accentuate her long legs, she sported four-inch black stilettos. Her mane of dark hair was softly curled and left flowing around her shoulders. Long black eyelashes, red lips, and rouged cheeks added to the drama. And she sparkled – from her earrings to her necklace to the jewels on the toes of her shoes. Helen introduced her to

Dirk, who never took his eyes off Louise as he grasped one of her graceful hands and brought it to his lips to kiss.

"Well, well, Dirk, aren't y'all the gentleman! This is my date, Jimmy."

Helen felt like a dowdy little mouse next to her dramatic friend, and she was uncomfortable with the way Dirk was fawning over Louise.

"Sure, hi there, Jimmy. Shall we get these ladies some drinks?"

Helen watched as the two men disappeared to the bar. Louise turned to her, "Well, he's one tall drink of water!"

"Yes, I told you he was handsome!"

"And such a gentleman." Louise fanned herself with her black clutch with the jeweled clasp.

"He does seem to be." Helen wasn't sure what to say. She was in awe of Louise but uncomfortable with the amount of attention Dirk was paying to her. "You look snazzy tonight."

"Oh, this, it's old. I just threw myself together. Do you think Dirk can cut a rug?"

"Beg your pardon?"

"You know, dance."

"This is our first time dancing, so I'm a bit nervous. But I hope so. Joseph and I loved to dance together."

"You need to get that Iowa boy out of your head. This here is a fine Southern man, and he deserves your undivided attention."

"You're right. Let's have fun." Helen could see the men coming back with their drinks. She had little experience with alcohol but didn't want to admit that she felt dizzy after a few sips of her Tom Collins. She recently moved from 7Up to more sophisticated offerings.

When Dirk led Helen onto the dance floor, she was pleased to discover he was an enthusiastic dancer, in addition to being a snappy dresser. They danced the jitterbug and swing.   With her tiny frame, he would toss her into the air or over his back. He twirled her around until her head spun. All thoughts of Iowa and Joseph melted. That night, she fell asleep without wondering where Joseph was and whether he was safe. Emily wrote that he was still serving overseas, even though the war was over. Typically, Helen fell asleep praying he wouldn't be a casualty of any danger. Even though she'd lost him, she wished him no harm, but tonight, he was far from her thoughts.

Helen didn't know a great deal about Dirk since she was keeping the relationship light. At least that's what she assured her mother.

"What does Mr. Betzini do for a living?" Mama asked. Helen could picture her back in Iowa, looking out the window at snow-covered hills.

"Dirk works in a factory. It pays pretty well. That's about all I know."

"What religion does he follow?"

"Oh, Mama, we haven't talked about anything that serious. We go to the picture show or dancing on Saturday nights. Just keeping it light."

"Does he know you're just keeping it light?"

"Mama, you're such a worrier. I'm having a great time, and I love this warm winter."

Truthfully, it is nice having a regular date again—someone to do things with. But I doubt that I'll ever love again.

"How are grandma and grandpa?"

"Your Grandma's health isn't what it used to be. It's ironic because I think bossing you around gave her a reason to live. Now that you're gone, Ma seems to have lost her interest in living."

"That is ironic. But please don't blame me, Mama. I need to have a life of my own."

"Sorry, dear. I didn't mean to blame you. Just needed you to know that your grandmother is getting on in years, and it's showing. Warren and I are planning to take a meal to them tomorrow."

"Well, send my love to them and tell them all is well in Texas."

There was no denying Helen was attracted to Dirk. When he looked deep into her eyes and kissed her, heat moved through her body right down to her toes, especially after a few drinks at the Fits and Starts Bar and Dance Hall. And he took liberties with her that made her uncomfortable, but she assumed it was because he was crazy about her. Dirk also carried a flask in his pocket and sometimes took another sip of whiskey on their way home from a bar. Helen tried to quiet the warning voice in her head about his drinking. And the jealousy that came out of nowhere.

On their next date, they went dancing again, and while Dirk was at the bar getting refills, another man asked Helen to dance. Helen was friendly and polite as she spoke to this stranger. When Dirk got to their table and saw her smiling, he set their drinks down, grabbed the man by his shirt front, and threatened him.

Helen screamed. "Dirk, stop! He was just being friendly."

"Well, let him be friendly with someone else. I don't like you getting 'fresh with other guys." The bar got quiet, and everyone stopped to see if there was going to be a fight.

Helen whispered in Dirk's ear. "I'd like to leave. Please, let's go now."

Dirk let the stranger go. "No, let's finish our drinks!"

After a few sips, she suggested they dance, hoping to lighten the mood. But Dirk was sullen and continued to scan the crowd for signs of the other man.

Helen realized things weren't better and smiled. "Shall we go now?"

Dirk slammed his drink onto the table, grabbed Helen by the arm, and hustled her outside to his car.

"Dirk, you're hurting me."

"You said you want to go home, so that's where we're going." He drove erratically back to the rooming house. When he stopped the car, she jumped out and dashed for her room, but her petite legs were no match for his lanky ones. He caught up to her and grabbed her arm again.

"Where do you think you're going?" he asked. He was getting angrier by the minute.

For the first time, Helen felt nervous around him. Instincts kicked in. *Stay calm. Sweet talk him.*

Helen turned to him and smiled despite her racing pulse. "I guess I'm just not feeling well tonight, Dirk. I'm sorry if I made you angry. That was not my intention. Forgive me?" She gave him a quick kiss and fled to her room alone.

Voices swirled through the night, arguing on both sides of her brain.

I need to break up with him.

But I like him, and we have so much fun.

He drinks too much.

But he's a great kisser.

He has a temper, and he could hurt me.

I'm used to dealing with Grandma's temper. I know how to calm him.

Chapter 12

Dirk's anger was…familiar. When she was little, Grandma caught her reading when she was supposed to be collecting eggs from the hen house. Grandma flew into a rage and took out a strap. She was about to hit Helen with it when Helen apologized sweetly and promised not to forget again. She forced herself to smile. It worked that time, and Helen quickly learned how to calm Grandma's rage by turning on sweet apologies.

Maybe I did something to provoke him. I'll try harder not to upset him.

The next day Dirk knocked on the door of her room. She was hesitant to answer at first.

"Helen, Kitten, please open up. I have something for you." She opened the door a crack, and Dirk looked sheepish as he held out a dozen long-stemmed blood-red roses. No one ever brought her roses before. They were fragrant, exquisite, and extravagant.

Dirk seized the door and flung it open. He held the flowers with one hand, captured Helen around the waist with his other, and held her firmly against him.

"Sorry, Kitten, I guess I had too much to drink last night. The thought of another guy getting near you made my blood boil. I promise it won't happen again." He pulled her toward him, and his lips brushed hers. She was too confused to resist.

He lured her into a deep kiss. "It's just because I'm so sweet on you."

He smelled so good – freshly showered and shaved. She loved the way his eyes smoldered when he smiled at her and looked over her slender figure. It felt so good to be loved. *Is that what this was? Love?* His kisses undoubtedly said he was crazy about her. He must love her.

"I'm sorry too. I didn't mean to make you jealous," she said as Dirk's lips nibbled along her neck, making her spine tingle. She was tired of wrestling with the voices in her head. She needed a long embrace and reassurance, and she got it.

"Let's spend the afternoon together, and then we can go out to eat tonight."

"Thanks, Dirk, that sounds swell." How could she resist such an offer? So much better than staying alone in her room on her day off.

Monday at work, Helen and Louise put in a new display of hats at the Foxy Lady. As they worked, they shared tidbits of their weekend.

"Did you see that gorgeous hunk of manhood, Dirk Betzini, again Saturday?" Louise tried on a sassy red felt hat as she spoke, then turned to Helen for approval. "What do you think?"

"Gorgeous as always, Louise. And yes, Dirk and I went dancing." Helen was straightening a ribbon on the band of a black hat.

"That's it? You went dancing? Y'all don't sound very jazzed."

"He blew a fuse when another guy asked me to dance. Dirk was getting us refills. When he came back and saw me chatting with this guy, he flipped out."

"He decked him?" Louise turned toward her, sporting a wide-brimmed navy-blue hat with a large feather on one side.

"Almost. We left shortly after, and he stayed mad all the way home. I've never seen him like that, and I felt…creepy."

"What do you think of this hat?"

"It's beautiful, Louise. But did you hear what I just said about Dirk?"

"Oh, Helen, he's just nuts about you, that's all. Probably had one too many. Has he apologized?"

"Yes, he brought me a dozen red roses yesterday and said he was sorry."

"Well, there you go. Nothing to worry about. He's a hunk that Dirk. You're lucky you saw him first."

"Yes, he's a dreamboat, but what a temper. I guess I'm just a worrywart!"

"Put the kibosh on that worrying, and don't let a good thing pass you by."

Helen took him back. Since they both lived in the same boarding house, it was difficult to avoid him, and she had to admit they had fun whenever they went out dancing.

Christmas was right around the corner, and Helen was feeling more than a little homesick. After a dull Thanksgiving alone in her rented room, she wanted to make Christmas Day special. The store was closed, naturally, but so were all the restaurants, coffee shops, and grocery stores. Still, the tiny oven and fridge in her room provided options. Although they'd only been dating a few months, she decided to invite Dirk to dinner.

The day before Christmas, she bought dinner rolls at the store, cleaned her room, and set out a wreath she made from pine cones. Red fabric adorned her tiny table, and she set out two white candles for ambiance. She baked Mama's favorite date cookies on Christmas Day and prepared a small ham with mashed potatoes and green beans. She still hadn't found a church to attend, and somehow the day felt flat without the beautiful service and music. Singing carols was one of her favorite traditions, and she loved singing them in chorus and with Joseph and his parents. A lifetime ago. The memory stabbed her heart. She could see his eyes the way he looked on her with love and made her feel so secure. But she'd better shake it off! No point dwelling on the past.

When Dirk walked over to her room, she greeted him nervously. Would he think celebrating Christmas was silly? Did he even believe in Jesus? They never spoke about religion.

They sat at her tiny table and enjoyed the simple meal. After dinner, he gave her a package, and she opened a pretty bracelet.

"Thank you, Dirk, it's beautiful. Since we've only been dating a few months, I wasn't sure what to get you, so I thought dinner would be my gift." She went to her tiny kitchenette to collect a tray. "And these date cookies." Before she turned back to him, he was behind her, encasing her in his arms and pulling her close. He nibbled on her neck and then sat down, pulling her onto his lap. "No problem. I don't have much of a sweet tooth. I figured you invited me in for something far more interesting."

After a bit of a struggle, his grasp on her lightened, and Helen stood up. "Let's not get carried away."

"That's exactly what we should do. Let's have a few drinks and get carried away."

"Sorry, Dirk. I'm not ready for that yet."

He stood and started to kiss her again. "I thought that's why you invited me to your room!"

She gently pulled away from him. "I'm sorry if I gave you the wrong impression. I wanted to celebrate Christmas."

"You sure have a funny way of celebrating!"

He left shortly after, and Helen was conflicted. She fancied him but didn't want to get entangled.

Helen and Dirk dated through the winter. Several times he became angry and grabbed Helen, threatening to hit her. She would shut him out, and then days later, he'd arrive with a piece of jewelry or flowers and apologize, promising to change his ways. Helen believed that people could change, so she never gave up hope that his temper would even out. Perhaps he, too, needed someone to show him more love. He certainly seemed in need of affection, as he couldn't keep his hands off Helen.

Dirk continued to shower her with gifts and attention. When he asked her to marry him that spring, Helen couldn't think of a reason to say no. Someone loved her, finally.

"Yes, I'll marry you," she hugged his broad shoulders when he presented her with a sparkling diamond. *Bigger than the one Joseph gave me. Now that we're getting married, he'll get his temper under control—no reason to be so jealous.*

"Let's not wait, Kitten, let's elope. I don't want to spend another night without you." He put the ring on her finger, pulled her close, and kissed her passionately. After a moment, Helen pulled back.

"Elope? When? And where?

"We can go to the courthouse Friday afternoon. Take the day off. Louise and Jimmy can stand up for us." He pulled her to him again and moved his hands up and down her spine.

"I always thought I'd get married in a church, Dirk." Dirk's caresses caused goosebumps to break out as she tingled from the sensations.

"You go to church?"

"Well, I know I haven't lately, but I keep meaning to find a church here."

"It takes months to find a church and a minister and all that. Let's just go to the courthouse. You can always find a church to attend later.

After we're settled." He kissed her in a way that told her the matter was settled.

She pulled back from his kiss and looked into his dark eyes. "I can't wait to call Mama."

"Why not call her after the wedding? She wouldn't be able to get here in time, and then you'd want to spend time with her." Dirk gave her his devilish grin. "Let's get out of town right after the wedding for a weekend honeymoon." He picked her up and spun her around.

She was breathless. "Honeymoon! I'll let you plan that. I need to find a dress."

"You've got plenty of nice dresses. Don't go to any expense. The honeymoon's the important part." He set her back on the sidewalk.

"But where will we live?"

"I found a house for rent not far from here."

"Already found a house? You were pretty confident I'd say yes."

"I was fairly certain you'd see things my way, yes."

"Didn't you think I'd want to see the house before you rented it?"

"No. It's just a house. What's not to like? If you said no, I'd move in and enjoy it until you came to your senses."

"I guess it's settled, then."

"It is. Get the time off work and ask Louise and Jimmy to come to the courthouse. That's it!"

Only five days until the wedding. At night she tossed and turned in bed, conflicted about a sudden marriage. Did they know each other well enough? She wanted to call Emily in Iowa to help her sort it out but didn't risk having her mother find out before the ceremony. Mama would likely try to talk her out of the wedding, and Helen wanted to make her own decisions to prove her independence.

Monday, at work, she ate lunch with Louise and flashed the ring for her reaction.

"Hot damn! That's quite a rock."

"Yes, rather extravagant."

"It's about time y'all got hitched!"

"About time? We've only been going together a few months."

"Enough time to know he's got the hots for you!"

"He wants to elope at the courthouse this Friday. Do you think you and Jimmy can stand up for us?"

"Sure, darlin'. I can knock off work early. It'll be our pleasure to see you two kids tie the knot."

Helen's forehead creased. "You do think I'm doing the right thing, don't you?"

Louise finished her lunch and reached in her bag for her nail file. "Helen, look what happened with that Iowa boy when y'all waited too long. Another sexy broad came along and snatched him. I say, 'strike while the iron's hot.' And that hunk is hot!"

"You're right. I worry too much. It's time to start living."

She pointed the file at Helen. "You know I love ya. But y'all are a bit of a fuddy-duddy. Probably from bein' from the farm and all."

"I can't look like a Fuddy-Duddy on Friday. Help me find a dress?"

"My pleasure. I'll have you looking like a red-hot mama."

"I was thinking something subdued but still stylish."

Louise leaned in. "Since it won't be in church, you don't have to worry about arousing the clergyman."

Helen burst out laughing. "Louise! Subdued."

The sun made a grand appearance on Friday, and Helen was glad she chose a lightweight suit for the ceremony. By the time of the late afternoon service, all of Austin would be steaming. She polished her nails, fixed her hair, and packed a sexy new nighty in her overnight bag.

Ready or not, by this time tomorrow, I'll be married.

They spoke their wedding vows in a flash, and it was over. Done. Married. Dirk invited Louise and Jimmy to have an early dinner with them before he and Helen headed out of town for the weekend.

Spending an entire weekend together made Helen realize how little they knew about each other. Conversations were stilted, and mealtimes were quiet. When she reached for his hand at dinner Saturday night, he smiled briefly but was preoccupied with the attractive waitress assisting them. A stab of jealously hit Helen. But she told herself he chose to marry her, so she shouldn't worry about other women.

Chapter 13

"I'm married, Mama! Dirk and I eloped. I'm Mrs. Betzini now. I didn't figure you could get here, so we just married at the Travis County courthouse."

"Married? When?" Cora collapsed onto the nearest kitchen chair.

"Last week. On a lovely April day."

"Oh, Helen, I'm so sorry I wasn't there."

"Me too, but I'll bring him home sometime soon."

"Yes, we're hoping to meet him. What did you wear?"

"A fitted cream-colored suit with a cream wool hat with a lace hatband."

"Sounds beautiful against your red hair."

"Thanks, Mama."

"Where are you two living?"

"Dirk found a little two-bedroom house to rent near work. He rented it before I said I'd marry him."

"Confident fella!"

"That's Dirk. Anyway, it's on a block with a row of houses. They're cute. Each one's painted a slightly different color, so I can tell which one is ours. They're all a stone's throw apart, so I'm hoping to meet some of the neighbors."

"That sounds lovely. I hope you find some other young couples. But Helen, why didn't you get married in a church?"

"We just didn't have time to book a church and a minister and all that."

"You're not….expecting, are you?"

"No, Mama! Why would you say that? Dirk was in a hurry to get married, and I thought, 'why not?' So, we did. He's so handsome. I can't wait for you to meet him."

"I'm looking forward to it."

Life was full of promise for Helen. She and Dirk enjoyed their evenings and weekends together, she continued to work at the Foxy Lady, and Dirk stayed with his factory job. Helen invited Louise and Jimmy to join them at the Fits and Starts Bar and Dance hall one Friday night.

Louise and Jimmy made it to the dance hall before them and already enjoyed a few drinks before Helen and Dirk arrived. Louise greeted them a bit too enthusiastically and then grabbed Dirk by the shirt front.

"Hey, cowboy, how 'bout if you and I dance tonight. Your little wife won't mind."

Her flirtatious moves rankled Helen, but Dirk was enjoying it, so Helen didn't say anything.

Finally, Jimmy took Helen's hand. "Well, Helen, how 'bout if I take you for a spin around the dance floor."

"Sure. What's good for the goose is good for the gander."

Jimmy wasn't as forceful a dancer as Dirk, but he guided Helen's lithe frame through the Lindy hop. As he swung Helen around, Dirk suddenly appeared and cut in. "No one dances with my wife but me."

Jimmy backed down. "I didn't mean nothin', Dirk. We were just having some fun."

Dirk grabbed Helen by the arm and pulled her out of the bar. She turned and shrugged at Louise as they made their exit. On the way home, Helen asked, "Why is it okay for you to dance with Louise, but not for me to dance with Jimmy? It was just an innocent dance."

"You're my wife, and Jimmy can keep his hands off you. That's it. It's not for you to question."

Helen kept quiet and turned her back to him when they went to bed.

Helen avoided Louise at work Monday. Louise found Helen sorting new blouses, and she picked up hangers to help. "Sorry I was flirting with Dirk at the bar. I thought if I could make Jimmy jealous, maybe he'd come up with a ring for me. Worked for you."

"I never purposely made Dirk jealous. You can have any man you want. If Jimmy doesn't want to get married, find someone else."

Helen stopped inviting Louise and Jimmy to join them on weekends, not wanting to rile Dirk's temper. She was careful not to speak to other men when they went out. Fear flattened the joy of dancing for her. She felt safer staying at home but also lonelier as her world shrunk.

One sunny Saturday, Helen bought flowers to plant in their front yard along the walkway. It felt so familiar to be spading black dirt. A young couple strolled by with a baby carriage. They stopped to introduce themselves, and Helen admired their little one.

"Who were you chatting with?" Dirk asked as Helen took off her straw hat and brushed the dirt off her knees.

"Mavis and Harry. They live next door and have the cutest baby. Let's invite them to come over and play cards with us some night."

"Why?" Dirk squinted his eyes and wrinkled his brow.

Helen kept her tone light."To be neighborly. To have someone to socialize with."

He took several steps toward her, and she craned her neck to look at him. "I don't need anyone else to socialize with, and neither do you."

Helen told herself he was just insecure, and things would change once he was sure of her love. She worked to make their home beautiful, sewing curtains, embroidering tea towels, and tatting lace doilies.

Nausea was her first clue that life would be changing. Helen could no longer choke down any breakfast before heading to work. And crushing fatigue finally sent her to the doctor.

A portly doctor with a kind face finished examining her. "Mrs. Betzini, congratulations. You're going to be a mother."

"Thank you! I was worried that I was sick, but this is such wonderful news."

He smiled. "Don't thank me. Take these vitamins and try to get more rest. Nausea should bet better in a month or so."

Helen was ecstatic at the thought of having a little one to love. She prepared a special dinner that night, and after they tasted a few bites, Helen burst out the news.

"Dirk, I have an exciting announcement. I went to the doctor today, and he said we're going to be parents."

"What? I never said I wanted to be a parent. How did you let this happen?"

"Me? Let this happen? It's OUR baby Dirk. Aren't you excited?"

"I never asked for some smelly, loud baby to disrupt my quiet."

Helen saw his bloodshot eyes and realized he must have been drinking on the way home from work. Certainly, when he sobered up, he'd understand what a blessing this baby is. She changed the subject quickly and placated him with a delicious dessert.

Dirk didn't mention the baby the next day or even the next month. Helen was afraid to broach the subject for fear of his reaction. But she longed to have him share in the anticipation for this new life.

As the baby developed inside, her stomach naturally swelled. One evening, as she was getting ready for bed, Dirk noticed her growing belly.

"I'm not sleeping with some pregnant lady!" he said. "You look fat!"

She thought he was kidding, but he stormed out. He came back hours later smelling of whiskey and perfume.

"Where have you been?" Helen demanded.

"Out looking for some fun. You're always sick, and now you're getting huge. I found a gal who looked a little more appealing." When he staggered toward her, she backed up with her hands balled in a fist behind her back.

Her eyes flashed furiously. "What? You were with another woman! How could you?"

"Get over it, Darlin. 'So what if I had a little fun?" He stepped toward her.

Rage replaced the fear she frequently felt. "Fun? Don't our vows mean anything to you? How dare you run around on me?" Cheeks flushed, her heart raced.

Dirk lurched forward and grabbed her by the shoulders. "Dare I? Don't you ever tell me what to do!" He threw her into a wall as if he was tossing a bag of garbage.

Helen crumpled into a ball of pain on the floor. Dirk walked out and slammed the door. Helen cried from the pain, humiliation, and the realization that he was not the man she thought he was. She stayed on the floor, wailing in near hysteria as her head pounded and her body ached.

Why doesn't he love me? Why doesn't anyone love me? She felt like her ten-year-old self crying alone in the attic when Mama was gone, and Grandma punished her harshly. There was no comfort and no one who cared about her. She was utterly alone.

She passed out on the floor. When she awoke hours later, she was lying in a pool of blood.

Helen went back to the doctor.

"I'm sorry, Mrs. Betzini, there's no heartbeat. You've lost the baby."

Helen bit her lips to keep from crying and looked away in shame.

"Did you have a fall?"

"Yes, I fell …down some stairs and hit my head."

The doctor nodded sympathetically. "Don't worry. You're young, and there's plenty of time to have a family."

Helen nodded and tried to smile.

Helen's senses were on high alert as she wondered when Dirk would reappear. Like a porcupine with quills raised and ready to fire, she jumped at every noise. Another argument like the last would certainly end their marriage. She took a few days off work to heal, but spending the days alone with her thoughts was torture. Part of her heart hoped he would come back and confess that he loved her, that he made a terrible mistake, and life would get back on an even keel. Certainly, he'd be sorry. But he was gone.

Chapter 14

"Hi, Mama."

"Helen, how are you, dear?"

"Okay, I guess."

"You sound tired. It must be the pregnancy. Are you getting enough sleep?"

"I- I'm not pregnant anymore. I lost the baby, Mama."

"I'm sorry to hear that, dear. What happened?"

"I fell, and I guess that caused it."

"Fell? Are you all right?"

"Yes, I'm just extremely disappointed."

"Of course you are. But many young ladies miscarry their first pregnancy, so please don't worry."

"That's what the doctor said."

"I'm so glad you went to the doctor. Did he say anything else?"

"No, just to get rest. I took a few days off work, but I can't stay at home alone forever."

"Alone? Isn't Dirk there?"

"Yes, I meant…alone during the day when he's at work."

"Well, please ask him to give you a big hug from me."

"I will. Thanks, Mama. I'd better go before I rack up a huge phone bill."

"So good to hear from you, dear."

Long-distance phone calls were always short because of the expense, and Helen suspected Dirk would hit the roof if he thought she'd told her mother too much. She desperately wanted to confide in her but couldn't bring herself to admit what was happening in her marriage.

She returned to work a few days later, and friends were sympathetic about the loss of her baby, although she told no one the truth of how it happened. "You're young. You have plenty of time to have more kids," everyone echoed the doctor as she bravely nodded. *But not this baby. This little one is gone forever.* The sadness penetrated her soul as the world moved in slow motion around her. She yearned for the tiny one who filled her with hope.

After working all day on her feet, she opened the front door, and Dirk was lounging in an overstuffed chair in the living room. Waiting for her. She gasped when she turned on the light, and their eyes met as she held her breath, wondering which Dirk arrived: the fun-loving, affectionate Dirk or the angry drunk who tramped all over her.

She was quickly relieved to see he was sober and calm. "Glad to see me?" He smiled suggestively.

Her eyebrows raised, but she said nothing.

"Sorry I messed up. Forgive me?" He remained seated. She stood speechless with one hand on the open front door, and the other instinctively covered her stomach. Was he kidding? Forgive him for betraying her, hurting her and their unborn baby?

When she said nothing, he quickly closed the distance between them. She held her breath and forced herself not to run or to show fear. He reached for the hand that held the door and gently pulled her toward him. He looked into her wary eyes.

"It was the booze, Helen. I'll stop drinking this time for good. Things'll be better."

She wanted to believe that. She also wanted someone to hold her, console her, and chase away the despair that wrapped itself around her head and heart.

Her blue eyes were clouded, her forehead was creased, and her lips twitched as she jutted her chin out defiantly. "I lost the baby." She needed him to know the consequences of his actions.

"Well, maybe it's too soon for us to have a baby." He reached into his pocket, took out a box, and opened it to offer her a jeweled necklace as a peace offering. She peered at it and looked away. Dirk pulled her closer and nuzzled her neck.

"Come on, Helen, you can't stay mad at me forever."

"I lost the baby." She repeated the words.

"Yeah, sorry, kiddo."

She may not stay mad, but she'd never completely trust him again. He slowly drew her back to him and even acted sorry that the baby died. But he took no responsibility for the death.

Helen was too embarrassed to tell her friends at work, or her mother, that her life was a sea-saw of emotion. Dirk promised to stop drinking, and for a while, he did, but the loss of the baby threw Helen into a deep, all-encompassing depression. With no one to confide in, she felt as if she was struggling to run underwater as she made her way through every day.

Helen wondered if Mama sensed that something was wrong when they spoke on the phone weeks later.

"Why don't you and Dirk take the train to Iowa for a few days? We'd love to meet him, and it'd be good for you to come back for a bit."

"Mama, you and Warren could come to Texas. Why don't you come south?"

"We will come and visit you sometime. But your grandmother is quite sick, and I think you should visit her."

"Why didn't you tell me about Grandma?"

"After you lost the baby, I thought you had enough on your mind. I don't know how much longer Grandma will hang on, and I know she'd like to see you."

"I don't know about that, but I'd like to see you and Grandpa."

She approached Dirk cautiously with her suggestion. "My Grandmother isn't well, and I'd like to go back to Iowa to see her."

"I thought you hated the old bitty."

"No, I didn't hate her. She was a difficult woman, but she mostly raised me, and I'd like to see her before she passes. And I miss my Mama. Don't you want to meet her?"

"Not really, but if you want to, I guess we can go for a few days."

"I think a trip will be good for us."

"Us? Maybe for you."

Mama and Warren met them at the train depot on a sunny spring morning, and Dirk was on his best behavior, polite and sober.

The cool air was a soothing balm for Helen, and as they drove to Greenberg to see her grandparents, she gazed out at farm fields, eager for sightings of new calves and colts. Helen was the first in the door, and the sight of Grandma took her breath away. Instead of stomping around the kitchen, Grandma Gertrude was slumped on the couch, her body shrunk, her feet in slippers. One side of her face drooped, and a tremor kept her hands in perpetual motion.

Helen was shocked. Gone was the woman who dominated their lives, and in her shell was a frail person who couldn't remember what she ate for breakfast or what day it was. But she hadn't forgotten Helen and was pleased to see her and to meet her new husband. Dirk was visibly uncomfortable with the cozy reunion and insisted on standing in the corner after the others found seats in the living room. As usual, the initial conversation revolved around the weather and their train ride to Iowa. Until a shrill siren sounded.

"What the devil?" An agitated Dirk looked outside to see what was causing the noise.

Helen laughed. "It's the noon whistle. Time for lunch."

"Noon whistle? People can't tell time here?" Dirk's tone was harsh.

Helen smiled at Dirk and tried to contain his growing irritation. "Yes, of course they can, but the whistles sound so the factory workers can stop for lunch."

"So does everyone in the town have to stop for lunch at the same time?'

Cora smiled at Dirk. "It's just a reminder, not a mandatory thing. But every time I hear the siren, it makes me hungry. Who wants lunch?"

After a simple lunch, Grandma turned to Helen. "I have something for you, child. It's in the top drawer of my dresser."

Helen got up from the kitchen and went into her grandparent's bedroom, opened the dresser drawer, and gasped at the sight of the tiny green cape she sewed for her doll so many years ago.

"I thought you must have thrown this away when it disappeared from the attic," Helen said.

"I was so angry when I found you'd taken that old piano cover without askin' me. I went to yer attic den and saw what ya did with it. I took it off yer doll cuz I wanted ta teach ya that it was wrong. But I never spanked ya 'cause ya did such a good job makin' it."

"I kept waiting for you to get angry with me. For days I shuddered every time you said my name."

"I know. That was yer punishment. To keep ya on edge so's you'd know ya did the wrong thing. But I was proud of yer handiwork. Yer stitches were so perfect, I jist decided to keep it. Now ya can have it back."

Helen was flabbergasted. This was the kindest thing Grandma ever said to her. "Thank you! If I ever have a daughter, I'll give this to her."

"Well, don't let her play with it 'til she's old enough not ta ruin it!"

"Yes, Grandma," Helen said, hiding her misty eyes. The bossy Grandma was still inside, but her compliment was a life-affirming gift.

"Dirk, I made this when I was just ten!" She brought it over for him to admire.

He looked at it briefly and handed it back to her. "That's nice, Helen." He gave a half-smile and looked around the room.

"I got somethin' else fer ya," Grandma said. "Look in my bottom dresser drawer."

Helen went to it and found the wine-colored piano cover and brought it to her. "This?"

"Yes, child. I want ya ta have it. Maybe someday you'll have a piano of yer own."

Helen's eyes were moist. She and Grandma loved beautiful fabrics and handiwork, and the piano cover was both. She held it to her face and recalled watching Grandma barter for it with the gypsy women who came to the door when she was a child. A lifetime ago. This was a connection to the Grandma she wanted to hang onto, not the side of her overshadowed by her anger at being saddled with a child.

After the long train ride back to Austin, life simmered into a routine of work and home. She started to feel settled, even safe, most days and began to heal emotionally

Dirk remained sober and polite for several months. Helen felt the worst was over for them. Marriage must be changing him, making him more steady. They even went dancing again on Saturday nights, although she was careful not to speak to other men.

Spring was always a time of hope for her, and even though it arrived sooner and with more intense warmth than the Iowa springs, she was happy to see the changes. She planted a little garden and spruced up the front walkway with flowers. The depression was lifting. When Dirk was gone, she enjoyed casual conversations with other neighbors, especially Mavis. Watching Mavis's little one grow increased the longing for a child of her own. But after the miscarriage, Helen wasn't sure she'd be able to have a baby.

At work, racks of colorful cotton dresses and floppy straw hats filled the Foxy Lady, brightening moods in the hope of a carefree summer. Helen and Louise rekindled their friendship, enjoying lunch together, keeping topics light. She didn't invite Louise to join them dancing but was happy for her companionship while working.

As summer wore on and the heat increased, she found more time to relax and work on embroidery and other needlecrafts she learned from

Grandma Gertrude, tatting doilies to dress up chairs, crocheting tea cozies and pot holders. At first, she blamed the heat for her morning nausea, but a trip to the doctor confirmed she was again carrying a child.

"Congratulations again, Mrs. Betzini. You should have a little one in your arms by next February or March."

Helen was elated. "That's such good news. Do you think I'll be able to carry this one?"

"I see no reason why not. Stay healthy and get lots of rest."

The doctor's words were a comfort, but now she needed to figure out how to break the news to Dirk, who may see this as an imposition. She decided not to tell him until she absolutely had to.

One hot September afternoon, Helen wearily opened the front door after work to find Dirk drunk and in a rage. The living room was in shambles, with lamps overturned and knick-knacks crushed on the floor. Helen's heart pulsed in her head, face flushed, and she thought of running but didn't. She felt she needed to make this relationship work now more than ever.

She took a breath and asked calmly. "Dirk, what's happening?"

"Well, darlin', I got fired today! The foreman's always had it in for me. I got in an argument with one of the guys who was being a complete jerk. He came at me, and I punched him in self-defense, but I'm the one who got fired."

Helen kept her distance but tried to offer reassurance. "You'll find another job, Dirk. I know you will."

You've got to.

"Oh, you know that, do you? You don't know nothin,'" he said as he glared at her. He took a few steps toward her, and Helen instinctively backed away. "I'm going out," he said, pushing past her and slammed the front door.

She let out the breath she didn't realize she was holding and steadied herself against the wall. Argument averted – at least for now. She paced the floors, wondering what to do. With all her heart, she wanted to run, but she took vows to stand by him, "for better or worse." *This is what that means, right? Stay with him, help him.*

Now certainly wasn't the right time to tell him she was pregnant again. After her last pregnancy, when would be the right time? *Certainly, after he sees a child of his own, he'll become attached.*

Just like my father was attached to me, she thought bitterly. I wonder what kind of a father Joseph would have made. The flash of Joseph's face jolted her back. *Forget him. He's out of your life.*

She pretended to be asleep when Dirk dragged himself in after the bars closed. She was afraid the sound of her heart pounding would tip him off, but he stumbled into bed and fell into a drunken stupor. Relief. Hopefully, she would leave for work before he awoke.

In the morning, she tiptoed through the house to get off to work without any trouble, skipping breakfast, which she was too nauseous to eat anyway. She hurried out the door and closed it without a sound. She relaxed a bit when she reached the Foxy Lady, but fear was never far from her all day. *Will he show up at the store and make a scene? What would my friends think if they discovered what was going on at home?*

Chapter 15

Days turned into weeks as she lived in fear and tried to keep conversations light while gently encouraging Dirk to look for work. She turned a blind eye to his nightly trips to the bar. *At least he's out of the house and won't notice my growing stomach.* After nearly two months of unemployment, Dirk surprised her by coming to the hat counter at the Foxy Lady. Her gathered dress concealed her bulging stomach.

"Well, you're lookin' fine, Kitten! Can I take you to lunch?"

He was clean-shaven, showered, and sober. His smoky eyes usually made her melt, but no more, as she cautiously agreed to lunch.

"I have news," he said as they sat at a nearby café and ordered sandwiches. "I've found me another job at a factory. A buddy of mine gave me a tip, and I went to see them today, and they offered me a job. I start Monday. Pay's about the same."

"That's wonderful, Dirk. I'm happy for you," Helen reached for his strong hand. The warmth was comforting, and seeing him smiling again made the knot inside her relax a bit. *Is this the charming man I married? Is he finding his way back to me?*

His sloppy joe sandwich arrived, along with her BLT, and they enjoyed the first bites as she wondered whether to share the news of her pregnancy. Dirk finally looked up.

"I'm sorry I was a bear these past few months. Things will be better now that I'm working again."

Helen smiled at him and nodded. He was in a good mood – and they were in public. She took a chance on the timing.

"As long as we're sharing news, I have something to tell you."

Dirk looked at her. "News? What news? Is this about your grandmother?"

"No, this is happy news. We're expecting again."

He sucked in his breath, and she smiled, hoping he'd be pleased. "Dirk, you're going to be a Daddy."

Dirk sat back from the table and stiffened his back. "I see. Are you sure the baby's mine? It's not like we've been together much lately, if you know what I mean."

She was insulted by the verbal blow but kept her temper in check. "Of course, the baby's yours. I would never cheat on you."

"When's it coming?"

"March. I'm about five months along."

"Five months, eh? You kept that one a secret."

She kept her tone light and tried to smile at him. "Just looking for the right time to tell you. I'm hoping this baby will bring us both a lot of joy."

"We can hope. Anyway, nothin' can spoil my good mood today. I've got me a job again."

Dirk started working again and kept his drinking to a minimum during the workweeks. Helen tried to focus on a healthy pregnancy without any major problems from Dirk.

"Merry Christmas, Mama."

"Merry Christmas to you, Helen. I hope you and Dirk got our packages."

"We did, and thank you. But I have some other good news."

"What's that?"

"I'm expecting again! Due in March."

"Congratulations, that's wonderful news. March! Right after your twenty-first birthday! Why didn't you tell me sooner?"

"Sorry, Mama. After the last miscarriage, I wanted to wait to be certain I'd be able to carry this one to term. Any chance you can come for the birth?"

"I'd love to, but Grandma isn't doing well, and I'm afraid to leave. I'm sure they have capable doctors and nurses in Texas. You'll be in good hands."

The pains started at work one spring day. Louise drove her to the hospital. How she longed for her midwife mother, but she was too far away to help. Louise called Dirk at his factory and told him the baby was coming.

"They won't let me into the room anyway, so I might as well enjoy myself while I wait for the news," he told Louise on the phone, and he headed to the bar after work.

Helen's labor was agonizing and lengthy. Finally, near morning, her little girl was born. They placed her in Helen's arms, and she kissed her face over and over, then checked for ten fingers and toes. "Someone I can love who'll love me back. I'll treasure you always," she whispered into the infant's ear as she nuzzled her close.

"Can I get your husband from the waiting room?" a nurse asked Helen.

"Yes, please do." She doubted he was there, but she wanted to picture Dirk asleep on a hard plastic chair in the men's waiting room. She asked nurses to check to see if a man was waiting in the father's room through the night. There was, but he was the wrong father. No one was there for her, but she hoped he might have arrived by now.

"I'm sorry, he must have slipped out for a bit," the nurse told her. She'd just come on duty and didn't realize Helen's husband hadn't bothered to come and see his newborn.

"Of course," Helen said. But secretly, she wondered if he'd abandon her.

Dirk took his time getting to the hospital later that morning. He stopped to buy flowers as a peace offering.

"So, what did you have?" he asked, standing at the door of her room. The light from her window was too much for his bloodshot eyes.

"*We* have a little girl," she said. "Where were you last night?"

"Out celebrating, of course." He gave a weak smile.

A nurse interrupted them. "Helen, may we bring your baby in?"

"I'd love that," she told her. Then to Dirk, she said hopefully, "You can meet her now."

The baby was brought in swaddled in a pink blanket, smelling of lotion. "Come and hold her, Dirk. Isn't she beautiful?"

As he came closer, he reeked of whiskey from the night before. Helen held her tongue, desperately hoping he would bond with their baby.

Dirk reached out awkwardly and held her. "What's her name?"

"I thought we should find a name together. What would you like to call her?"

"You pick. Whatever you name her is fine with me." He held her awkwardly at arm's length, but Helen remained hopeful.

"How about Bonnie Ann? I had a teacher in high school who was important to me. Her name was Bonnie, and Ann is my mother's middle name."

"Sure, Bonnie Ann sounds fine. Here - take her back." He handed her off like a football being passed. "Well, enjoy your baby." He left in a hurry.

Helen snuggled her tiny one and kissed her head. Bonnie grasped Helen's pinky finger. "You can count on me. I'll always be there for you." The joy of motherhood was tempered with the knot in the pit of her stomach. The knot that was her marriage. She believed that marriage was forever, even though her parent's marriage wasn't. When do you know forever isn't possible?

After several days in the hospital, Dirk brought Helen and Bonnie home. He visited a few times but wasn't interested in holding Bonnie Ann for more than a moment. The heaviness of the March day clouded Helen's mind, and the bitter wind chased all joy from her heart. But now that she was home, she could share her news with Mama.

"I have a little girl, Mama! I, er we named her Bonnie Ann."

"Congratulations! That's beautiful. What a wonderful blessing."

"Yes, but I wish you were here."

"Were there complications?"

"No, just a long and painful night."

"I'm sorry, dear. But it sounds as if everything turned out fine."

"Yes, Bonnie's fine, but Dirk's not interested in her."

"Some men aren't interested in babies until they're bigger and can respond to them more. Be patient."

"I'll try. I'd better not rack up a phone bill. Bye, Mama."

Helen was cheered momentarily speaking to her mother, but the days and weeks slowed to a crawl as she danced between Bonnie's needs and Dirk's moodiness. When the phone rang a few weeks later, she was delighted to hear her mother's voice again.

"Hello, dear! How's little Bonnie?"

"Mama! It's so good to hear from you. Bonnie's doing pretty well – nursing and putting on a bit of weight."

"And how about you?"

"I'm exhausted from the nightly feedings, but I do love her so much."

"Of course you do! So how is Dirk adjusting to fatherhood?"

"He seems so agitated when she cries. Especially at night. Most nights, I sleep in a chair in her room so she won't wake him."

"Get your rest, child. Birthing takes a lot out of a woman, and you need time to recover. Not just a few weeks, but months."

"Mama, ever the nurse. I'm so tired most of the time, I feel like I'm in a fog."

"Ah, the baby blues. Hopefully, it'll pass if you get more sleep."

"I wish you were closer. You have so much experience with babies, and I have none."

"You'll be a great mother, but I do ache to hold Bonnie. Any chance you can come for a visit in a few months?"

"Oh, I'd love that. Maybe we could drive out in the country to see farms in the spring with all the baby animals grazing on the hills. I even missed the snow this year."

"You're more than tired. You're delusional!" Mama teased her. "Truthfully, I do enjoy a fresh coating of snow. Right now, most of it has melted, and the snow crocus are popping their heads out. Any chance Dirk would consider moving to Iowa? I'd love to be able to see you and Bonnie more."

"I didn't think I wanted to move back, but having a baby has changed my heart."

"I'm glad to hear that. But, Helen, I know this is terrible timing, but I do need to tell you something."

"Is it Grandma?"

"Yes, dear. She passed away last night in her sleep. It's too soon for you to travel, but I wanted to let you know what happened."

"I'm sorry, Mama. I know you loved her."

"And she loved you, in her way. I know she could be difficult, but I couldn't have survived without her."

"What will Grandpa do?"

"He'll soldier on. He's still in good health and has always worked hard, so I think he'll be okay for a while in his house. I'll bring casseroles over for him."

"You sound like you have it all planned out. Shouldn't you be in a state of shock?"

"I'm still absorbing the shock in my own way. Grandma has been sick for a long time, and as a nurse, I have more experience with life and death. I hope you allow yourself time to grieve, Helen, even if you aren't here. Take some time to recollect her good qualities and pray for her soul."

On a beautiful, warm spring Sunday, Helen and Dirk were eating grilled cheese sandwiches and tomato soup for lunch on their modest patio, while Bonnie blissfully slept in a bassinette in the shade nearby. There was little conversation between them, but the silence was companionable. Helen popped into the kitchen when they finished, brought out a warm apple crisp, and served Dirk a generous portion. The scent of cinnamon and sweet apples usually made him smile, and he was in a reasonably good mood, so Helen broached what was on her heart.

"I was thinking about growing up on the farm the other day, and I miss it."

"Miss it? I thought you hated the farm!" Dirk shoveled a heaping spoonful of apples in his mouth.

"I hated being so lonely all the time, but I loved the animals and watching the earth change through four seasons every year."

"Four seasons. Ha! You mean early winter, mid-winter, bitter winter, and a month of summer?" Dirk laughed.

She smiled. "Winter's not that bad. There's beauty and rhythm to life in Iowa."

"So much beauty y'all couldn't wait to get outta there."

"Now that Grandma Gertrude's gone, Grandpa's alone. I'd like to be closer to help him." As she spoke, Dirk made quick work of the dessert.

"Well, you'll never get me to live up north. I can't stand the cold, and I'm sure not going to move to a God-forsaken place that has snow half the year."

"Not half the year, more like a quarter of it."

"Forget it, Helen. The answer is NO." Dirk slammed his hand on the table as he stood, and his metal chair tipped over backward. The racket woke Bonnie, who started wailing.

Helen sighed but stayed seated and took another bite of the sweet apples.

"Well, aren't you going to get your baby?"

"She's our baby, and yes, I'll get her. I just wanted to give her a moment to see if she'll go back to sleep."

"Pick her up. I can't stand all that crying. And clean this dump! You're home all day. The least you can do is keep the house neat."

He stormed into the house while Helen collected Bonnie and brought her inside to nurse and rock her. When she tiptoed into the living room after putting her back to sleep, Dirk was gone.

Chapter 16

Figures. Not even a note. Just gone. She was relieved. Now she could enjoy Sunday afternoon in peace. When had things gotten this bad? *What wife is happier when her husband is out? And what condition will he be in when he finally comes home? This can't be the way marriage is supposed to work. Sundays used to be a day of fun when we were first together. It wasn't just Bonnie that's changed things between us, his drinking and jealousy were the first markers that life was off-kilter. Why hadn't I listened to the warnings inside me?*

Helen never experienced deep, lasting happiness, and she wasn't sure she could identify the feeling. Were Grandma and Grandpa ever happy? They went to church together every Sunday, but there were never signs of affection between them. What about Mama and Warren? Yes, they appeared happy, but she was rarely around them for long. How does it work on a daily basis?

Maybe happiness is too big a goal. I'd settle for not living in fear. Did she have the strength to make a change on her own, and was it wrong to leave someone you no longer loved? Could she actually escape without a death sentence?

Who could she confide in? Certainly not her childhood friend, Emily. What would she think of her now if Helen confessed how her life careened out of control?

Taking care of the baby was rewarding but also isolating, and she felt imprisoned by her marriage. When she told her manager at the Foxy Lady she'd be staying home with her new baby and not returning to work, he suggested she work on Saturdays. She was excited about the idea, but Dirk was not, saying there was no way he would watch "her baby." On her low wages, it didn't make sense to hire a sitter. As much as she loved Bonnie, conversations with her were a few years away, and Helen longed for the camaraderie from the clerks at the store.

Perhaps a visit over coffee would ease her loneliness. Helen called Louise and invited her over for coffee while Dirk was gone. A rush of excitement washed over her as she brushed her hair and put on a fresh blouse and a touch of lipstick before Louise arrived that afternoon.

Helen grabbed the door before the doorbell awakened Bonnie. "Louise? How are you?"

"Hi-de-ho, darlin'! Haven't seen you in a month a Sundays."

Helen invited her into the modest living room where vertical blinds, only partly open, cast bars of light onto the sofa. Helen dashed into the kitchen and brought out two cups of coffee and a plate of lemon gingersnaps.

"Y'all look beat, if you don't mind my sayin 'so."Motherhood is exhausting, but I adore her."

"Is that why y'all aren't back at work? That baby takin 'all your time?"

"Well, Bonnie's part of it. Along with the housework, laundry, and cooking for Dirk."

"How is that dreamboat of yours?"

Helen looked away. "He's fine…I guess."

Louise punctuated her words with a cookie. "I hope you're keeping him happy, if you know what I mean. Such a fine specimen. Better be careful, or another woman will get her paws on him." A sparkle flashed as a bar of light from the afternoon sunshine bounced off her hand.

Helen reached for her. "Louise, did you and Jimmy get engaged?"

"No, silly, I threw him over. Found myself a sugar daddy. Take a gander at this rock."

"Wow! It's beautiful! But what happened to Jimmy?"

"I realized he'd never be able to provide for me in the way that I deserve. Don't get me wrong, your little house is sweet and all, but I want the finer things in life. I just wasn't willing to settle for less."

"So, what's his name?"

"Roberto Bernardi. As soon as his divorce is final, we're going to tie the knot."

"He's married?"

"Yes, for the moment. His kids are nearly grown, so I won't have to deal with children."

"Grown? Louise, how old is he?"

"Forty-seven. He owns the fancy Italian restaurant in town, Mama in Cucina. It means Mama's in the kitchen! But they won't get me in that kitchen!"

"But… he's old enough to be your father!"

She giggled and admired her ring. "Don't be such a fuddy-duddy!"

"What do your parents think about him?"

"My parents! Why would I tell them? We'll probably just go to the Justice of Peace the way you did. Your marriage worked out fine, so I'm sure ours will too."

"Yes, well, I hope so."

"Must be off. I have a manicure scheduled for this afternoon. Get some shut-eye, darlin'! Don't want to show Dirk those dark circles."

Helen shut the door and wondered how they'd ever been friends. Their conversation did nothing to ease her worries.

When Bonnie was about two months old, Helen was looking forward to the weekend. Dirk was still at work, but he was happier lately, and since it was his birthday, she made a cake, popped it in the oven, and marinated a steak, ready to grill. A rare treat. Perhaps she wasn't trying hard enough to make their marriage work. Maybe Louise was right. What man would love her with circles under her eyes and baby drool on her blouse? She hoped a birthday celebration would bridge the divide. He still wasn't interested in Helen physically, but she was too tired to return affection anyway and was glad he wasn't pushing intimacy. He was humming that morning in the shower and was pleasant at breakfast, but she didn't dare comment on it. If she tiptoed around the landmines of his moods, maybe things would improve, and she wouldn't feel so trapped.

All the windows were open to encourage the breeze to cool her home from the warmth of the oven. While Bonnie napped, there was a knock on the door from the Western Union delivery man.

"Telegram for you, Ma'am. Sign here."

Her hands shook as she closed the door and opened the telegram. Had something happened to Mama? She read:

"Karen, meet me at San Marcos Main St. Hotel. Room booked for the weekend. Love, Dirk."

Karen? Her mind was still in a fog as she slowly realized the telegram was delivered to the wrong address. They brought it to the "sender" instead of the person he meant to receive it. Karen – whoever she was.

She slumped onto a living room chair. *That explains his happiness these past few weeks - he's met someone else. Someone who isn't tired from nursing a baby in the middle of the night and who doesn't jump every time he comes near. Someone lovable.*

She could hear her Grandmother telling her that she never wanted to have her around. Then her mother explaining that her father hadn't wanted her and left her behind. She replayed the phone call from Joseph all those years ago saying that he found someone else. Joseph. The one she thought was the love of her life. And even he abandoned her. She sat trancelike, taking in her new reality.

What have I done to deserve this? Wasn't I a faithful and patient wife? Didn't I work until I was ready to deliver and still did all the cooking and cleaning? Why doesn't he love me? Why didn't Joseph love me?

Too embarrassed to tell Mama or friends the truth, her world shrunk as Dirk mentally and physically backed her into a corner like a frightened animal. Much like the attic corner of her youth, only now she had someone else to consider. She sat, and energy began to course through her as she formulated a plan.

I'm not going to wait for more pain and humiliation. I'll leave him.

Money! She needed cash to get away once and for all and was grateful her frugal grandmother taught her to squirrel it away. She turned off the oven and left the cake to rot while she searched the house. An old cookie jar, socks in her top drawer, and dollar bills stuffed inside the toe of a shoe yielded a tidy sum. In the back of her top dresser drawer, her hands landed on the tiny locket Joseph gave her when they were first dating. Why had she kept it? She opened it and gazed at their picture, then tucked it into her suitcase, not able to part with it, even though she knew they had no future together. She thought of how naïve she had been and how hopeful. Would she ever feel that optimistic again?

No time to waste, she opened Dirk's dresser drawers, digging to find whatever money he might have stashed. Her hands shook just to look inside his things. She thought about how he guarded his possessions and his privacy. Now she understood why he did it. He was leading a double life. *Well, no more. Today the misery ends. My sentence is up, and I'm breaking out.*

The local bus company told her the next ride to Iowa was Saturday morning at ten. Since Dirk now planned to go straight to San Marcos for his affair and wouldn't be home overnight, she figured she was safe waiting out the night.

She dragged her suitcase out from the closet and set it on the bed, then hurriedly went through her dresser to choose what would fit in the lone bag. Necessities only and warm clothing. She'd sell the jewelry he'd used to lure her back each time he strayed. She added Bonnie's things and the tiny hooded cape she made many years ago from Grandma Gertrude's old piano cover. She held it to her nose and breathed in the faint scent of the farmhouse. She turned it over and over in her hands, admiring the tiny stitches. *I made this.* Where was that girl who made this delicate cape with the perfect stitches? That lonely little ten-year-old who hid for hours from a grandmother who made it clear she didn't want her around. As she pondered her pain, she sat on the bed she shared with the man who was more of a jailer than a lover.

She hadn't grieved for Grandma Gertrude, and her conflicted feelings remained bottled inside her. Deep down, Grandma must have cared for her. She took the time to teach her to sew, embroider, crochet, and do other needlecrafts. *Grandma said she was proud of me for doing such a good job making this cape, even if I took the old fabric without her permission. The kindest thing she ever said to me.*

  Mama, where are you? I'm in trouble. She longed to hear words of comfort. Tears threatened to spill, but she pushed them back. *Be strong, Helen. Now is not the time to grieve. Get packed.* Fear propelled her as she leaped up to gather more clothes and finish packing. Inside the closet, she didn't hear him come in.

Chapter 17

Dirk saw the suitcase, clenched his teeth, and growled at her. "Just what the hell do you think you're doing?"

"I think I'm the one who should be asking questions," she replied as she moved out of the closet toward an open window. "Who is Karen?"

"What? What crazy idea are you talking about now?"

She whipped the telegram out of her pocket, and he grabbed it from her hands.

"Karen is none of your business."

"None of my business? We're married. Your business is my business." She kept her voice under control, but her insides were shaking. Confrontations never ended well.

"Not where Karen's concerned." His voice escalated.

Edging toward the door, she tried to escape, but he blocked her.

"So, you admit you're going away with her this weekend?" Part of her still hoped it was a misunderstanding.

"I don't have to admit anything." He came closer to tower over her, and the scent of whiskey wafted in the air. "Looks like you're the one who is planning a weekend affair." He sneered at her, grabbed her suitcase, and threw it across the room, spilling the contents.

She stepped away from him. "I'm leaving you. I've suffered enough of your abuse." She didn't realize she was shouting, but at this point, she didn't care who found out. So what if the neighbors heard them through the open windows? There was no point keeping this broken marriage a secret any longer. Could she reach the phone on her nightstand? He saw her glance at it and snatched it, and threw it across the room.

"You've had enough. What about me? I told you I never wanted to sleep with a pregnant lady, and you kept getting pregnant. Now we've got this damn baby crying at all hours!" He grabbed her and slammed her into the wall, and she cried out from the pain but stood her ground.

"Damn baby? How dare you? Bonnie's our child, and she deserves to be loved."

"Well, I didn't ask for a baby, and I never wanted to be a father."

The shouting awakened the sleeping infant in the next room.

"That was pretty obvious, but don't worry, Bonnie doesn't need a drunk for a father." Her face burned, and her heart pounded in fear and rage.

"So that's what you think of me. A drunk, huh?" A vein popped out on Dirk's forehead as he grabbed her by the shoulders and shook her.

"Let go of me! I need to get my baby." She hollered.

He did, but only for a moment. Dirk snatched the BlackJack nightstick that he kept by his bed in case of burglars and swung at her. She ducked, but as his anger escalated and his eyes got wilder, he swung again, and Helen screamed while Bonnie shrieked from the racket.

"Help, please help me," she called toward a window. She tried to get out of the bedroom, but he pinned her in a corner, like a cowering animal. When he swung the steel stick, she could only turn and the rod connected with her shoulder. "OWWWW. Help me, please."

"No one's going to rescue you! There's no point screaming. No one loves you, and no one ever will." She could smell the alcohol on his breath as he stooped to shout in her face. His pupils were dark, his eyes wide with a maniacal stare.

Despite the intense pain in her shoulder, she kept fighting him and screaming for help. Since she couldn't get around him, she sunk onto the floor, hoping to crawl away, but wasn't fast enough. He swung again and, this time, struck the side of her head. Blood gushed out. *I can't bleed to death. My baby needs me. Please, God, help me.* As Bonnie continued to scream from her nursery, Helen was out of options and feared he'd kill her baby next.

She felt dizzy from the loss of blood and shock from the pain but begged Dirk again. "Please, just let me go! I need to get our baby!"

But the alcohol-stoked rage only intensified his anger. "You want me to let you go, huh?"

"Yes, please. My baby needs me."

"Baby! I told you I never wanted children, but you just had to have your way!" His nostrils flared, and he bared his teeth.

"She's your baby too, Dirk! Please stop this!"

"Stop saying that! After I finish you off, I'm going to take care of her next."

Helen shrieked again with what little strength she could muster. "Help! Please, someone. Help me."

Dirk was in a sort of trance. He raised his nightstick again to hit her, and she feared he'd kill her with the next strike. Her hands covered her head, hoping to minimize more damage. Suddenly there was noise from the other rooms.

"Stop! Police!" Two burly officers burst into the house and quickly found the bedroom where Helen crouched on the floor. "Drop it! Don't move!"

Dirk threatened to hit Helen again, but one officer grabbed his arm and wrestled the nightstick out of his hands while the other officer cocked his gun trained on Dirk. "Call an ambulance when you get the cuffs on."

Bonnie screamed from all the commotion.

"Have you got anyone to look after your baby?"

Helen could barely speak. "Yes, Mavis is next door to the East. Please bring her to me now, though."

The officer retrieved Bonnie and gingerly put her in Helen's arms to comfort her tiny one. The police waited until an ambulance arrived to take Helen to the hospital.

Mavis came to get Bonnie and looked around in disbelief. "I didn't know what was happening, but I called the cops. Thank goodness they got here in time."

"Thank you, Mavis."

"I should have come over, but I was afraid he'd kill me too," she whispered to Helen.

Dirk overheard as he was led out of the room and spit at Mavis. "I'd gladly kill you too."

One of the cops grabbed Dirk and led him toward the squad car. "That's enough! You've done enough damage."

As they were loading Helen onto a stretcher, the first officer approached her. "Do you want to press charges, Mrs. Betzini?"

Helen glared at Dirk. "Yes, I sure do! Please keep him away from my baby and me."

"Let's go, mister, you're under arrest," the officer said as they pushed Dirk into the waiting patrol car. But as they did, he shouted at Helen, "I'll never forgive you! This isn't over!"

"Hey! That's enough! This may not be over. If she dies, it'll be murder."

Murder? Helen wondered. Would she make it through the night?

Helen gasped as she bolted upright. Get up! Get out! Last night's terrifying nightmare roared through her mind. The confrontation, stitches, and his arrest. She tried to stand, but the room spun, and her head ached. Crows outside egged her on. Get up! Get out! They echoed the frantic voice in her head. Hurry! Escape before Dirk bails out of jail. If only there'd been a bus heading north last night.

The night before, Helen took a cab home from the hospital after they stitched the wound in her head. She collected her infant and fearfully approached her house. Her hand shook on the doorknob as she wondered if he'd be waiting for her. But that was ridiculous. Dirk was in jail. Wasn't he? How long could they keep him?

The aroma of something sweet wafted toward her as she wondered if someone was cooking. She stopped. What was that smell? Oh yes, the half-baked cake she left in the oven. Half-baked, like their marriage. A bitter irony.

Once inside, she surveyed the rooms, bolted the door, and settled Bonnie into her crib. Picking up the clothes Dirk threw all over their bedroom made her dizzy, but she pressed on. She finished packing, set an alarm, and collapsed for a few blessed hours, praying for protection as she fell into a fitful sleep.

Now, upon waking, every muscle ached, but she pushed through the pain. Her mirrored reflection revealed the bald spot where they shaved her hair to sew her skull. Shaky hands dabbed makeup over the dark spots on her cheek. She dressed in a skirt long enough to hide the purple splotches on her legs and a blouse with long sleeves—no need to arouse pity or curiosity.

She dashed into the nursery, reached into the wooden crib, and her head spun again. Helen steadied herself before she scooped up her sleeping infant. Pain shot through her shoulders from the assault with the nightstick, but she was tough, and she was alive. A lifetime of anguish prepared her to be strong.

"Wake up, little one," she coaxed, stroking silky cheeks. She nursed Bonnie, then dressed her and, balancing her on one shoulder, picked up the heavy black phone, and called her neighbor.

"He's on the way, baby girl." Her head throbbed, but she tugged on a felt hat to hide the stitches. And her pride. She was breaking out of this prison and hoped she never had to face Dirk again. She was shocked her marriage was ending but also apprehensive about her future. No time to think about it as she wrapped Bonnie in a soft pink flannel blanket, tied a white bonnet on her, and grabbed the diaper bag, purse, and small suitcase. Everything else she left behind. As she waited for her ride and walked from room to room, she realized there were few happy memories from the brief time she lived in Dirk's house. He had chosen it, practically imprisoned her in it, and nearly killed her. Once she escaped, she never wanted to be detained there again.

Helen and Bonnie were first on the bus. She chose the last bench in the back to keep an eye out. Her nerves were firing. *Please start this bus, please start this bus, we've got to get out of here*, she silently prayed. Bonnie was oblivious to the danger that might descend at any moment. Would he bond out of jail this early? Would Dirk have time to get his gun? Her insides quivered at the thought of what he nearly did last night. And might still be planning to do today. How could he hate her that much? Wasn't she a faithful wife who tried to make him happy?

Look alive, Helen! Keep watching. It felt like an eternity waiting for the scheduled departure. Other passengers filed on, filling seats. Her eyes darted from them to the window. She fussed with Bonnie's hat to shield her from the bright Texas sun pouring through the East window. They were heading North – to a new but uncertain life.

Helen continually scanned the street below. And then she spotted him, and her heart nearly stopped.

Chapter 18

He was racing frantically toward the bus, and she gasped as their eyes met through the window. Her stomach soured, pulse raced. His dark brown eyes were fierce, his jaw visibly clenched. How had she ever loved him? Trusted him? Was she so desperate for someone to love her? She pushed Bonnie further on her lap to shield her from whatever was about to happen while trying to steady her breathing.

Dirk charged onto the bus and stormed back to the last row, his cowboy boots thundering noisily. The stubble on his chin and dark circles under his eyes added to his menacing appearance. The night in jail only stoked his anger, but did he have time to get his gun?

All six feet, three inches of him, towered over her in the narrow aisle as she instinctively leaned away and clutched Bonnie.

He sneered with squinted eyes. "What the hell do you think you're doing?" His greasy, wild black hair fell across his face. He stunk like a tavern after closing hours.

"I'm leaving you." She struggled to keep her voice even as her insides shook in spasms.

The bus driver clomped down the aisle. "Hey, Mister, where's your ticket?"

Dirk ignored the question. "Oh! You're leaving me? Is that what you think?"

She said nothing but nodded, trying not to let him smell fear.

The bus driver tapped him on the shoulder. "Fella! What's going on here?"

Dirk shrugged him off. "None of your damn business!" He pushed his face into Helen's.

"You leaving for good? Or is this some little female game?"

"I'm leaving and filing for divorce." She struggled to sound calm and tried to speak quietly. Passengers nearby were looking up from their books, craning their necks toward the unfolding drama.

"Listen, buddy, this is my bus, and I don't want trouble. If you don't have a ticket, get off the bus."

Dirk glared at Helen for a long moment. "You were a terrible wife."

She didn't take the bait and willed herself to look strong and held his gaze. She didn't want to look down for fear he'd notice Bonnie. Would he be capable of hurting an innocent child?

"You go runnin' back to your mama. Divorced just like her. Won't that be a shocker in small-town Iowa?"

The driver intervened again, grabbing Dirk's arm. "Come on, that's enough. Get off this bus!"

He didn't budge, but she kept her face calm and hoped he'd forget the squirming infant in her lap.

He shrugged off the driver and glared at her for what felt like ages. He finally leaned closer and poked her injured shoulder. "I... never... loved... you. No one ever will. No wonder your pa took off without you."

The words washed over her without penetrating her psyche. She held her breath, trying not to make a sound that would ignite his volatile temper.

"OK, that's enough, Mister. Get off this bus, or I'll call the cops."

"Alright, alright, I'm going." But he leaned back to Helen one more time. "Good. Good riddance. Go back to that God-forsaken state. And take your baby with you! Let's see how you manage on your own." He spat the words in her face. She turned away from the force of his anger but said nothing. He turned with a final sneer, pushed the driver, lumbered down the aisle and off the bus.

She watched his back retreat, and her heart pounded in her chest, and her hands visibly shook. Would he come back with a gun?

The bus driver watched her for a moment. "You OK, Ma'am?"

"Yes. Yes, thank you. I, I'll be fine as soon as this bus gets going." She lifted Bonnie's sleeping face and kissed her cheeks. Holding Bonnie calmed her. So soft, so innocent – with no idea of the danger they just escaped. His words stung, but she already realized he didn't love her. They were attracted to each other, but he couldn't have loved her and treated her with such contempt.

Helen looked around, embarrassed, and tried to hide her face, but her heart still hammered, and her insides quivered. The other passengers kept sneaking peaks at her, some sympathetically.

The driver snapped the door shut, and within a moment, the bus chugged to life. Was it over? She still shook but realized he hadn't fought her leaving. Would she ever again have to endure his torments?

As the bus pushed farther from Austin, another reality settled in. Life as a single mother. Like mama. She resented her father for abandoning them. Why didn't he love them enough to stay? Maybe she was unlovable? She longed for a conventional family and married Dirk, hoping to create a happy, secure home, but now that dream was shattered. What did she do wrong? What signs had she missed?

Bonnie would grow up without a father. Salty tears trickled down Helen's cheeks, stinging the open wounds. Bonnie deserved a father's love, but how would Helen ever trust another man?

No more pretending. The night before, when she returned from getting stitches, she called Mama and confessed the mess of her marriage.

"I wondered what was going on, Helen. You didn't seem happy. There was a nervousness about you whenever Dirk was in the room. I didn't want to pry, but now I wish I had."

"I'm OK, Mama. I just needed a few stitches."

"He could have killed you, Helen! Are you sure he'll be in jail all night?"

"Yes, the officers said the soonest he could post a bond to get out of jail would be in the morning."

"I'll be praying for your safety. Stay alert, and I'll see you in a few days. I can't wait to meet Bonnie, but I'm so sorry you had to endure his wrath."

Wrath was right. As she thought about it now, the full extent of what happened played again in her mind. *Why does he hate me? What did I do to deserve it?* Then the record player in her brain played back painful moments as if from a "greatest hits album." Hits of a different sort.

She heard Grandma Gertrude telling her, "I didn't ask to have you around. You're a bother. I raised my own, and now I'm stuck with you."

Joseph's words played next, "Take off the ring I gave you. I'm seeing someone else."

Dirk's "Good riddance. I never loved you."

Even Mama's "I need you to live with your cousins during the school year." And later, when Mama said, "I'm moving in with Warren when we're married, but I want you to stay with Grandma and Grandpa."

What would Mama think of her now? Would she be ashamed to have a daughter who was involved with a violent man?

No one wanted her. But why? She fell asleep with the rhythm of the bus. Exhaustion was the only escape from her cruel reality.

Mama was at the bus depot, pacing as she waited to see her daughter and granddaughter. Helen and the baby were the last off the bus. When Mama spotted them, her hand flew to her mouth in shock. Helen pulled her hat low on her face, but Mama could see her swollen and bruised features.

She gingerly hugged Helen's shoulders. "I'm so thankful you are alive."

"Me too, Mama. Here's your granddaughter, Bonnie Ann." She pulled the blanket back to show Bonnie's tiny face.

Mama saw strangers staring at Helen. "She's beautiful, but let's get to the car where she's out of the wind."

"I must look like I was in a train wreck. A train wreck of a life."

"Nothing you can't recover from, Helen. With God's grace." Mama put her arm gently around Helen's waist, and they walked to the safety of the car.

Over the next few days, Mama tended to Helen's wounds and snuggled Bonnie.

"I'm so sorry I wasn't there for you, Helen, and that you got tangled up with Dirk."

"It's not your fault, Mama. I'm a grown woman."

"Yes, you are. But I should have guided you more. Most of my life, I thought I avoided men, and that's not healthy either."

"Did you date when you were in school?"

"Oh my, no. Ma told me that my sister Margaret was the pretty one, and I was the brainy one and that men didn't like brainy women. I kept to myself in school, convinced no one would ever love me."

"That's how I feel. That no one will love me."

Cora reached out and stroked her cheek. "I love you, Helen! And I believe one day you'll meet someone who'll appreciate the beautiful and talented woman you are. But for now, you need to heal."

"Did it take you a long time to heal after my father left?"

Cora's hand recoiled, and she looked away. "No! I was so relieved to erase him from my life, I didn't care that he rejected me. The difficult part was losing Ruby, and I've never gotten over that. Having her snatched from me was cruelty beyond comprehension."

Helen's brow furrowed. "Was anyone charged with poisoning him?"

"No, the county sheriff never investigated further. They simply closed the case."

"How odd."

"Yes, but Kentucky has their own system of justice."

"Mama, did you ever love Frank?"

Cora spoke softly and shook her head. "No, I didn't even like him."

"So, how did you end up married to him?"

She hesitated for a moment and then took a breath and looked at Helen. "I never wanted to tell you this while he was alive, in case you had a chance to have a father-daughter relationship, but now that's he's been dead for a few years, you might as well know the truth. He forced himself on me while I was a teacher in the Kentucky mission, and when I found out I was expecting, I went to Frank's father for advice. He and the local minister forced Frank and me to marry."

"So Ruby was the product of a rape?"

"I don't like to think of her that way. But yes, hers was a violent conception. I tried to appreciate your father as a child of God after being married so we could make it work, but we were just too different. And, like Dirk, Frank drank to excess, was unfaithful, and could become violent."

"I always thought there was more to the story. How horrible for you."

"Yes, but I survived, just as you will survive your disastrous marriage. I'm so grateful that I have you – even from an unhappy union. You have always been a blessing to me, Helen, and you're stronger than you think, my dear."

"When I was terrified, I thought of Grandma and how strong she was, and I prayed for some of that strength. It's a relief not to see him every day and to wonder what kind of mood he's in."

"Why didn't you tell me what was going on?"

Helen looked away. "I thought I was supposed to make my marriage work, no matter what. I didn't want everyone to see me as a failure or as someone unlovable. But I guess it didn't matter because that's how I feel now."

Cora again reached out and gently stroked Helen's arm. "You need healing from more than bruises and cuts. Be patient, but also be careful. Men who drink to excess and exhibit extreme jealousy are often dangerous. You've narrowly escaped one. At least I hope you're finished with him."

"I definitely am. He was so much fun when we first met. Handsome, a great dancer, and wow, could he kiss."

"He lured you in."

"I thought he loved me. After every fight, he brought me flowers or jewelry. Sometimes he showered me with gifts."

"But did his behavior change?"

"Sometimes he'd stop drinking for a few months, and then things got better. But something would set him off, and I'd be walking on eggshells."

"How did he convince you to marry him?"

"He stopped drinking for a few months and was full of fun. He suggested we should get married, and I thought he'd stay sober if we did. I thought marriage would help him settle down."

"Marriage rarely changes a person's personality."

"Yes, I see that now. The happiness didn't last, and he started drinking again, and when I got pregnant, Dirk became a different person. Angry and physical."

They sat together for a few moments, lost in thought, until Cora quietly asked. "What happened to your first pregnancy, Helen?"

Helen looked into her mother's eyes and wondered whether she should tell her the truth. Would the ugliness be too much for her? She finally looked down and whispered. "He threw me against a wall and stormed out. I awoke in a pool of blood."

"Why didn't you tell me?"

"Too embarrassed. I didn't tell anyone. I… I thought it was my fault."

"Your fault? That you were carrying his child? How could that be your fault?"

"I know how it sounds, but I was so isolated and confused. Dirk didn't allow me to talk to anyone or socialize, and every time he was upset, he convinced me I did something wrong. My world revolved around pleasing him and keeping his anger at bay."

Cora spat the words in anger. "And this is how he thanked you! By trying to kill you."

Helen rubbed the back of her neck. "But I'm alive, Mama. I got away."

Cora pulled her into a hug. "Yes, and I'm grateful to God. I only wish we could be certain we'd never hear from him again."

"Me too, Mama. I told the police to press charges, but he was out on bail by morning. I doubt he'll contest the divorce."

"Such nasty business, all of this."

"And here I am, a single mother, just like you were."

"Bonnie will be a huge blessing to you."

"She already is. I was so afraid Dirk would hurt her on the bus."

"What a terrible ordeal."

Again, they sat with their memories and worries. But Helen had more questions, and now that her mother was finally sharing family secrets, she wanted to keep the door open.

"Mama, why did you and Frank come back to the farm?"

"We were still married, living in Kentucky during prohibition when some hooligans set our cabin on fire because they thought I turned them in for bootlegging, but I didn't know anything about them. I barely escaped with you and Ruby."

"Where was Frank?"

"Supposedly out playing with his band. He didn't come home for several days. After the sheriff cleared him, we needed someplace to live. Grandma and Grandpa sent us the train fare to come back to Iowa. We had no other option, and I hoped we could help my parents run the farm and that Frank would settle into a routine."

"So, what happened?"

"Frank detested the farm, the animals, the smells, and my parents. He escaped one night with Ruby and went back to Kentucky. You know the rest. Painful memories."

"Mama, it took you decades to find a good man. Do you think I'll be alone forever?"

Cora stroked Helen's cheek. "I don't know, dear. For now, focus on yourself and your daughter. Who knows what God has in store for your future?"

"Future? I feel lost. How am I going to support myself and my daughter? I've made a mess of my life."

"Pray for guidance, Helen. You'll find your way."

Chapter 19

Helen hadn't lived under the same roof with her Mama for ages. When the
Great Depression hit, Grandpa took a government job that meant he could
no longer take Helen to school on his beloved horse, Lady. That meant
Helen lived with her cousins during the school years. Her grandparent's
farm was too far a distance to walk, and none of them could bring her to
school, so she and her cousins would walk to school together. When her
grandparents sold the farm and moved to the town of Greenberg, Helen
was close enough to walk to high school, so she stayed with her
grandparents and mother until her mother married Warren.

Helen realized her mother loved her, but she longed for more time
with her growing up. For most of her formative years, she felt like a rag
doll tossed back and forth between her grandparent's and Aunt Alice's
home.

And now Helen was staying in Warren's – and Mama's home, but
it wasn't familiar.

When the bruises on her face lightened, Helen took Bonnie to
meet Grandpa. Grandma's Iris were in full bloom next to the front steps,
and buds on the rose bushes peeked out under the sunshine. When she
opened the porch door, happy memories of dates with Joseph flooded
back. For a moment, his cheery smile flashed across her memory. *Was that
in this lifetime?*

Helen hugged Grandpa's bony shoulders. *Has he shrunk?* Gone was the strong, stout man who cut wood, milked cows, and corraled cattle.

They settled onto familiar, worn chairs, and Helen pulled back the blanket covering her infant.

"She looks like you did as a baby, Ole Bean."

"Grandpa, no one has called me that for years!"

"It'll always be my pet name for ya."

"I'm sorry I wasn't here for Grandma's funeral."

"I understand, Ole Bean. You were quite a distance away. Now let me hold my great-granddaughter." She handed Bonnie to him, and he kissed her tiny forehead. Bonnie's eyelashes fluttered open, and the two gazed at each other until she drifted back to sleep. The gentle grandpa that took Helen to school on the back of his horse was still there.

"Where's Bonnie's dad?"

"Still in Texas, Grandpa."

Grandpa nodded. "I see."

"He turned out to be a different man than I thought he was. A drinker."

"Sounds like that fella yer mama got involved with."

"Frank?"

"Yup. Same sort."

Grandpa asked Helen about her life in Texas, and she tiptoed through the details of it. *He needs to understand why I left Dirk, but not the nitty-gritty parts.*

Helen got up and walked around the living room of their modest home. The curtains were drawn, and the windows were shut, leaving a stale smell that clung like an unwelcome guest.

"Let's let in a little light and some fresh air." While Grandpa held Bonnie, Helen opened a few windows. She walked through the house and upstairs into her old lavender bedroom and stopped near the full-length mirror she used to hem the emerald green skirt for the winter dance. There was the bed where she dreamed about a future with Joseph and the pillow she cried into all night when he told her he found someone else. The memory stabbed her heart. Maybe being back in this house wasn't what she needed. It was easier not to think about Joseph when she was so far away in Texas. *Forget him. He's a married man. Focus on your daughter.* Now she needed to find a way to shake the love she felt for him, but it wrapped itself around her heart like a grapevine around a tree trunk.

She wandered back downstairs and stepped into the parlor where she and Grandma Gertrude did so many needlecrafts. But there was a new addition - Grandma had an electric sewing machine. Such an extravagance for her frugal grandmother.

The noon whistle blew throughout the town, and Helen smiled when it startled her.

"It's lunchtime. Can I fix you something to eat, Grandpa?" She went into the kitchen and was stunned to see dirty dishes littering every counter and piled in the sink. The fridge was a minefield. Sour milk, rotten fruit, and a bowl of something unrecognizable covered in green mold.

"Grandpa, what are you eating?"

He shrugged his shoulders. "I'm not hungry. With Gertrude gone, I jist don't know what to eat. I know she could be difficult, but she took care of the both of us all these years."

Helen threw out the rotting produce, cut the mold off the end of the cheese, and found some stale bread. While Grandpa held the baby, she washed the dishes and cleaned the sink.

"Let's go to the market." As they walked the aisles of the local grocer, her brain buzzed. Grandpa wasn't doing well, living independently, and Helen felt out of place at her mother's home. Perhaps she and Bonnie could move back in with Grandpa. But she would need an income—a way to make money from home. The plan needed time to percolate. She promised to visit again soon.

"Mama, Grandpa's not eating, and the house was a mess. I don't think he should be living alone."

"I try to check on him a few times a week, but it's difficult since he lives so far away. I've talked to him about moving in here with Warren and me, but he likes his independence."

"I'm wondering if I should move in with him. He'll still be in familiar surroundings. I can stay in my old room with Bonnie."

"Don't you worry that having a baby around will upset him? Be too much for him?"

"I think his being alone is what's upsetting him. Bonnie's a good baby. She nurses well, naps long, and doesn't fuss much without a good reason. I think he'd enjoy her, but it has to be his decision."

"How will you support yourself? Working at the Five and Dime store won't provide enough income for you and Bonnie."

"No, and I don't want to be away from Bonnie for long. But I'm working on a plan."

A few days later, Helen brought fresh groceries when she and Bonnie visited Grandpa.

"Don't be spending yer money on me, Ole Bean. I know you don't have any income right now."

"No, I don't, but I do have an idea. What would you think about Bonnie and I moving in with you?"

"Well, I guess you could have yer old room if that's what you want."

"I don't intend to freeload, Grandpa. I see Grandma left an electric sewing machine, like the one I learned to sew on in school. I could do sewing, mending, and alterations for others, and I could use the little parlor where Grandma Gertrude did her sewing. I mean, if it's OK with you."

"Well, it sure will perk up this house to have ya here. I can help watch Bonnie while ya sew if that helps."

"That would help a lot! Grandpa, my skills are pretty basic. But there is a one-year course in tailoring, sewing, and pattern making at the community college nearby. A course is starting in the fall, and I'm going to apply for a scholarship. Classes will only be a few hours each day, and I can sew for others in the evenings or early mornings."

"Well, OK, but what about Bonnie? I don't mind watching her for an hour or so…."

"No, don't worry. I'll find someone to care for Bonnie. You and Grandma took care of me for all those years, and I don't expect you to do that again."

Grandpa was delighted when Helen and Bonnie Ann moved in. Their presence transported him past his depression and grief over the loss of Grandma. Helen chased the cobwebs of the past by sewing slip covers for the sofa, giving walls a fresh coat of paint, and making new cape cod curtains for the kitchen and drapes for the living room and parlor. The summer months sped by as Helen resuscitated the old house and took on a few clients.

Then one evening, the phone rang. The familiar voice left her weak.

Chapter 20

"Hi Kitten, do you miss me?"

The blood drained from her face. Her knees went weak as she stood and strained to look out the window.

"Where, uh, where are you?" *Don't betray me, voice. Stay calm.*

"You didn't answer my question. Do y'all miss me?"

Was he in Iowa? She didn't want to antagonize him, but he needed the truth. There was no way she would ever go back to him. Grandpa was napping, so she kept her voice low so as not to awaken him. "I'm quite happy now."

"Well, Kitten, I miss you. Come back to Texas."

Never. She never wanted to see his face again or let him near her baby. "So, you're in Texas?"

"Where y'all need to be, seeins how you're still my wife."

"I'm not going back. I want a divorce."

"Well, actions speak louder than words, and I haven't gotten any divorce papers. I figured you must be pining for me. "

"My lawyer must've gotten behind. I'll make certain those papers get to you as soon as possible."

"Is that what you want?"

Was he kidding? "Yes, absolutely! It's what I want."

"I've stopped drinking, Helen. I'm a changed man. Let's give it another shot. We took vows, after all."

Fear turned to anger. Her hands gripped the phone cord. "Vows that you repeatedly broke with other women. And then you nearly killed me!"

"Now you're exaggerating. I may have roughed you up a bit, but I was mad that you were leavin. I've forgiven y'all for pressing charges against me."

"You've forgiven me? Are you kidding? I still have blinding headaches and stitches in my head as a reminder of the beating. I haven't forgiven you, and I certainly haven't forgotten your abuse."

"Where's that sweet little lady who always forgave me before?"

"She's gone. I'm never coming back, Dirk, so face reality."

The line went dead. He hung up on her. Was this the end? A chill ran through her.

Helen called her lawyer the following day and explained that they needed to complete the divorce in a hurry. He told her the papers were delivered to Dirk by certified mail to sign and return. Weeks ago.

So, Dirk lied to her. Again. Helen hoped their conversation would convince him to sign and return the papers.

Focus. Create a new life. She needed to earn a living but still didn't know whether she'd receive a scholarship to pay for classes she desperately needed. She was starting to take in a few sewing jobs, but they were barely enough to meet her expenses. Sure, Grandpa didn't charge her rent, but she needed to earn enough for food, clothes and hoped to save enough to purchase a car. She took the jewelry from Dirk to a local shop and sold it all to supplement her income.

Life was complicated, especially with blinding headaches. But she was happy to be back in Iowa for springtime with everything in bloom. When they drove through the countryside to visit Mama, she and Grandpa took measure of the corn and soybeans and watched for calves and colts grazing with their mothers. Grandpa passed judgment on whether there was enough soil moisture for the crops and familiar sights took on new significance.

Perhaps seeing high school friends again would help her reach back and recall when she was fearless and hopeful. Traits she longed for now. After several weeks, she found the courage to reach out to Emily and decided to tell her the truth about what happened to her in Texas.

The two lifelong friends met at the Five and Dime. Helen arrived early and lingered near the entrance for a moment visualizing the last time she was there. The soda fountain was the same, but the fashions changed. The manager recognized her.

"Helen! Were you away at college?" he asked.

"No, I was in Texas." Helen kept her tone light. *I got quite an education, but not on paper.*

"I was sorry to hear your Grandmother passed away."

Helen nodded. "Thank you." She turned and spotted Emily breezing in.

"Emily, I love your hair!" Emily's normally straight blond tresses sported long waves. Coral lipstick accentuated her pouty lips, and black mascara added a sophisticated touch. Her light blue sundress showed off a bit of summer sunshine.

"These perms are the latest thing. But of course, you never needed to add more curls. I do love your hair shorter, Helen!"

"Thanks, it's easier this way." Helen's lemony sundress accentuated her red hair along with the sporty sunhat she bought while working at the Foxy Lady and managed to fit it into her suitcase when she escaped Texas.

They ordered root beer floats, then settled into a corner booth. Their conversation quickly deepened from hairstyles to the details of Helen's failed marriage.

"Men are nothing but heartbreaks. I'm staying single. I'd rather be alone the rest of my life than to ever be with someone like Dirk again."

"I had no idea you were going through all that. Why didn't you ever call?"

"It's hard to explain – even to myself. At first, he was charming, attentive, and we had so much fun dancing. Gradually Dirk became jealous if I even spoke to another man. And sometimes, if I spoke to women. He watched the phone bill each month and expected a report on what I spoke to Mama about. I was afraid if I called you or anyone else, he'd become enraged. After Bonnie was born, I left my job, so without my own income, I felt more and more dependent on him."

"So, you have a daughter?"

"Yes, my dear, sweet Bonnie. She was born in March."

"Still tiny, then. I'd love to see her."

"Thank you! I'll have you over soon. We're living with Grandpa now that Grandma is gone, and I'm using her sewing machine to take in some alterations."

"Will Dirk want to see his daughter?"

"Dirk didn't want children, and I'm hoping he'll give up all rights to her in the divorce."

Emily reached for her hand and squeezed it. "How horrible for you. I can't imagine anyone walking away from a daughter!"

Helen's eyes widened, and she withdrew her hand and stirred her float. "You mean like my father walked out on me?"

Emily sucked in a breath. "I'm sorry, Helen. I forgot."

"It's okay. Frank wasn't part of my life, so I guess I never knew what I was missing."

"He was a fool. He missed knowing what a wonderful person you are. And now Dirk will never know Bonnie."

"Thanks, Emily. But maybe I've spared her from a lifetime of broken promises. If she expects nothing, she'll never be disappointed."

"Sounds a bit harsh. Is this your new philosophy?" Emily looked at her with concern.

"I have to wrap myself in a cocoon so I won't get hurt again. I don't have the energy for it now that I'm a mother, and I can't take risks."

Emily nodded. "Do you think the divorce will be final soon?"

"I hope so. Dirk has the papers. Just has to sign them."

"Helen, why isn't he in jail?"

"As part of the divorce settlement, I agreed to drop the charges against him if he'd relinquish his parental rights."

Emily nodded thoughtfully. "Let's hope this will close the door on that chapter of your life."

"Yes, that's what I want. Now, how about you and Jacob? What's happening in your life?"

"Jacob is finishing his engineering degree in June, and we're planning to marry next summer. I finished the courses for my elementary teacher's degree and will be doing my student teaching this fall. I can't wait to work with children."

"That's wonderful, Em! I'm so happy for you. I may be taking college classes this fall. I applied for a scholarship, and if I get it, I'll take tailoring and dressmaking classes at the community college."

"That's fabulous. I'll pray you get it."

Helen swirled the straw around in her float. "Have you seen any of our old friends?"

"You mean like Joseph?"

"Well, yes. Does Jacob stay in touch with him?"

"He ran into Joseph once in Des Moines. He's out of the service now." Emily raised her eyebrows and waited to see if Helen would respond.

"Wow. I'm not sure I want to know how he's doing."

"Still too painful? "

"Is he still married to that floozy? What was her name?"

"Lucy. I don't know. Jacob didn't say."

"You're right. It's too painful. I don't want to talk about him." *Or think about him.*

They moved on to lighter topics and other town gossip.

Chapter 21

Helen's step was lighter as she walked home. Home. Yes, she did feel like she was home again. As she walked in the door, Grandpa was trying to soothe Bonnie, pacing back and forth, his huge hands nearly covering her tiny body.

"Oh, Grandpa, I thought she'd stay asleep!"

"Just woke up. Been doing pretty well until a few minutes ago."

"I'll change her and nurse." Helen took Bonnie upstairs to tend to her, then brought her back to see Grandpa.

"She's a good little one. Like you were, Ole Bean."

"Thanks, Grandpa. I appreciate your watching her so I could see Emily."

"Did you sort things out?"

Helen put Bonnie on a blanket on the carpet and gave her a squeaky toy to grip.

"What do you mean?"

"Whether you're goin 'back to that fella or not."

"Which fella?"

"That Dirk, in Texas. Never told me why ya left him."

"I told you he was a drinker. But I wanted to spare you the details, Grandpa."

"Ya don't need ta spare me. If ya don't mind talking about it, I'd like ta know what happened ta my granddaughter."

"He was a troubled guy. Drank too much and was violent when he did."

Grandpa's face grew somber. "Did he hurt ya?"

"Yes, in many ways. Dirk was unfaithful and flaunted it, and when I finally said I was leaving, he nearly killed me."

"I've noticed the scar on your head."

She gingerly touched the spot where her hair was just growing back in. "He beat me with his nightstick. I got stitches here the night before I left Texas."

"Helen, in my 75 years, I've seen a lot. Misery, wars, the Depression. I know you were often unhappy as a child, and I don't ever want to see you hurt again."

"Thank you, Grandpa. You always stood up for me."

"I always will. But if you're going to live here, be honest with me. That fella could still be a danger, so if he calls, ya need to tell me."

"He did call. About two weeks ago. He tried to get me to go back to Texas, but I told him I wanted a divorce and he should sign the papers."

"Has he done it?"

"Not that I've heard."

Grandpa's eyes pierced hers. "Don't let down yer guard."

"I won't. I didn't want to upset you, but I see what you're saying."

"The same sorta fella that made yer Mama's life so miserable."

"You mean my father?"

"Well, if ya can call him that."

Helen was thoughtful. "It's odd we both got into the same trap."

"But are ya finished with him?"

"Yes! I've sent divorce papers."

"Is he finished with you?"

"Don't say that, Grandpa. It gives me chills."

"Ya need to be careful until you're sure he's gone. Yer pa was a miserable sort, but he never tried to kill yer ma. This Dirk character sounds more dangerous."

"I'll be careful. I didn't want to drag you into this, but I feel better now that you know."

Helen pushed a small sign deep into the front yard of Grandpa's house. It read: Rip N Stitch Tailoring and Alterations. A small ad in the paper encouraged more business to trickle in. She used her more formal name, Mrs. Betzini, in her ads and with clients, hoping to sound more business-like. She was happy to be able to work on small projects even before her courses began.

One afternoon, Grandpa put Bonnie in the stroller so Helen could complete a dress for a client. She was lost in thought working on the tricky sleeve when the doorbell rang. She absent-mindedly swung open the front door. And blinked. Dirk.

She gasped. "What are you doing here?"

He grabbed the door so she couldn't close it. "Is that any way to greet your husband?"

Helen took a step back and kept her tone light. "Ex-husband. Why are you here?"

He grabbed her wrist. "I missed you. Come on, Helen. You can't expect me to stay away forever!"

"Why haven't you signed the divorce papers?"

"I want you back. I've stopped drinking, this time for good." Dirk took another step toward her and put his free arm around her waist. "Come on, pretty lady, give me another chance." He leaned in to kiss her, but Helen turned her head away.

"So that's the way you want it? Playing hard to get."

Helen strained to get out of his grasp. "I'm not playing. Our marriage is over."

"We have a child together. Shouldn't I be allowed to see her?"

"You never wanted anything to do with her before."

"I'm a changed man. I miss you and… and…."

There was something strange about his eyes. His pupils were dilated. "You don't know her name."

"Betty! Her name's Betty."

"No, it's Bonnie. Now leave before I call the police."

"Police! For what? Since when can't a father see his kid?"

"You gave up all parental rights when I agreed to drop the charges against you."

Dirk tightened his grip on her. "Come on, Kitten, I wasn't thinking straight. I've changed my mind."

She yelled in the hopes a neighbor might hear her. "Let go of me! And don't call me Kitten. My name's Helen!"

He pushed her inside and shut the front door. "Come on, Helen, give me a break! Things will be different this time. Just come back to Texas."

"Dirk, it's over! Now let go of me and leave this house."

He leaned in closer. "I came all this way, and this is the reception I get, Kitten?"

"Don't call me that. I'm not your Kitten. I didn't ask you to visit. I asked you to sign the divorce papers."

Just then, the front door flew open, and Grandpa barreled in, leaving Bonnie outside in the stroller. His calm voice betrayed the danger he suspected. "Hello there, what's going on here?"

"None of your concern, old man. I'm just here to see my wife."

Grandpa kept walking toward the kitchen and casually asked. "Helen, did you ask him to visit?"

"No, Grandpa, he won't leave."

Grandpa snatched the phone off the kitchen wall and dialed 9-1-1. "Police, we have an intruder." He listed the address and hung up.

Dirk stepped toward him but wasn't quick enough to stop the phone call.

"Hey, what's the meaning of that! I just wanted to see my daughter."

"Take your hands off my granddaughter before I get my rifle."

Dirk dashed outside and snatched the infant from the stroller. He ran to his car and carelessly tossed Bonnie onto the front seat, and took off. Helen tried to run after him, but the car got away too quickly. Moments later, a police car screeched to a halt in front of them, and she and Grandpa promptly filled him in and gave him a description of Dirk's vehicle.

Grandpa put his arm around Helen, who was in near hysterics. "Don't worry, Ole Bean. They'll catch him." Helen phoned her mother and asked her to pray. Then she and Grandpa paced back and forth inside their home, not wanting to be far from the telephone.

Within 20 minutes, the phone rang. Police had Dirk in custody, and Bonnie was safe with them. Grandpa and Helen wasted no time driving to the station to collect Bonnie. She was crying but was otherwise unharmed. Helen clung to her. The police sergeant told them there was already a warrant for Dirk's arrest stemming from another assault in Texas. They could add kidnapping, resisting arrest, and speeding to his rap sheet. In addition, they were testing his blood for illegal drugs. This time he said Dirk Betzini would be in prison for a long while.

Helen was shaking but asked to see Dirk while he was safely behind bars. Grandpa held Bonnie while an officer led her back to the damp, smelly, concrete cell.

"What were you thinking? How dare you take my daughter!"

"I figured you'd follow me back."

"To Texas?"

Dirk shrugged.

"You know nothing about caring for an infant. Nothing to feed her. You could've killed her."

"Don't be dramatic!"

"Let me make this very clear. You need help, which I cannot give you. I never want to see you again. Sign the divorce papers and give up your parental rights to Bonnie." It felt like an eternity until he answered.

"Yeah, fine. I never wanted to be a father. I'll sign the damn papers." Was there sadness in his voice? She didn't care. All she wanted now was to close the door to this terrible marriage. She turned her back on him and walked away.

Within minutes of getting home, Cora and Warren walked in.

Cora's voice shook as she put her arms around Helen and Bonnie. "Thank God you're safe. We couldn't lose another child."

Helen realized her mother was reliving her own nightmare of Ruby's kidnapping. "She's okay, Mama. And I don't think we'll have to worry about him again."

Helen hoped she was utterly and finally rid of him. But would she ever be free from the nightmares and headaches?

Chapter 22

"The maple tree out front is starting to turn, Grandpa." Helen, Bonnie, and Grandpa were enjoying breakfast outside on the porch before the fall semester began.

"Yer Grandma loved that tree. Every year she'd wait for the leaves ta turn red."

"They're like roosters announcing the daybreak. Only maples announce a whole season."

Grandpa chuckled. "You ready to be a student again, Ole Bean?"

"More than ready. I can't wait! Hopefully, I'll learn skills that'll help me earn a living. How to create clothes with all the finishing touches. I do love to sew." Helen was taking tailoring and pattern-making courses at the community college.

"You git that from yer Grandma. She always loved ta sew and do needlecrafts. She could be hard on ya, but she taught ya how ta do fer yerself."

"I did learn a lot from her. Thanks for reminding me, Grandpa."

Stepping onto the campus and into a classroom was exhilarating the next day. Once again, she was turning a corner, finding a new direction she hoped would be a permanent improvement. A nursery on campus was available to take care of Bonnie, so Helen was never far from her, which eased her worries.

Helen absorbed the information quickly and found the classes engaging. The teachers treated students like adults, a welcome change from high school. As instructors discovered her natural gifts and encouraged her, Helen's confidence grew, and she found herself eager to greet the challenges of each new day. Fear of the future, which was her constant companion, was fading as she embraced her new life.

After morning classes, she collected Bonnie and spent the afternoon sewing for clients or school projects. She hoped Grandpa enjoyed a few hours of quiet each day, but she kept a keen eye on his health, encouraging him to eat well and take his evening constitutional, as he called his nightly walk.

Tailoring class was especially challenging, but the techniques were opening new avenues of possibilities. Instead of simply mending suits and jackets, she would now be able to create them. Her instructor, Mr. Hibbs, singled her out numerous times with compliments.

In October, Mr. Hibbs held a jacket Helen was making and exclaimed, "Class, look at the delicate basting stitches."

Helen pushed her hair behind her ears and bit her lip. Yes, she was pleased, but being singled out brought jealousy, which she experienced in high school after winning singing competitions.

Weeks later, Mr. Hibbs again asked the other students to examine one of Helen's projects. He beamed at her and held the Saffire blue wool dress she was making. "Look at Helen's bound buttonholes."

The other students crowded around her table to examine the technique.

He pointed to the bodice. "And the covered buttons are the perfect finishing touch."

"Thank you."

"Your work is so precise, Helen."

Helen blushed deeply from all the attention.

As the first semester was drawing to a close, Mr. Hibbs invited her to his office. She nervously approached, hoping there wasn't a problem with the men's suit she was working on for her final project.

He was sitting behind a small desk in a cramped office, with fabric and sewing supplies scattered on a side table and a packed bookshelf shoved against one wall.

"Come in, Helen, and have a seat."

Helen shrugged out of her winter coat and sat on the edge of her chair. "Thank you. I brought my final project."

"Splendid! Yes, I see you're making a man's suit. Is it for your husband?"

"No. I'm not married."

"So, for a gentleman friend?"

"No, no. For a client."

"Client?"

"Yes. I do sewing and mending to support myself, and I gave one of my clients a discount if he'd let me make a suit for him and use it for my final project."

Mr. Hibbs tugged at the sides of his mustache. "How fortunate for your client. The wool you chose is exquisite."

"Did you want to see it again, Mr. Hibbs?"

"Certainly."

Helen fumbled with the tote bag and pulled out the nearly finished suit. "I still have to attach the collar."

Mr. Hibbs reached for it and examined her work. "The lining looks perfect. Your client should be pleased to have a new suit in time for Christmas."

"Yes. That was my hope."

He sat back and fiddled with his tie chain. Then looked at Helen.

She studied the pile on his desk for clues. "Was there anything else?"

He looked hopeful. "Well, yes. I was wondering if you'd like to go for coffee?"

"Oh!"

"I realize this is unusual, but the semester is almost over, and I don't believe you'll be retaking my class."

"No, right."

"I'm not breaking any regulations if we simply enjoy coffee together."

"OK. Yes. I guess that would be nice."

They agreed to meet a week later at a local cafe. Helen wasn't sure if this was a date or if he had other business to discuss with her. She made sure her white blouse was free from splattered baby rice cereal.

Mr. Hibbs was in his usual three-piece suit and tie as he waited at a table. He spotted Helen, jumped up, and helped her out of her coat.

"Thank you, Mr. Hibbs."

He spoke quietly into her ear as he pulled out her chair. "You're welcome, but please call me Edwin."

The intimacy of the gesture startled her. "Edwin, then." She settled into the chair.

Once seated, he tilted his head and grinned at her. "That forest green looks sharp against your red hair."

"Thank you. It's one of my favorite colors. And with Christmas near, I thought it would be festive."

The conversation went from hesitant and stiff to an easy exchange of ideas. No business propositions, just a pleasant coffee date. She assumed she wouldn't hear from him again and was surprised when he called and asked her to dinner days later.

"Emily? I'm wondering if you'll watch Bonnie for me Friday night?"

"Of course, I'll watch her, but what's the scoop? Gotta date?"

"My tailoring instructor asked me out, and I don't want to leave Grandpa with Bonnie."

"Tailoring instructor? How old is he?"

"He's 30."

"Single?"

"Yes, of course. Never married."

"Does he know about Bonnie?"

"No, we've only had coffee. He'll likely run scared once he hears about my past, but I thought it'd be fun to have an evening out before that happens."

"Good for you! What's he like?"

"A bit formal, but nice. Nothing serious, just a night out."

Friday night, Helen and Emily were playing with Bonnie as they waited for Edwin.

"The gig will be over as soon as he meets my little rascal."

"Have some faith, Helen. He sounds like a great guy."

"So far, yes."

The doorbell rang, and Helen took a deep breath before answering it.

"Hi, Edwin! Come on in. Let me introduce my Grandpa John, my best friend, Emily, and my daughter, Bonnie."

"Daughter?"

"Yes." Her face warmed to a deep red as she lifted Bonnie for a better view.

Edwin reached for her and caressed Bonnie's chin.

"How old is she?"

"She's nine months. One in March."

"She looks like you. She's lovely."

"Oh, thank you!"

"Well, shall we go? Very nice to meet you all."

Edwin held the door of his blue 1946 Chevy Sedan for Helen to take her seat, and Edwin went around to the driver's side.

As they drove to the restaurant, he turned to her. "You're a mother!"

"Yes!"

"I hope you don't mind my asking but are you a widow?"

"No, I'm divorced."

She let that sink in for a few moments and then added, "I was married to an abusive alcoholic. He was bad news."

"Is he out of the picture?"

"I hope so. Last I knew, he was in prison."

"I had no idea."

"Look, Mr. Hibbs, er Edwin, I understand if you want to cancel our dinner."

"Why would I want to do that?"

"It's a small town, and I don't want you to ruin your reputation."

"For being seen with you?"

"Yes."

"Are you planning to dance on the table at dinner?"

Helen giggled. "No."

"Then I don't think anyone will notice us having dinner together. This isn't the 1800's after all. Not even the 1920's! So, let's enjoy dinner."

The restaurant was casual and served staples that were popular with locals. Wide egg noodles made in their kitchen, topped with roast beef swimming in a rich, brown gravy. Other menu favorites were pork chops and mashed potatoes, chicken and dumplings, creamed corn, and pies that featured whatever fruit was in season. When winter rolled in, pumpkin, squash, and coconut cream pie graced the menu. They sat on wooden benches in cozy booths with soft, warm lighting while discussing movies and books they enjoy. Although Helen currently had little time for reading, she enjoyed the light conversation. But something about Edwin made her feel as if she needed to sit straight and keep her elbows off the table, which she did.

After dinner, he drove her home, walked her to the front door, and put out his hand to shake hers.

"Thank you, Edwin. That was a delicious dinner."

"You're welcome. We'll have to do this again." Helen nodded and went inside.

Grandpa was in his room, but Emily was waiting for her. "Well, how did it go?"

"Fine."

"Fine? Only fine? Doesn't say much."

"He's nice. We had an interesting discussion, but no fireworks."

"Did he kiss you?"

"No. Handshake. I doubt if I'll hear from him again."

"You think he'll be scared off by a child?"

"I don't know. Maybe. Edwin seems to like me, but he's 30, I'm 22, and he's never married. I expect he's looking for perfection, and he won't find it with me."

"Aren't you the cynical one!"

"Just realistic, and I'm not looking for another relationship. I've got enough going on with the course work, my sewing business, and caring for Bonnie and Grandpa. Should I go on?"

"No, I see your point."

Just then, Grandpa walked into the room. "What's this? I hope you're not letting an old man stand in the way of your happiness?"

"No, Grandpa. I just meant I have a lot of responsibilities right now, and I'm not looking to start a new relationship."

"Ready or not, if the right fella shows up, give him a chance."

"Same for you, Grandpa. If a nice lady shows up, don't chase her away."

Grandpa chuckled. "I don't see that happening, but I'll keep it in mind."

"And I don't think Edwin is right for me. Probably no one is."

Emily sighed. "Well, just in case you need another break from the lonely hearts club, let me know, and I'll gladly watch Bonnie again. Now, I think I'd better head home before the snow starts."

"Stay safe, young lady. We're looking for a storm tonight. Could drop a foot a snow."

"Thanks, Mr. Harper. I'll stay safe."

"There are a few hours before the fun begins. I do love the first snowfall, and I can't wait to show Bonnie."

Chapter 23

The magic that is winter appeared overnight. Helen awoke several times to look out the window and watch the flakes fall. By morning, their corner of the world was covered in a heavy, wet overcoat. Snow clung to every branch and bush, tree and trellis. Sunbeams peeking out of clouds made everything shimmer. As soon as Bonnie awoke, Helen wrapped her in a blanket and brought her to the window.

"Snow, baby. That's snow."

Bonnie smiled and cooed, a bit confused.

At breakfast, Grandpa, too, was energized by the snowfall. "I needs to git out and shovel the walk as soon as we're done eatin'."

"I'll help, Grandpa. I can wrap Bonnie in blankets and put her in the stroller for a bit. I can't believe how much I missed this the last two years!"

Helen pulled on a stocking cap, coat, scarf, and boots and then dressed Bonnie in her warmest snowsuit. By the time she worked her hands into gloves, she was starting to sweat. She opened the door, and a blast of cold air welcomed them. They had barely begun to shovel when a blue 1946 Chevy Sedan pulled up, and Edwin popped out, carrying a shovel.

"Need any help with your walks?"

"Edwin! What a nice surprise. Sure, dig in!"

The three of them cleared the walks quickly, despite the heavy snow.

Edwin leaned on his shovel. "My mother always says, 'Many hands make light work.'"

"Mine too! Now that the walk's cleared, let's build a snowman… for Bonnie."

"I haven't made a snowman since I was a boy, but I'm keen."

Grandpa took Bonnie inside to warm up for a bit while Edwin and Helen rolled three large balls into a proper snow creature. Edwin found small branches for the snowman's hands, and Helen popped inside for a scrap of fabric to use as a scarf and a carrot for a nose.

Edwin appraised their creation. "Hmm, we still need two eyes. I don't suppose you have any coal?"

"Not since we left the farm. Maybe two coat buttons would work?" Helen went inside and brought a bundled-up Bonnie out with her to see the snowman as she put the buttons in place.

With outstretched arms, Edwin asked. "May I hold her?"

Bonnie was a bit unsure, but she responded to his smiles once in Edwin's arms and tugged on his mustache.

"You're beautiful like your Mama, little one."

"Oh! Well, thank you! Of course, I think she's adorable, but it's nice to hear it from others."

"Mothering must be a lot of work."

"It is, but watching her grow and change is rather magical. Learning new words or doing something to surprise me makes it all worth it."

"She's lucky to have such a wonderful mother."

Helen's cheeks warmed, despite the cold. "Thanks. Um… Would you like some cocoa? I think you've earned it and not just for saying I'm beautiful!"

Edwin chuckled. "I can't stay. I promised my mother I'd clear her walk and run some errands for her. She might say 'many hands make light work, 'but she really means my hands make her work light." He handed Bonnie back to Helen and kissed them both on the cheeks before driving away.

Helen watched him drive off, feeling a bit dejected.

"Did yer fella leave?"

"He's not my fella, Grandpa. Just a friend. And yes, he had things to do, but I was so happy for his help."

"That snow sure is heavy with moisture."

"I hope it didn't hurt your back, Grandpa."

Grandpa yawned. "I'm still strong as an ox, and don't you forget it, Ole Bean."

Helen chuckled. "Ox, is it? Well, I think the old ox needs a rest."

"Yeah, just going to catch a few winks."

"I think Bonnie could catch a few winks too. That fresh air made her sleepy. And I need time to sew."

While the other two napped, Helen worked on the quilt she was making Grandpa for Christmas. Her mind wandered back to her first Christmas with Joseph. It felt like a lifetime since she felt the thrill of being loved by him. Thoughts of Joseph still landed in a soft spot. Why had she loved him so fiercely? Young love? First love? Naivety? She missed the way he laughed and the way he made her feel. As if the world was a gigantic jolly place waiting for them to conquer it together. But it was impossible to imagine him without thinking about their break-up, which inevitably brought raw emotions of rejection.

That rejection propelled her to Texas. At first, she felt so independent and full of hope as a working woman in Texas. Earning her own money and managing her life. But then Dirk came along and tapped into her vulnerability. The need for love. First, the thrill of his raw masculinity was a powerful draw, and eventually, the terror of his erratic behavior nearly cost her life. Dirk's reluctance to accept fatherhood overshadowed even the exhilaration of becoming a mother. And now, she was a single parent in a world that only approved of two-parent households. Her life was a roller coaster.

Ever the worrywart, she couldn't help wondering if she was giving Bonnie enough love and attention? Were her classes taking too much time from Bonnie? Helen realized her mother must have grappled with the same questions when she left Helen with Grandma and Grandpa to get an education. That education saved Mama and Helen. During the depression, they never starved like so many others. They struggled, yes, but they survived. And she and Bonnie would survive. Wouldn't they? She wanted to feel that optimism now but instead felt cautious. However, Helen was still determined to make Christmas a time of wonder for Bonnie.

Helen awoke earlier than usual Christmas morning and dashed downstairs to turn up the heat, plug in the Christmas tree lights, and put the coffee on to boil while preheating the oven. She made Grandma Gertrude's famous caramel roll recipe the night before and left them to rise in the fridge. All she had to do now was pop them into a warmed oven, and they would be Christmas magic. Mama and Warren were coming over for breakfast to watch Bonnie open her gifts, and Helen wanted everything to be perfect. She whipped up an egg casserole to complete the meal, just in time.

Bonnie was chattering to herself upstairs in her crib as Helen opened the door and greeted her enthusiastically. "Merry Christmas, my little one!"

Bonnie somehow must have known this day was special. She was standing in her crib babbling when she saw her mother and put her arms out.

Helen smothered her with kisses and then changed her into a festive red corduroy dress with white tights and white high-top shoes. Bonnie was starting to pull herself up, and the shoes gave her more stability.

"Grandma and Grandpa Warren are coming today! And I think Santa came last night."

"Sah sah?"

"Yes, baby, Santa Claus brought you a present."

"Sah sah?"

"Never mind. You'll understand soon enough. Let's go look at the tree."

She carried her downstairs and showed her the lights and the presents under the tree. Fortunately, Bonnie had little experience with gifts, so the wrappings were safe from her curiosity.

"Merry Christmas, Grandpa! Mama and Warren should be here soon."

Grandpa kissed Helen on the cheek. "Merry Christmas, Ole Bean."

He reached for Bonnie, kissed her, and lifted her above his head. "Merry Christmas, Bonnie. I'm so glad you're here." He brought her into the living room and showed her the nativity scene on a side table. "Today is Jesus' birthday."

"Sus sus?"

"Yes, Jesus."

Helen grinned at him. "She's a regular parrot today."

Minutes later, Mama and Warren arrived laden with gifts and trays of cookies.

Mama shrugged out of her coat. "Smells wonderful in here, Helen. Are those Grandma's caramel rolls I smell?"

"Of course! What else would I make for Christmas? And yum! Your date cookies. Can't wait."

They enjoyed a hearty brunch and then set about opening gifts in the living room just as the doorbell rang.

"You expecting anyone?" Mama said.

Helen hurried to answer it. "Not me, but I'm glad I got dressed." She swung open the door "Edwin! Come on in."

He stood on the doorstep. "I can only stay a moment. I wanted to bring you one of my mother's fruitcakes."

"Would you like a cup of coffee?"

"No, I'm afraid I have deliveries to do for my mother. I just wanted to wish you a Merry Christmas."

"Thank you. That was very thoughtful."

"It's my mother's tradition. She loves to make these fruitcakes, and it's my job to deliver them. Have a wonderful day." He thrust the heavy cake in her hands, and he was off.

Helen shut the door and brought the fruitcake inside.

Mama's eyebrows arched. "New boyfriend?"

"Just a friend. Edwin. He was my tailoring instructor. We've only gone out a few times, so nothing serious."

"Still, that was a nice surprise."

"I'm sorry I didn't think of something to give him. It was so unexpected."

"Did you invite him in?"

"Yes, Mama, of course. But he has to deliver fruitcakes for his mother."

"Does he live with his mother?"

"No, but he's an only child and his father's deceased, so she relies on him a lot."

Warren lit his pipe. "He sounds like a good son."

"Let's finish opening presents." Helen needed to change the subject before they started digging for information about her love life, or lack thereof.

The spring semester started in the middle of January, and Helen was eager to begin classes again in design and dressmaking. She was determined to make each project more perfect than the last.

A few weeks into the semester, Miss Olson, the stylish instructor for dressmaking, announced an optional contest through McCall's, the nationally known pattern company. The challenge was to design a woman's dress and create it from a man's suit. Helen shopped the used clothing store, found a zoot suit in lightweight navy-blue wool with a herringbone pattern, and then brought it to Miss Olson's office after class to ask for advice.

"I'm thinking of making a dress with several gores for fullness and long sleeves. Do you think I'll have enough fabric?"

Miss Olson's manicured hands pulled the suit inside out as she examined it. Standing close to her, Helen realized she was likely only a few years her senior.

"This zoot suit is a great choice. The wide trouser legs should yield enough to create the gores. And you can easily get the bodice and sleeves out of the jacket. The lining is in good shape, so you can reuse it as well. But you'll need to carefully match the herringbone pattern as you sew each gore."

"I will. I'll also trim the shoulder pads but will use the same ones. And instead of a zipper closure, I'm planning to make bound buttonholes and use large pearl buttons."

"Bound buttonholes. Elegant, but they can be tricky. The execution of your design is going to be a lot of work."

"I know, but I can see it in my head, and I seriously want to try for the prize money. I learned bound buttonholes in my tailoring class, so I'm hoping I can make them perfectly."

"Mr. Hibbs spoke highly of your final project in tailoring. If anyone can complete this, you can. You have a determined spirit, Helen."

"Thank you. I've had a few rocky years, and I'm trying to make a better future for myself and my daughter."

"You've certainly found your niche. And I understand you're dating Edwin, eh, Mr. Hibbs."

"Nothing serious. We've just had dinner a few times."

"He's quite the catch if you can tolerate his mother."

"You've met his mother?"

"We dated for nearly a year."

Another student knocked on the door. "Miss Olson, do you have a minute?"

Helen retrieved her project. "I'd better go. Thanks for the advice on the dress."

Helen carefully ripped the suit apart at the seams and laid out the pieces to measure and plan. She created a pattern based on her measurements, then used it to make a dress out of lightweight cotton she could wear in the summer to be positive the pattern worked. It did, but she lost confidence and set it aside.

She and Edwin were still dating every few weeks. Their relationship was rather formal, but she enjoyed his company. At dinner one evening, as she wrestled with a tough pork chop at the local restaurant, he asked about her project.

"How's the competition garment coming along?"

"I made the pattern and used it to make a dress out of less expensive fabric. It fit, but now I'm nervous about cutting into the beautiful wool."

He took a sip of his red merlot wine. "The fit can change dramatically with different fabrics. And you may need to finish the seams more carefully to make sure the wool doesn't unravel. I'd be happy to take a look at it."

She frowned. "Is that cheating?"

Edwin set his wine glass on the table. "Only if I do the work for you. Free advice is allowed."

"Okay, yes. I'd love your advice. The project is on my work table at home."

Emily agreed to stay a few minutes more and watch Bonnie, and since Grandpa was in the living room reading, Helen and Edwin went into the small parlor she used for her business.

"This fabric is exquisite, Helen. Great choice. Why don't you try the first dress on so I can see how it fits?"

Helen went into the bathroom to change, then self-consciously modeled it for Edwin.

He studied the fit and had her turn around several times. She felt her face flush under his scrutiny.

"The skirt pattern is fine, but you should let out the bodice about 1/8 inch on each seam to allow for the bulk of the fabric."

She let out a breath and crossed her arms in front of her. "Okay, sounds doable."

Edwin reached for her hand and drew her closer. She took a step toward him.

He caressed her cheek. "You're so pretty when you blush! I love your freckles."

"The curse of the red-heads."

"Not a curse at all." He kissed her gently on the lips.

She stepped back and giggled.

"You're laughing at me?"

"No, your mustache tickled my nose."

"I'd better go."

"You don't have to. I'm just about to put Bonnie to bed, and we could play cards."

"No, I promised Mother I'd stop by and listen to a musical program on the radio with her."

"Another time, then."

Chapter 24

Emily came back downstairs with Bonnie. "He's already gone?"

"Yes. He gave me a few pointers on my project, though."

"Let me guess - he had to do something with his mother?"

"Yup! This time it was a musical program. The dinner wasn't great either. The pork chops were dry and overcooked."

"So, not a great evening."

"Not terrible, just nothing spectacular. I was grateful for Edwin's advice on my dress, but I never feel completely at ease around him."

"Could be because you don't spend much time together."

"Or because he's so formal. How is your Jacob, by the way?"

"Changing the subject? Jacob is great. Heading into his final semester."

"You are, too, right?"

"Yes, I love student teaching at the elementary school. We had so much fun getting ready for Christmas."

"I'm so happy for you both. And to think, we'll all be graduating this spring, even if mine was only a one-year course."

"As long as it leads to your happiness, that's what matters."

"You're such a good friend."

"Well, I hope you think enough of our friendship to be my matron of honor."

"What? You set the date?"

Emily put her hand out and wriggled her fingers. "We finally got officially engaged!"

"Finally is right! I'm so happy for you two. I can't believe I didn't notice sooner."

"You were preoccupied with Edwin."

"When is the wedding?"

"The first Saturday in October."

"Well, I'm not exactly a maiden, but I'd be honored to stand up for you two."

"And there's one more thing… Will you make my wedding dress? Of course, I'll pay you, but it would mean everything to wear a dress sewn by you instead of a store-bought gown."

"Emily, I'd be thrilled to make your gown. Are you sure you don't want someone with more experience?"

"I want you. I've seen your work, and I want my dress made by my long-time friend."

Helen was misty-eyed. "I'm honored on both accounts. And thank you for giving me so much advance notice on the dress. I'll start thinking about designs."

Emily hugged her tightly. "You have a lot going on with the contest and your classes, so we can think more about the dress after we all graduate."

"And then we'll plan a shopping trip to Des Moines for the fabric." Helen was glad for a creative project she could put her heart into and keep her mind off men.

Edwin's advice restored her confidence, so Helen felt ready to carefully cut out the pieces, matching the herringbone pattern where seams would meet. She worked on the dress in the evenings when Bonnie was in bed, glad winter snow meant there was no garden to beckon her outside.

By the end of February, Helen finished the dress, showed it to Edwin, and mailed it into McCall's headquarters, relieved and happy with the results. Edwin suggested they enjoy a celebratory dinner together, which they did.

Edwin held his wine glass high and offered a toast. "Whether you win or not, your design was beautiful, and so was the execution of your dress."

"Thank you! And I appreciated your advice."

"I doubt you needed it, but I was happy to offer it anyway."

"On another topic, Bonnie is turning one March fifth, and I wondered if you'd like to come to a casual birthday dinner for her?"

"How nice! I'd love to."

After dinner, Edwin drove her home and once again ended the evening with a chaste kiss, leaving her standing on the front porch wondering if their relationship would ever amount to anything.

"Hey Mama, I hope you and Warren can come to Bonnie's first birthday party."

"I wouldn't miss it! What's the noise in the background?"

"Grandpa and Bonnie are playing in the living room. No one can make her giggle like he can!"

"This is so good for him – and all of you. It's been a long time since I heard him laugh. How is business?"

"Crazy busy since Christmas. Lots of alterations on clothing gifts. Now I'm starting on a few Easter dresses, and I even have an order for a wedding gown."

"I'm so proud of you, Helen."

"Thanks, Mama. It means a lot to me."

Helen served ham loaf with a sweet and sour glaze, mashed potatoes, biscuits, Jell-o salad, and canned green beans from last year's garden. But the main attraction was Bonnie's birthday cake. A two-layer confection frosted with a seven-minute boiled white frosting and decorated with animal crackers and gumdrops.

Bonnie was the center of attention in her high chair, and she made the most of her special day entertaining them with silly faces and blowing raspberries. When they finished dinner and presented her cake, her eyes lit up at the sight of it. The cake was her first taste of sugar, and she made a face after her first taste, and they all laughed. But with everyone watching, she used both fists to stuff as much as she could into her mouth and was soon covered in frosting.

Helen laughed at her antics. "Not very ladylike, Bonnie."

Cora fetched a clean washcloth. "I'll mop her up when she's finished."

After dinner, they gathered in the cozy living room, and Helen handed Bonnie the first gift. The wrapping paper enchanted Bonnie until she discovered the stuffed bear inside and hugged it to her as they all clapped. Helen also made her a crocheted lamb and a new dress.

Edwin's gift was next, a top that spun when you pushed on the handle.

Mama and Warren splurged on a babydoll with eyes that opened and shut and a wardrobe of new clothes for Bonnie to grow into.

Bonnie was confused with all the attention and stimulation as they showed her one new item after the other. She kept the stuffed bear in the crook of her arm, which made Helen smile.

Finally, Mama handed Helen a wrapped gift.

"This gift's for you. A baby's first birthday is truly a celebration for the parent who survived a baby's first year, and you deserve recognition for all you've gone through. These are tools for your trade Helen."

The package was heavy. Helen tore off the wrapping paper, and inside was a set of new scissors, including cutting, pinking, and embroidery shears.

"Thanks, Mama. These are perfect." She hugged her.

After picking up the wrapping papers, Helen said, "Can anyone stay for a game of cards? I think Bonnie is about ready for sleep."

"Sounds like fun. Okay with you, Warren?"

"Sure. What about you, Edwin?"

"Sorry, I promised Mother I'd pop over there tonight." He gave Helen a quick kiss and left.

Cora looked at her daughter. "Sorry, dear. He's certainly devoted to his mother."

Helen shrugged. "Yes. And I doubt that will ever change."

As she drifted off to sleep, Helen reflected on the year since her baby's birth. Grandma's death, escaping from Dirk's rage, moving into Grandpa's house, taking college classes, and now starting her own business. She loved being Bonnie's mother and delighted in every new tooth, word, and step. But there was an ache in her heart, a sense of emptiness. Was it selfish to want more? She enjoyed Edwin's cordial company, but his kisses never gave her the same heady dizziness she felt with Joseph. Probably just first love flutters, she decided.

Helen still hadn't heard about the pattern competition and assumed McCalls chose someone else's project, but she pushed it out of her mind.

Her goal was to make her business a success, with or without the prize money.

One sunny May morning, she put Bonnie in her stroller and started along Elm Street to work out the kinks in her shoulders. Mornings began with the sunrise, so she could sew for a few hours before Bonnie awoke. With breakfast over, they were off to look for daffodils, a sure sign of spring, before she'd head to campus—only light sweaters today, with a bonnet for her baby. Spring, with its abundant sunshine and apple-green leaves, chased away the last remnants of winter. She took a deep breath, and the scent of manure made her wrinkle her nose. Greenburg was close to farm fields. The awful smell brought conflicting memories of springtime on the farm. The joy of baby animals, yes, but also the reality of fertilizer and outhouse odours. It was a lifetime ago since they'd moved away from the farm. The move was life-changing for her. She was close enough to walk to school and then found a job at the Five and Dime store as a young teen. For the first time in her life, she had spending money and could invite friends over. Her teen years were filled with skating, bowling, and movies with friends, especially Joseph. But no time for sentimentality today. She shook her head back to reality. Life was heading in new directions, and she felt a surge of energy thinking about the possibilities. Spring was propelling her forward. She'd been back in Iowa just over a year, but she was pleased with all the positive changes in her life.

As much as she enjoyed her college classes, completing them meant more time to work on her business. And maybe her relationship with Edwin would blossom over the summer. She liked him but didn't feel a magnetic pull toward him, which perhaps meant she was maturing a bit. She was drawn to both Joseph and Dirk physically, and both relationships ended in disaster. Different kinds of disasters, but both left her shaken to her core. Some days she still wished she understood why Joseph fell for another gal while he was engaged.

I'll probably never know. But no point dwelling on that and spoiling this beautiful day. She took a cleansing breath to blow out the cobwebs of memories that might cloud this day, then threw back her shoulders, quickened her pace, and looked around. What, or rather who was that in the distance? She squinted against the sun to get a better look. Could it be? What was he doing?

Chapter 25

She squinted again, then stared before she was sure it was him. Joseph. What was he doing on that ladder? Not wanting to be detected, she inched forward, trying not to make a sound.

It looked like he was working on a house two doors away, engrossed in something. She froze for a moment and stared at the familiar profile. His straight nose, full mouth, and angled chin. The curly blond hair and muscular build. Her heart raced as she realized how much she missed even the sight of him. But she hesitated a millisecond too long. He looked over. *Maybe he didn't see me.* She turned the stroller around and headed in the opposite direction, her heart thumping.

"Helen," he called as he raced off his ladder. "Wait." He caught up to her and peeked at Bonnie in the stroller. "Hi! I was hoping I'd run into you, but I didn't know how to arrange it."

Helen backed up and shook her hair. "I don't think it's appropriate for us to talk."

"Because you're still angry with me?"

Eyebrows raised, she cocked her head to one side. "Because you're still married." *And maybe I am still angry. Why wouldn't I be?*

Joseph pulled one hand through his unruly hair. "Look, Helen, I'd like the chance to talk to you. Not here on the street. Can I pop over after work?"

Her eyes flashed. "Won't your wife be expecting you?" Helen was sarcastic and bitter. She didn't mean for her words to take on such an edge, but yes, she was still hopping mad.

He shook his head. "I, I don't have a…a wife anymore."

"Did you run out on her too?" Now she was swinging!

He looked at her and leaned forward. "Actually, she ran out on me. Are you happy?"

Helen just stared at him. A tiny chink in her armor cracked.

He blew out a loud sigh. "Could we please not have this conversation here? I'd like a chance to talk to you in private."

Helen wasn't sure she wanted to talk in private with Joseph or any man but wanted to hear what he had to say. Didn't she? She'd been angry at him for four years and in love with him for six years. Was it worth hearing him out?

She put a hand on her hip. "Come over after you finish work. But only for a few minutes."

She wasn't going to make this easy for him. And did he think she was just going to listen to his story and feel sorry for him? Never. She was angry. And the more she thought about how he broke their engagement, the angrier she got—calling her instead of telling her in person! Taking up with a floozy when he was already engaged! Putting her through the public humiliation of the break-up right before graduation. No, she was not going to get sucked into any sob story of his. No matter how badly he was hurt, he deserved it. He needed to suffer.

So why was she seeing him? And why did her heart do flip-flops at the thought of talking to him again? Four years had passed since she last saw him. Well, four years, two months, and six days since he called to ruin her life. While she vigorously brushed her hair and changed into a silky blue blouse that revealed a bit of cleavage, she clung to her anger. No one was going to feel pity for her. She was doing fine and didn't need him to turn her life on its head again.

But she was a mess. A bundle of nerves by the time he rang the doorbell. Oh, the emotions that evoked. The memorable dates that started with the sound of the doorbell and his handsome face at the door.

Grandpa took Bonnie out for a stroll so they could speak without interruption. Joseph was sweaty from work, and his hair was a mass of curls from working outside all day in the wind and humidity.

She invited him into the parlor that she used as her sewing workroom. They sat in straight-backed chairs facing each other. Now that they were alone, Joseph didn't seem to know where to begin.

"So, you have a little one?" he asked.

"Yes, Bonnie Ann. She's a year old. Grandpa's out walking her. I hear you have kids."

"Three, well, really two."

"Which is it? Three or two?"

Joseph's hand made a pass through his hair and rubbed one eye. "One of them isn't actually mine."

"Isn't ACTUALLY yours? Just sort of? How can that be?"

His hands flattened against his thighs as if he was about to stand. "It's difficult to explain."

She wasn't sure she wanted to hear more about that. Years without speaking to each other was making it difficult to begin. That and the anger Helen was still feeling. Did she want to have this conversation?

"So, where's Bonnie's father?"

"In Texas, where I hope he stays forever. Where's your wife?"

"Ex-wife. She took off for California with the kids. Then filed for divorce. I think she's already married again."

"Look, Joseph, if you've come here looking for sympathy, you won't find any. You walked out on me years ago. Since then, I've been through hell and back, and I'm not sure this is a good idea."

"I'm not looking for sympathy, Helen. I was hoping to explain what happened."

"I know what happened. Another gal came along, and you dumped me and broke our engagement. Now she's dumped you, and you're feeling sorry for yourself."

He let out a breath. "There was more to it. I was young and stupid."

"Yes, we were both young, and I was stupid to get involved with you."

Joseph studied the ground and nearly whispered. "I'm sorry you feel that way."

Helen's eyes were still shooting arrows. "How could I feel any different?"

"No, you're right. I'm not explaining myself very well."

Helen waited, perched rigidly on her chair.

Finally, Joseph stood. "Look, maybe we could go out for coffee sometime."

"I don't know what good it would do." Helen wasn't going to thaw out anytime soon. Helen opened the front door. Joseph looked at her for a moment as he stood in front of her.

"You're still incredibly beautiful, Helen."

She looked away, and he walked through the door. She closed it and stood at the door, wondering what she was supposed to do with the information and the compliment. For years, he never left her thoughts, but neither had the hurt he caused. She needed to move on.

But now that he was working at a house on her block, how would she avoid him? She was determined not to be a prisoner in her neighborhood. What was he doing anyway?

The next morning, she and Bonnie headed out again for their walk. She heard a whistle and ignored it. Then he whistled again. "Hey, Helen, good morning." He was scrambling down off his ladder. *Does he think I'm going to be drawn in by an immature whistle? Ha. Think again.*

"Good morning," she said stiffly and kept walking.

The third morning, he again turned and greeted her while standing on his ladder, and she stopped for a moment.

"What are you doing to that house anyway?"

"I'm an electrical contractor. Learned the skill while I was in the service, and now that I'm out, I work on private homes and businesses."

"When will you be moving on to another project?"

"Couple more days. Sick of seeing me?" The sun shone through his blond curls and cast a golden glow around his face. His smile made her weak in the knees.

"Yes, as a matter of fact, I am!" She took off down the street, pushing her stroller. The sooner he moved on to another project, the sooner she could forget him. How was she supposed to get him out of her mind when he was there every day in HER neighborhood?

She went by the house on the fourth day, and he wasn't there. She stopped and stared at the house. *Didn't he say he'd be here for another day?*

She craned her neck but didn't spot his truck. *Why do I care anyway?*

"Looking for me?" He startled her from behind. She jumped and turned around to see him. "Had to get some cable from my truck."

"I, I, uh was just admiring these daffodils. You parked in a different place."

"Same flowers that were here yesterday. And yes, my truck is back there," he said, pointing to a side street.

"The daffodils looked more beautiful today. Without you in the way."

He grinned and bent down to look into the stroller. "Hi, Bonnie Ann." Then straightened, cocked his head to one side, and smiled at Helen. She tried not to admire his dancing blue eyes and the cleft in his chin. The magic look that used to melt her heart. What a fool she'd been. Not anymore.

"Are you going to shun me forever, Helen of Troy?"

"That's the plan, yes. Now excuse me." And she strutted off, pushing Bonnie in the stroller, heart pounding.

On Sundays, Helen and Bonnie took Grandpa to church. Sometimes Mama and Warren drove over to attend with them. At first, Helen squirmed in the pews, feeling out of place since she hadn't darkened the door of a church for several years. Hadn't even gotten married in a church. But she agreed to bring Grandpa, which was his one request when she moved in with him again.

Music was the first part of the service that spoke to her heart. She loved singing growing up – especially in high school. The words to the hymns held new meaning to her now that she understood how precious life was and how quickly it could change. As Pastor Gerald spoke of God's love and mercy, it resonated deep in her frozen heart. Could God forgive her for turning her back on him? Week-by-week, the pastor's words chipped away at the iceberg inside her.

There was a brief graduation ceremony for those who took the one-year course in tailoring and dressmaking just before Memorial Day. The ceremony was only for the students and teachers, which included Edwin. After the ceremony, he gave her a book on sewing embellishments.

"I know how you love to add your special touches to garments, so I thought you'd enjoy this."

"Thank you! What a thoughtful gift."

After her graduation, Cora and Warren invited Helen, Grandpa, and Bonnie to their home to celebrate Helen's accomplishments.

Cora held a glass of wine. "I want to toast you, Helen, for your progress not only in your classes but also your business."

"Thank you, Mama. Now, if you don't mind my bragging, I have a bit of news. At our school ceremony, they announced I won the McCalls competition and a prize of $25!"

The Greenberg newspaper and the Des Moines Register ran stories about the local woman who won the national McCalls competition, which kept customers calling and business growing as word got out that Helen was an excellent seamstress. She made little dresses with pinafores for Bonnie and embroidered tiny flowers and designs on Bonnie's dresses and bonnets during quiet times. And sometimes found herself thinking of Grandma while embroidering. Despite Grandma's temper and impatience, they spent many evenings together sewing, crocheting, doing embroidery, and other skills she was drawing on now. Good memories with Grandma which Helen wanted, no, needed to tap into.

With business growing, the range of client requests also grew. Some required only a few hours of mending or simple alterations, but others needed complicated adjustments to garments. Or entirely new creations. Projects were piled high on the work table with clothes in different stages of completion. Most customers were happy for her services and understood her waiting list was several weeks long, but then there was Bertha, or rather, Mrs. Schmidt.

Bertha blew in like a fierce windstorm after she read the article about Mrs. Betzini's business. She arrived without making an appointment and carried in bags full of suits and dresses she wanted Helen to alter. Bertha said some needed new zippers, others had missing buttons, but all of them were tight.

"Mrs. Betzini, I need your help. Something happened to these over the winter."

Helen tried to understand the issue. "Tell me what needs to be altered."

Bertha reached into the bag and pulled out a dress. "This must have shrunk in my new clothes dryer. I need you to let it out."

Helen examined the dress and found there were no seams large enough for the necessary changes. She measured Bertha and then measured the dress.

"I'm afraid this dress is about two sizes smaller than your measurements."

"That's impossible. I just wore this last fall." She reached into the bag and pulled out another dress. "This one needs a new zipper."

Helen took the dress and worked the zipper successfully. "It seems to be working now."

"Is there anywhere I can try this on and show you?"

Helen showed her to the bathroom, and Mrs. Schmidt came out wearing the dress, and as she turned around, Helen could see her girdle where the zipper wouldn't come together.

"See what I mean? The zipper doesn't work."

Helen yanked and pulled on the zipper, but it wouldn't budge. "Mrs. Schmidt, this dress is too small. The zipper won't work because both sides of it need to touch, and they are several inches away from that."

"Too small, eh? Well, can't you fix it?"

"I could add side panels to the dress, but I don't have the original fabric, and I'm afraid it would look odd."

One by one, they went through the bag of ill-fitting clothes. Helen tried tactfully to help her understand the problem was caused by more than the dryer. She needed a new wardrobe.

"Why don't I make you a new summer dress, and if you like it, you can order more." Helen took her measurements and packed her dresses back into her bag.

"Fine! But Mrs. Betzini, nothing in pink. The color makes me look pale."

"I should have it finished in two weeks. I'll see you then."

Chapter 26

The newspaper announced the July 4 celebration in Greensberg was approaching, and this year the festival would be grander than ever. Many businesses planned to build floats or drive cars, bicycles, or horse-drawn buggies with signs to promote themselves. With soldiers home and the war in the rear mirror, there was a significant push to rebuild the economy. Houses were assembled in neat rows, businesses sprang up in downtown districts, and optimism filled the air. Helen wanted to be part of this. Grandpa said she could drive his Ford Coupe, and she made signs for both sides of it. She asked Edwin to drive the car in the parade so she could hold Bonnie and wave and toss out candy and fliers.

She dolled up Bonnie in a red dress with a white pinafore. A navy-blue bonnet edged in delicate white lace kept the sun off the tot's face. Bonnie was a crowd-pleaser smiling and giggling as their decked-out car slowly made its way along Main Street.

Helen had a great time showing off her baby and promoting her business. Until she spotted Joseph, who stood alone by a light pole. He took off his cap and waved it as she went by, and their eyes connected for a flutter of a moment, setting her heart to race. Her smile froze for a second until she recovered her composure, and the car crawled slowly forward. *Why can't I get over him? What power does he have over me?* She hoped Edwin didn't see her reaction.

Don't get swept away again by emotions. Stay focused. After the parade, she, Edwin, and Bonnie walked around Main Street Square and sampled offerings from food vendors. Their next stop was the petting zoo, where Bonnie wanted to touch all the farm animals, especially the baby goats who ran to her bleating and begging for treats. Edwin was gentle and patient with Bonnie's changing needs. Seeing him hold her hand and kiss her cheeks, Helen wondered if he could be a father to Bonnie. The problem was she didn't see herself married to him, but perhaps she was afraid to get emotionally involved with anyone.

While watching the world from her daughter's eyes, she had the unsettling feeling someone was watching her. Or was she on the lookout for him? *Forget him, Helen.*

After a full day of adventure, Helen put her baby to bed for the night. Grandpa said he would listen for her so Helen could join Emily and Jacob for the fireworks. Edwin declined to join them, saying he promised to watch the fireworks with his mother from her balcony.

Helen found them at the park, and to her dismay, Joseph was with them. Jacob hadn't mentioned Joseph was joining them. Like old times. Only those days were gone and would never return. Since the four of them went roller skating and took in Saturday night pictures at the cinema, too much pain transpired.

They laid out a few large blankets to wait until dusk for the official fireworks. Emily and Jacob sat together on one, leaving Helen to sit next to Joseph on the other. She hesitated as Joseph sat.

"Come on, Helen, I won't bite," Joseph said.

Okay, I can do this. I'll show him he has no effect on me. No big deal.

"Promise?" she said and plopped next to him. The sun was just setting over the town, leaving streaks of orange and pink painted across the sky. Fireworks would start after it was completely dark. At least the planned fireworks.

Joseph picked a piece of grass next to the blanket and chewed on it. "Your baby sure was a show stopper in the parade today."

"Thanks." *Don't try to charm me.* "She's a happy little one. Easy to please."

"Motherhood suits you," he said.

"It's the best part of my life." She kept her eyes focused on the sky as silence as heavy as rain clouds enveloped them.

"Who was the guy driving you around? New beau?"

"Yes, not that it's any of your concern. He was my tailoring instructor."

"How long have you been seein' each other?"

She looked away and fiddled with the blanket. "Since December."

"You serious about him?"

Her eyes flashed. "Why do you care?"

"Just curious, Helen."

"He's a nice guy. Decent."

"Decent! Well, that's great."

Tension hung between them as Helen shifted her attention to people in the crowd. She smiled, waved, and nodded towards clients, former school chums, or folks she recognized from church—anything to keep from looking at Joseph.

"The sunset's bringing out the red in your hair."

"Thanks, I think."

This small talk was painful. When would the show begin? In silent anticipation, they watched the last streaks of color fade to indigo as the moon peeked through the trees, casting a lacey pattern over their blanket and faces.

She was relieved to hear the first boom and see a blaze of fire followed by plumes of crimson and blue and sat back on her elbows to watch the sparkles and shimmers ignite the sky and then fade to dust. Lush rings of color exploded into soft speckles, creating a velvet-like effect. She stole a glance at Joseph, and when their eyes met, she quickly looked away and tried to focus on the fireworks in the sky and not the clash of emotions inside her.

When the finale erupted and filled the night sky with red, white, and blue swirls and stars, she was relieved - and disappointed. She hopped up and quickly said goodnight to her three companions.

Joseph followed and reached for her elbow. "Let me walk you home."

She pulled back. "No need, I'm just a few blocks away." She didn't wait for objections but sped off briskly.

Edwin invited Helen and Bonnie to the county fair in early August, where there were dozens of different animals on display for Bonnie and needlecrafts, quilts, and clothing displays for Edwin and Helen to admire. They purchased corn dogs from a food vendor and wandered through the exhibits of items competing for ribbons.

"You should enter something next year, Helen. I'll bet you'd win a blue ribbon."

"Thanks for your confidence. I'll think about it. What about you? Why not enter a suit you made, Mr. Tayloring guy."

Edwin laughed. "You're right! Even though I'm not trying to build a business, I should enter for the fun of it."

As they moved to the exhibit of baby animals, Bonnie reached for the baby chicks. With a volunteer assisting, children could hold and caress a tiny ball of yellow fluff. Bonnie was nervous, so Helen held the chick and let Bonnie stroke it.

"This brings back memories. Grandma raised chickens on the farm."

A familiar voice chimed in. "I remember you talking about the farm."

Helen stood and nearly dropped the chick. "Joseph! What are you doing here?"

He smiled and waved at Bonnie. "Same as you, enjoying the fair. Hi Bonnie."

Helen's cheeks flamed. "Um, Edwin, this is Joseph, a high school friend."

The men shook hands. Edwin asked, "You here alone, Joseph?"

"Yeah, just wanted to take in the fair."

Edwin smiled. "Why don't you join us?"

Helen gasped. "No, he doesn't want to! I mean, we'll probably be interested in different displays."

Edwin furled his eyebrows and studied her.

Joseph chuckled. "You're right, Helen. I was heading to the home industrial displays, which would bore you silly."

"Yes. Right. Goodbye, Joseph." Helen put the chick back, turned, and walked away.

Still holding Bonnie, Edwin followed for a bit before speaking. "Helen, why were you so rude to that man?"

She pushed her hair behind one ear. "Was I?"

His eyes studied her. "Yes, and you seemed nervous. Are you afraid of him?'

She looked away. "No, nothing like that. I just didn't want to see him."

A knock at the door interrupted her work one warm August afternoon.

Joseph was wearing his work clothes and his most charming smile. His wind-blown curls added to his rugged appearance. "Excuse me, ma'am. I understand you do mending and alterations, and I need your services." He crossed into the entry, carrying in a pile of work clothes. "These work pants need patches, and I have a pair of trousers that need to be hemmed."

Helen was ruffled at the sight of him but smiled. *Okay, I can handle this. Just a business transaction.* She led him into her work room and noted where to sew patches, but the dress trousers might be awkward.

"You'll need to try the trousers on so I can mark the hem." She pointed him to a bathroom, and when he emerged, she had him stand on a chair while she got her pincushion.

"Business going well for you?" He was nonchalant as he stood quite still on the chair.

"Business is brisk. I work long hours while Bonnie's sleeping, but I enjoy the independence."

"You won't poke a pin into me, will you?"

She smirked despite her determination not to be charmed by him. "Not if you stand still." Her hands shook a bit, being so close to him, but she worked quickly to finish.

"How's your Grandpa doing?"

"He's out for a walk, but I think he's adjusting to having a baby around again. He needs someone here to look after him." *Keep chatting, Helen. Just like before. Just easy chats, and he'll be gone in a few minutes.*

"I was sorry to hear about your grandmother."

"Thank you, but we both know she could be a pain in the neck. I was in Texas when she passed."

"I thought she was going to skewer me the first time I met her."

Helen giggled at the memory. "Ha! A charmer she was not!"

She finished pinning the pants, and Joseph jumped off the chair and changed back into his work clothes.

"I'll have everything ready for you in three days," she said as she handed him the bill. "You can pay me then." The longing to hug him surprised her, but she kept her distance.

"Swell!" He smiled. They stood looking at each other for a long moment.

Helen finally opened the door. "Goodbye."

Joseph took a step to leave and then stopped at the door, paused, then ran his hand through his hair as if he had more to say, let out a breath, and bounded down the front steps.

Helen fussed over her stitches while working on his clothes and worried he'd think her skills were inferior. *That's silly, Helen. What does he know about sewing!*

Three days later, he appeared again after his workday to collect his clothes. He took a moment to look over his pants, and she held her breath, hoping he'd be happy. *He's just a customer, of course, you want him to be pleased with your service.*

He handed her the money, and their hands brushed against each other. He grasped her hand gently and said, "Helen, please give me a chance to explain."

"It won't do any good." Her heart was too wounded ever to trust him again.

"All I'm asking is for you to hear me out. I don't expect you to take me back, but I'd at least like to be on friendly terms. I mean, if it's okay with Edwin." He looked into her eyes and delivered a smile even an ice queen couldn't resist.

"I don't have to get Edwin's permission – or anyone else's."

"So, if it's not a problem, why not give me a few minutes."

She sighed. "Come back tonight after the baby's in bed. We can go for a walk."

Chapter 27

Helen changed into an ivory blouse, a royal blue skirt, and comfortable wedged shoes perfect for an evening stroll. Grandpa greeted Joseph warmly as he answered the door. Bonnie was already asleep in her crib.

They walked to the park near Main Street, where they watched the fireworks together just weeks before. A place they frequented many times – a lifetime ago. The familiarity of it calmed Helen's nerves. Why was she so hesitant to hear what he had to say? Afraid to hear she wasn't good enough? Pretty enough? Worthy of love?

They found a bench and sat under the dusky sky as the sun painted a picture of orange sherbet with streaks of raspberry. The park was deserted, except for birds chattering in the evergreen trees and the occasional rabbit or squirrel scurrying about rustling through the bushes. Joseph took a breath and started awkwardly.

"When I moved away after graduation, it was a difficult transition. I had never lived alone before. I was always surrounded by family and friends… and especially you. I couldn't come to see you often due to the gasoline rationing. And, well, I was lonely."

She looked at her hands, not wanting to see the pain in his face. "I was lonely, too, without you. But I stayed true to you."

"Yes, I can't excuse my behavior, but I want you to understand. I was heading for the service soon and wondered if I'd come back wounded or die overseas. The worry consumed me."

Helen nodded. She worried about the same things.

"A woman at work, who was several years older than me, decided to take her lunch with me every day. We'd chat about work and our lives. She was flirtatious, and I was young and stupid. She was the one who first asked me to dinner at her place. I was lonely, so I went. I thought it was just a dinner, so what could it hurt?"

"And all the while, I was spending evenings alone with my grandparents."

"I know it was wrong, but we were so young when we got engaged. I never spent much time with other girls, and I started to have doubts."

"You doubted I was the right girl for you?" This was difficult to hear. But at least they were talking.

"I doubted our relationship, not you. I started to think you were too good for me. I hadn't had the chance to date other people. This gal, Lucy, was far more experienced. She drew me in. And when I'd go home to visit you, things were so awkward between us. Probably because I was so conflicted."

"Things didn't seem the same, but I thought the distance between us was to blame. I never suspected you were seeing someone else because I trusted you so fiercely."

"At first, we were just friends having lunch together, so I didn't mention it to you. But things escalated, and she invited me to her apartment. Then after only being with her a few times, Lucy told me she was pregnant."

"That's when you called me to break off our engagement?"

"Yes, I felt trapped and panicked, but I thought marrying her was the right thing to do. I waited a few months to be sure she was pregnant."

"Sounds like you didn't completely trust her, even then."

"I didn't, and I still hoped I could somehow fix things with you. But when she started to show, I realized it was true, and I had to marry her. The next thing I knew, I was called up to the Air Corps."

"I heard you served for several years, even after the war." *I prayed for your safety.*

"I came home on break and met our first child. But somehow, she had two more kids in the three years I was gone. The last child isn't the same race, so I know she doesn't belong to me."

"Did Lucy admit it?"

"She didn't have to. It's obvious to anyone who has eyes. I don't think she was ever faithful to me. I got out of the service, came home, and confronted her, and she packed the kids and took off one day while I was at work. When she got to California, she sent divorce papers."

"Nice lady!"

"She was a piece of work. Always lying and changing her stories. I knew before we married I didn't love her, but I thought we should marry for the child's sake. I wanted to provide for my child."

"Did you terminate your parental rights?"

"No. I still want to be a presence in their lives, but they're so far away!"

"Just like my father was far from me growing up. And now Bonnie's father is out of her life."

"Has he given up his rights?"

"Yes, thank goodness. He's a dangerous man, and I don't want Bonnie ever to meet him."

"Dangerous? What happened?"

"Let's not talk about it now."

She looked up, and blinking stars made her feel insignificant against the vastness of the night sky. The irony of their situations stared her in the face. Tears puddled in Helen's eyes, and she hoped he wouldn't see them in the dark, but when she looked at Joseph, she could see the sheen of moisture in his eyes.

"I made a mess of things, Helen. I'm sorry I wasn't man enough to be faithful to you!"

"I made my own mistakes. And you're right. We were both young and inexperienced."

He sighed and reached for her hand, and she didn't pull it away. "Do you think you'll ever be able to forgive me, Helen?"

Helen shook her head and whispered. "I don't know."

"Can we at least start over and be friends again?"

"Yes, I think that's where we should start. As friends." Helen squeezed his hand. As they stood, Joseph pulled her into his arms, and as they hugged, some of the hurt eased, loosening the knot inside a bit. It felt so good to be in his arms again, and she wanted to nuzzle into his neck, but Helen was cautious. She lost her heart to Joseph once and nearly lost her life with Dirk and now had to protect herself. And Joseph needed to prove he was trustworthy. She pulled away, and they walked home in silence. When they reached her porch, she held out her hand to shake his, but Joseph brought it to his lips and kissed her hand as he looked into her eyes, leaving her heart tingling from his touch.

Sunday morning, the church was stuffy with heat and humidity. Windows were opened to catch any available breeze but attracted more black flies than relief. Helen's yellow sundress was a little more casual than the dresses she usually wore to church, so she donned a straw hat, which later felt like a steam oven on her head.

The pastor's message was on love. How ironic, she thought as she tried to focus on Pastor Gerald's words while balancing a squirming toddler in her lap. Bonnie's cheeks were flushed, and she had long since pulled off her white bonnet, exposing tight ringlets. Helen blew gently on her face to cool her, but Joseph's image dominated her brain.

When her attention resurfaced, the pastor's words were even more thorny to understand. "God loves each of us, and we should try to hear His "I love you" in our hearts."

Helen struggled with the idea of listening for God's love. Love, in general, was a mystery. She never felt deeply loved. The two men who professed to love her, Joseph and Dirk, both betrayed her. And she'd been dating Edwin for months, but there was no declaration of love from him. He was a kind man and pleasant company, but nothing more.

"Think of God as your father because he loves you infinitely more than your earthly father," Pastor Gerald continued.

My earthly father! Ha! He said he loved me when I met him but never did anything to show me love. No visits, letters, presents, phone calls. How was I supposed to feel love from him?

Mama was the closest person to her in her youth, yet she was rarely there. She was affectionate when Helen was little, on the occasions they were together. Helen had an ache in her heart as she recalled times when she clung to Mama's waist, crying and begging her not to leave again. But as the county midwife, Mama had little choice. Her job kept her away long hours and sometimes for days as she attended to women and babies. As an adult, Helen realized how difficult this was for Mama and how torn she was. Especially leaving Helen with Grandma, who told her regularly, she was not wanted and was a bother. Grandpa was kinder but worked long hours on the farm and later building roads, but he had trouble expressing love and affection.

She pondered the message after the service as she prepared lunch for Bonnie, Grandpa, and herself. Yes, something was missing from her life, but there was nothing she could do about it. She couldn't rewrite the script of her youth. How was she supposed to feel God's love when she hadn't known love on earth, and why had a message about love sent her into a funk?

She vowed to help Bonnie feel loved and would never make her baby girl feel she was a mistake or an imposition. Later, as Helen altered a suit for a customer, the pastor's message wrapped her in a heavy mental blanket. *What does it feel like to know love? Will I ever experience it?*

Helen shook off the pastor's words as a new week began. Monday, Bertha Schmidt was coming to see the new dress, and Helen hoped it fit.

Mrs. Schmidt arrived a bit late on Monday morning, a bead of sweat on her forehead.

"Good morning. I hope you like the fabric I chose." Helen held a mint green dress in cotton seersucker.

"It looks enormous! It'll swim on me. Mrs. Betzini, what were you thinking?"

Helen kept her temper in check. "I thought a dress with a little wiggle room would be more comfortable in this heat. Mrs. Schmidt, why don't you try it on?"

Bertha went into the small bathroom to change and came back to show Helen.

"It's too big! And I don't like the color. What size did you make this?"

"Your measurements show you're a size 18, which is what I made. The fit looks perfect."

"I wear a size 14! Not 18. Are you trying to insult me?"

"No, of course not. Size is only a number. I think the dress is flattering on you."

"Flattering! What an insult."

"Mrs. Schmidt, the color goes well with your complexion, and the style makes you look slimmer."

"Slimmer? Are you saying I'm overweight?"

"No, of course not. I think the dress looks very nice on you."

"You're only saying that because you want to be paid! Well, I'm not going to pay you." Bertha went back into the bathroom to change. She came out and thrust the dress into Helen's hands. "You can keep this."

After she stormed out, Helen called Emily to vent.

"This angry woman just refused to pay me for a dress I made her. None of her clothes fit, but she won't face the fact her figure has changed."

"Changed? From what?"

"Mrs. Schmidt clearly forgot to stop celebrating the holidays last January and packed on the pounds all winter and spring."

Emily giggled. "I wouldn't worry about it too much. You can't please everyone, Helen.

"I do intend to please you, though. Want to pop over and go over the designs for your wedding dress?"

"Yes! I can't wait to see them."

Within minutes, Emily arrived, and she and Helen analyzed the three designs Helen created. After Emily selected her favorite, Helen carefully took all the needed measurements and then poured them both a glass of lemonade. They went into the living room for a chance to chat.

Emily took a sip of her cold drink. "Where's your grandpa and Bonnie?"

"He took her to the park since I had a client coming over."

She nodded in approval. "Wonderful man, that grandpa of yours. Speaking of wonderful men, what's happening between you and Edwin and Joseph."

"Well, you got right to the point! I wish I knew. Edwin is kind and respectful. He's thoughtful and great with Bonnie."

"But what about you? Is he great with you?"

"I like him, but I don't think about him when he's not around."

Emily's eyebrows raised. "Who do you think about?"

"You know darned well. It's still Joseph. I can't seem to shake him."

"Why fight it?"

"After what happened, I'm not sure if I could ever trust him again. But we went for a walk last week, and he explained how he got trapped in that marriage. Do you know, one of the kids who she claimed was his isn't even the same race?"

"Horrible. What a betrayal."

"He didn't blame everything on her, which I respected. He admitted his part in the affair. I know he was young and stupid, but if I get involved with him, will I always be on my guard that he's having another affair?"

"But what if you pass up the chance for happiness out of fear?"

"It makes my head hurt to think about it. For now, I'm just going to worry about Bonnie, Grandpa, and your wedding dress!"

Emily brightened. "And your matron of honor dress. Don't forget it!"

"Haven't started it yet, but there's plenty of time. Your dress is my priority."

Chapter 28

Each day after bending over her sewing machine, she could barely raise her head. The quiet time sewing gave her time to think, but the cares of the day crowded out any lasting peace.

Her shoulders ached as she reached to lift Bonnie, and as she caught a glimpse of her reflection, she saw the posture of a 90-year-old. The "dog days of summer" ushered in a steaming combo of heat and humidity, making their "feels like" temps read in the tropical range. Living in the sauna with small fans as the only relief shortened tempers, swelled ankles, and made sleeping nearly impossible. And lack of sleep meant more crankiness. She longed for a blissful escape.

"Hot enough for you?" or "Hot enough to fry an egg on your head?" were endlessly repeated around town when she did errands. Ugh. She tried to manage a smile when an old-timer said this when she was in the grocery store, but the tired cliches made her groan.

Helen complained to Grandpa about the heat one evening as she was sweating into the frying pan as she browned hamburgers, potatoes, and onions for supper.

"Heat and humidity are good for the corn," he reminded her.

"Why aren't you sweating? "

"Used to it, I guess."

She and Bonnie had permanently beaded foreheads. Naps were shorter, which meant less time to sew and more time keeping Bonnie cool while simultaneously keeping tiny fingers out of whirling fans.

"Hi precious one," she said as she lifted Bonnie out of her crib. "What a short nap, little lady. Shall we play in the water?" Bonnie lay her head on Helen's shoulder, still shaking off dreamland. Helen hugged her fiercely and kissed her cheeks, feeling a flood of love for her toddler. "I love you, Bonnie," she said as she held her, swaying gently back and forth.

Helen found the large metal tub she kept on the porch for their outside playtime and set it on the lawn. She filled it partway with cool water and stripped Bonnie to her diaper. Bonnie was fully awake now that she noticed the tub and her favorite rubber ducky. Helen added some dish soap and flapped her hand in the water to create bubbles.

Sitting on the lush grass, Helen admired Bonnie's strawberry blond ringlets and flushed cheeks. She kissed her tiny hands and looked into her chocolate brown eyes. "Say, Mama," she begged, but Bonnie was too preoccupied with the bubbles.

While they were playing, Joseph drove up. His face was beet red from the sun, and his clothes were soaked from a long day wiring a house.

"Hi Helen! I have an idea to take our minds off this blasted heat. Are you in?"

"If it's ice cream, yes, we are."

"Sorry, no. I have a surprise for tomorrow I think you'll both love. Can you be ready by six tomorrow night?"

"A surprise, huh? I've never liked surprises. How do I know this one will turn out well?"

"Trust me. Or don't. But be ready tomorrow night." He swiped the back of his hand over his forehead. "My shower's beckoning."

As he turned and walked back to his car, Helen couldn't help notice the bulging biceps under his work shirt. She always admired his broad shoulders, and the years of hard work looked good on Joseph. *What would it feel like to…? Snap out of it, Helen.*

Surprise, huh. What should she wear? Where were they going? Who else would be there? She finally decided to wear a light blue cotton dress she made to match her eyes. She painted her toenails deep red after a cool bath. *It's a treat to pamper myself.*

She brushed her hair, put it in a loose bun, and then fastened the pearl-like buttons down the front. *No, hair's too fussy.* She pulled the pins out and shook her curls loose. *Too wild.* Next, she pulled one side back and tucked a white gardenia from her garden behind her ear. *Hope he doesn't think I'm trying too hard. It's fun to dress up. That's all this is.* Her white sandals would keep her feet cool. On impulse, she reached for the atomizer and finished with a light spray of rosewater. She chose a soft pink cotton dress for Bonnie with white shoes and a white sweater, in case there was a chill later on. *Wishful thinking. It won't cool for months.*

Joseph smiled approvingly when he caught a whiff of Helen's cologne. "Someone smells fresh, and I love the flower in your hair. I did tell you we're going canoeing, right, pretty lady?" He winked as they walked to his car.

"No mention of water, but any chance we can get a hint?" Helen was never good with surprises.

"We'll be there in 20 minutes, and it begins with the letter 'c,' but we've ruled out canoeing.'" He started the car, and they were off.

"That's a relief. I'm dressed completely wrong for canoeing."

He grinned at her and kept driving. "Yes, I noticed. That's a pretty dress on you."

"Oh, uh, thank you. Climbing? Are we going to climb a big hill?"

"No again."

"Good. Bonnie's not in the mood for a big climb tonight."

"Oh, Bonnie's not, huh? What do you think your toddler wants to do tonight?"

"Chew. She's teething again and would like something to chew."

"We might find something to chew, but that's not our main objective."

Helen grinned. "That leaves out a candy factory with chocolate and caramel. How about coach – a ride on a horse-drawn coach."

"You're getting warmer. There will be animals."

"Animals, hmmm. A farm or zoo would have animals, but they don't start with 'c.'"

Joseph raised his eyebrows and smiled. "You'll see soon enough."

Within minutes they stopped in a parking lot next to an enormous tent set in an empty field. They scrambled out of the car, and the music ringing from the tent drew them closer to a clown who beckoned them inside.

Helen couldn't contain her excitement. "Circus! Bonnie, we're going to see a circus!" Bonnie's eyes widened as Helen showed her the tent's bright lights, and they sniffed the scent of popcorn and peanuts.

Joseph beamed. "Surprised?" His pleasure at pulling off the mystery was evident.

"Yes. I've never seen a circus!"

Inside they scrambled to walk across the hay-strewn tent floor and found seats in the bleachers. Joseph bought them popcorn. "Something for Bonnie to chew, just as I promised."

Helen, Bonnie, and Joseph sat mesmerized at the sight of six elephants decked out in bells and red garlands. Acrobats dressed in airy costumes rode and sometimes danced atop the enormous creatures. When the elephants formed a line in perfect order and got on one knee, the crowd went wild, and Joseph put his arm around Helen's shoulder and gave it a slight squeeze.

"Having fun?" He had to whisper in her ear because of the crowd noise, making goosebumps break out on Helen's arm.

"Joseph! This is wonderful. Thank you so much," she whispered and smiled at him as he removed his hand from her shoulder to focus on the next act.

Next came a set of four white tigers and a trainer who was unafraid of their potential power as he commanded them to do tricks. There was a collective gasp when he put his head inside the open mouth of the largest tiger. When miniature horses arrived, ridden by monkeys with fringed hats riding atop decorative saddle blankets, they quickly became a crowd favorite. Helen whispered in Bonnie's ear to tell her the names of each animal.

When the trapeze acts began, Bonnie sat back on Helen's lap, and they all looked in amazement at the performers' agility and grace. Helen covered her baby's ears for the final act when they shot a man out of a canon.

"How do they do it without killing him?" She whispered to Joseph, who laughed and shook his head. She wanted to lean against him but held herself still.

She had to admit Joseph was making a valiant effort to smooth out their friendship. But she kept herself from showing affection and didn't want to give the impression this was a date.

Bonnie fell asleep in the car on the way home.

"That was so much fun, Joseph. Thank you! What a wonderful surprise."

"So happy you and Bonnie liked it. Perhaps you ladies will let me surprise you again."

Helen grinned and raised her eyebrows. "Perhaps."

When they arrived at her house, Joseph dashed around the front of the car and said, "Let me carry the baby." Carefully he lifted Bonnie, and together they tiptoed into the house and upstairs to her room. He gently lay her in the crib. They both watched the sleeping toddler for a minute.

"She's a lovely baby," he whispered. "I long for my kids."

Helen nodded. She would ache to be away from her little one and realized how difficult it must be for him. They walked to the front door. The house was still with both Bonnie and Grandpa sleeping. She smiled, remembering the first time they were on a date when Grandma turned on the porch light above them so they wouldn't kiss. Butterflies of nervousness flitted in her tummy now as Helen wondered if Joseph would reach for her. It felt so natural being with him again, but she kept her guard up to protect her heart.

She grinned at him and spoke quietly, not wanting to awaken Grandpa. "Thank you again, Joseph. What a wonderful surprise, even though there was no chocolate." She stuck out her hand to shake his, and again he took it, pressed it to his lips, and delicately kissed each of her fingers.

"Good night, Helen of Troy."

How would she ever sleep after such a magical evening with him? She was beginning to see him differently now and realized he wasn't the 18-year-old who broke her heart. He was a mature man with his own experiences and heartbreaks that only added to his allure. The more she got to know this Joseph, the more she longed to be with him.

Chapter 29

She shut the door behind Joseph and leaned against it, longing to see him again. Soon. *I'm supposed to be mad at him. Isn't this the jerk who broke my heart? Maybe he's matured?* She went to bed, confused but with a warm glow inside her from spending time so close to him. After all the years of missing him and despite the anger and hurt, she never stopped loving him. And now, he was finally in her life again. Wasn't he? Even if they could never be more than friends, she was happy to enjoy his company. But would she be satisfied just being friends?

She was still enjoying Edwin's company. After a lunch date, he suggested they stop at his mother's house so he could change a few lightbulbs for her. Emily was watching Bonnie so Helen could have a break. Edwin and Helen planned to go swimming after the quick errand, and since Helen had never met his mother, she secretly wondered if this was a sign that the relationship would get serious? She wasn't sure how she felt, except curious about the woman who kept Edwin at her beck and call.

Edwin called out as he entered the house. "Hello, Mother, I'm here." They went into the living room together and found her sitting on the sofa. Edwin's mother looked over, and her face contorted.

"What? What is SHE doing here?"

Edwin was confused. "Mother, this is Helen."

"That's Mrs. Betzini! The one who refused to alter my clothes."

He looked at Helen, whose eyes were wild.

"Mrs. Schmidt? Bertha?" Then Helen turned to Edwin. "She refused to pay for a dress I made her. The only client who's ever refused to pay me."

Edwin looked back and forth between them. "Do you two know each other?"

Bertha said, "What are you doing with a married woman?"

Helen put her hands on her hips and looked at Edwin. "I thought your last name was Hibbs!"

"No, I mean yes. Hibbs was my mother's first husband. And Mother, Helen isn't married. She's divorced."

"Damaged goods!"

"How can you say that, Mother, when you were divorced twice! And if you needed clothes altered, why didn't you ask me?"

"What mother asks her son to alter her clothes? I needed a woman. But this imposter kept telling me she couldn't fix my clothes."

Edwin turned to Helen. "Why couldn't you help her?"

"She's trying to fit into a size 14 dress when she measures size 18. I made her a dress according to her measurements, and she threw it in my face."

"Oh!"

"Yes, and you told me your father passed away!"

Edwin was getting rattled. "He has. They divorced when I was a child, and he died later. Technically it wasn't a lie."

Bertha was still slumped on her couch. "You said you were dating someone named Helen. You disguised her real name."

"I didn't mislead you. Helen is her name. She uses Mrs. Betzini as a business name."

"So that's a lie too?"

Helen was infuriated. "No! Mrs. Betzini is my legal name. And Helen is my first name."

"And where is your husband, young lady?"

Helen's lips tightened into two narrow lines as she spat out the words. "My ex-husband is in prison, where he belongs."

Bertha's hand flew to her heart. "Prison! Son, who have you gotten involved with? Isn't Betzini a mafia name?"

"No, Mother, stop! This has nothing to do with me. I'm not involved with anything. We're just having fun."

Helen was white with rage. "Well, thank you for clarifying our relationship." She bolted out of the house and sprinted along the sidewalk.

Edwin followed and caught up with her.

"Please, Helen, let me drive you home and explain."

"Why do men always need to explain? Why can't they just be honest."

"I'm trying to be honest. Please, let's talk in the car."

They drove to her house, and Edwin turned off the motor and reached for her hand, which she reluctantly relinquished.

"Helen, please let me explain. I meant to say I wasn't involved in anything illegal. My mother gets things so twisted, and then I get confused and say the wrong thing. I'd like to continue seeing you. I enjoy your company."

"I enjoy you too, but I don't think it's enough for me. Our relationship doesn't seem to be going anywhere."

"I assumed after a painful divorce you wouldn't want anything serious."

"You're partly right. But in all honesty, someone else has come back into my life. My first boyfriend. We were all set to get married, and things went terribly wrong, and we broke up."

Edwin pulled his hand back. "The man we ran into at the county fair?"

"Yes, Joseph. We married other people when we were teens, and we're both divorced now. I still have feelings for him, so it isn't fair of me to continue to see you as I'm sorting this out."

Edwin sighed. "Now, who wasn't honest? When were you going to come clean with all this?"

"Come clean? We had no agreement not to see other people. As you said, we were just having fun."

"I was a fool. I should have told you how much I care for you, but I thought it would scare you away."

"It might have. Or your mother would've scared me off. She's a lot to deal with, Edwin."

"Yes, she is. I try to be a good son because she's alone in the world. But she doesn't understand I need a life away from her."

"You're a good son, but if your mother is always your first priority, there won't be room for anyone else."

"And now is it too late?"

"I'm afraid it is. I can't see a future for us. I'm sorry, Edwin."

He nodded thoughtfully. "Well, if it's too late, I hope we can end as friends. You'll always have a soft spot in my heart, Helen. And I'll miss Bonnie."

"Thank you, Edwin. Yes, I don't want you to hate me. You're a wonderful man, and you'll make someone happy someday. Someone besides your mother."

"Understood. She's a bit overbearing."

They hugged a final time, and Helen got out of the car and went inside.

Emily was picking up toys in the living room. "You're home early. I thought you were going swimming?"

"Me too, but we needed to run a quick errand."

"Oh well, did you have fun?"

"No! We just broke up. And get this! The horrible woman who stiffed me on the dress is his mother!"

"How did it happen? I mean, how did you have her as a client and not realize she had the same last name as Edwin?"

"Because they don't have the same last name. He has the name of his father, who was her first husband. And he referred to me as Helen when he spoke about me to his mother. But when she hired me, I used my professional name, Mrs. Betzini."

"Confusing."

"You should have heard the fireworks when Edwin brought me home to meet her. She was rude and insulting!"

"So, you threw him over because of his mother?"

"Well, no. The relationship wasn't going anywhere, and I told him I needed time to sort out my feelings about Joseph."

"Whoa, Helen. You dodged a bullet. Imagine having a mother-in-law like her?"

"No wonder he's still single. Such a nice man, but his mother runs his life."

"Helen, maybe it's time for you just to step back from men. Figure out what you want."

"I suppose so."

Emily's voice lightened. "Then you'll have time to finish my wedding dress!"

Helen laughed. "Ah. Your true motivation. Don't worry. You'll have your dress in time. Now tell me how the rest of the wedding plans are going."

The heat finally subsided as marigolds and asters bloomed in the colors of the fall leaves. At church a few weeks later, Pastor Gerald quoted scriptures about a season of forgiveness. He spoke about the danger of hanging on to anger. "It's time to heal our hearts by forgiving those who've hurt us."

Helen thought holding on to anger was protecting her from future hurt. Now her pastor was saying she needed to forgive those who wronged her. She had a laundry list of pains and people she held responsible.

After lunch, she pondered what it would feel like to forgive. Where would she begin when it was all too overwhelming? Shouldn't she just focus on raising her daughter? *I must need a nap! My head hurts from trying to figure it all out.*

She sat by the window staring at the crimson maple leaves on the tree in the front yard and the dramatic contrast against the brilliant blue sky. A familiar black Ford pulled up and parked in front of the house, shaking her from daydreams, and she quickly pulled the curtain shut. She waited until the doorbell rang, counted slowly to ten, and opened it, not wanting to appear too eager. Joseph beamed when he saw her.

"Let's go for a drive. The fall colors are at peak, and I know of an orchard where we can pick apples and pumpkins."

Helen chewed on her lip and looked at the pile of clothing, waiting for her to work her magic. "It's tempting, but I should work today. Don't want to hold my customer's clothes hostage. And Bonnie needs a nap."

"Those clothes won't even miss you. Get Bonnie. The drive will lull her to sleep. Let's enjoy this Sunday afternoon. When winter sets in, we'll wish we'd spent more time outside while it was warm."

"Why does that make so much sense?" She chuckled. "Let me grab sweaters." Grandpa was resting, so she left him a note: "I'll be back in time to make supper."

She only saw Joseph once after their evening at the circus, and she didn't want to admit how happy she was to see his rugged face. His broad shoulders looked inviting in the red flannel shirt atop his well-worn jeans.

Bonnie smiled as Helen tied her white bonnet under her chin. "Yes, my little one, we are going on an adventure."

Joseph reached for Bonnie. "Can I carry you to the car, big girl?" Bonnie surprised them by putting her hands out for Joseph and rewarding him with a smile.

He quickly lifted her toward him and took a moment to hug her close. "Hello, baby doll. Have you missed me?"

"You talking to Bonnie or me, you charmer?" It warmed Helen's heart to see how tenderly he carried her.

"Both! Have you missed me, Helen?"

"Maybe just a little, my friend." She emphasized friend, but who was she reminding?

They settled in the car and started driving over hills Helen called "God's country." As they reached the top of a bluff, they stopped by the side of the road to ooh and awe at views that looked like oil paintings—the brilliant fall leaves in crimson, eggplant, and gold mixed with lush evergreens.

"Hard to believe we get to see this every year," Joseph said. "I could never live somewhere with only one season."

"Like California?" Helen prompted him. She needed to know. Would he be leaving to be closer to his children?

"Yes, like California. I do think about seeing my children more often, but I don't know if I could ever live there."

"When I lived in Texas, at first, I loved the warm winters. It's so easy to get around without all the snow and ice. But I also missed the excitement of the first snow, the exhilarating fresh air, ice skating, and making snowmen."

Joseph nodded. "It's what we grew up with. What we know and love."

They found the apple orchard, and each picked a bag of apples, then headed to a pumpkin patch and found smooth round pumpkins perfect for pies and decorations. They loaded their produce into the trunk of his car, and as they were driving back to Greenberg, Bonnie fell asleep.

"I have a blanket in the back. Let's stop for a while and let Bonnie sleep."

Helen agreed. She didn't want their time together to end.

They found a remote spot on the top of a hill, spread the flannel blanket under a massive oak tree, and lay Bonnie on it in the shade to finish her nap. Helen and Joseph sat near Bonnie and munched crisp apples, and let the warm day work its magic on them. For the first time in years, Helen realized she was entirely at ease. *Perhaps I'm starting to trust him.*

Monarch butterflies and iridescent dragonflies danced around them, their colors glistening like stained glass in sunshine. After a few moments of easy chit-chat, Joseph's face turned serious. "Please tell me what happened in Texas, Helen. You always change the subject when I bring it up."

Helen shook her head. "It's painful to talk about."

"Was he unfaithful to you?"

Her voice lowered with a bitter edge. "That was only the beginning of it!"

"I've shared my story with you, Helen. Whatever happened, it won't change my feelings for you."

Chapter 30

Helen looked away. The beauty surrounding them made her grateful to be alive, and perhaps it was time to trust him with the truth. How was she so stupid to get involved with a man like Dirk?

"Dirk abused me – in many ways. He was a large, strong man – at least a foot taller than I am. At first, he would just grab my arm or shoulders, and I thought it was because he was drinking."

"He was an alcoholic?"

"As it turned out, yes. But I didn't realize it. I was too immature and inexperienced to see the signs. The first time he seriously hurt me, we were already married. He slammed me against a wall." Her voice softened to a whisper. "I was pregnant, and later that night, I lost the baby. I, I assumed it was from the abuse." Her face clouded over from the memory.

Joseph watched her intently, his forehead creased. "I'm so sorry. I didn't know you lost a baby." He reached out and gently placed his hand on her shoulder.

His soft touch gave Helen confidence to continue. "It should've been my wake-up call, but he came back after a few days with a gift and begged me to forgive him."

"So, you stayed with him?"

"Where else could I go? I knew almost no one, and I thought I couldn't run back to Iowa. Besides, I took a vow and thought I had to honor it."

Joseph nodded. "I thought the same thing. I was willing to stay with Lucy, even when I learned she cheated on me because we took vows. But in the end, she was the one who left and divorced me." He shook his head at the irony. "So, what changed your mind about leaving him?"

"I couldn't take it anymore." Did she have the courage to tell Joseph everything? "Dirk was furious when I finally said enough."

"This was after Bonnie was born?"

"Yes, she was about two months old."

"Did he try to convince you to stay because of the baby?"

"Ha," she said bitterly. "He never wanted a baby and insulted me when I got pregnant again and said he didn't want to sleep with a pregnant woman!"

"So, he stepped out on you, and you decided to leave?"

Helen couldn't stay seated any longer. She hopped up and paced back and forth near the blanket. She clenched and unclenched her hands as she spat out the memory. "No, I stayed much longer, like an idiot. I stayed through the humiliation of his running around and bragging about it. I was so happy to be having a baby of my own, but because I was expecting, I didn't think I should leave him."

"What changed your mind."

Helen took a big breath in and slowly blew it out. She had only told her mother the details of those last terrifying hours. If she told Joseph now, would he think badly of her?

Joseph stood and faced her. "Helen?" He reached for her hand and held it. She looked at him and saw concern in his eyes. Maybe the nightmares would stop if she confided in someone.

"After Bonnie was born, I got a telegram meant for another woman. Dirk planned to meet her for a weekend in a nearby town. That was the last straw for me. I started packing to leave. I decided I'd taken enough, and I'd start over no matter what."

Joseph nodded in encouragement. She let go of him and shook her hands, and nervously pushed her sleeves up to her elbow.

"I checked on the bus times to Iowa, and there wasn't a bus until the next day. I assumed Dirk wouldn't come home from work since he was meeting another woman, so I started packing. But he came home and surprised me." Her voice was shaky as she recounted the horrific details. "He flew into a rage when he saw I was packing. But I was angry too. When I showed him the telegram, I thought he'd be embarrassed. But instead, he went nuts."

There was a tightness in his eyes, and his nostrils flared with anger. "What'd he do?"

Helen was pale as she stared into the air in front of her. She took a deep breath and continued. "He, he picked up the nightstick he kept by the bed and …beat me. Neighbors heard my screams and called the police. As I was lying on the ground bleeding from a blow to my head, the police barged in and stopped him from killing me. He said he was going to kill Bonnie after he finished with me," she sobbed out the words.

Joseph pulled her against him. His strong arms were comforting, but thinking of that terrifying night brought shivers down her spine.

Joseph spoke through clenched teeth. "Helen! How dare he! How could anyone assault you?" He held her out and looked at her again. His eyes were dark from concern and rage.

Her breathing was jagged. "He, um, he was drunk."

"That's no excuse. Did you press charges?"

Helen's insides were shaking at the memory of her terror. "Yes, but he was only in jail for one night. I was sitting on the bus with Bonnie in the morning, waiting to leave, when he stormed onto the bus and confronted me.”

"What? He bonded out?"

"A friend helped him bond out of jail. I prayed he didn't have a gun, but I was sure he'd kill me rather than let me go. To my surprise, after he threatened me, he backed down and let me leave."

"I could have lost you forever," Joseph pulled her toward him. "Was that the last you heard from him?"

She regained control of herself. "No, actually, he called once last year and tried to sweet-talk me to come back to him. But I didn't entertain it for a moment. Any love I may have felt for him had long since died. Then he showed up a month later and tried to kidnap Bonnie. The police got him and arrested him on a laundry list of charges, including possession of illegal drugs."

"Where is he now?"

"Still in prison. Police had enough evidence against him to put him away for years, and I got him to give up his parental rights as part of the divorce."

They embraced long enough to slow their breathing and calm the frayed nerves. Then Joseph held her at arm's length. His eyes were wide, and his brow was creased.

"Helen, what drew you to him, if you don't mind my asking?"

"He was charming at first and showered me with gifts and attention. He could be great fun when we went dancing. But he had a dark side I didn't understand. I thought his jealousy and drinking would stop once we were married."

"You wanted to marry him?"

"I didn't think about it, but when he asked me, I couldn't think of a reason not to. I know it sounds silly, but I was quite alone in the world in

Texas. And I had a girlfriend who kept telling me what a fine southern gentleman he was."

"Some gentleman. He nearly killed you!"

"I should have listened to my inner self. I had a lot of doubts, but I pushed them away."

"I know what you mean about doubts. Have your wounds healed?"

"I still get headaches, but the worst wounds are emotional. I have terrifying nightmares. I don't ever want to get caught up in another dangerous relationship." Her eyelashes were wet with tears, and her mouth was ruddy from biting on it as she tried not to break into sobs.

"I feel sick thinking about what could have happened." His hand swept over her cheeks, and his thumb brushed her lips. Helen shrugged and struggled to stay in control. Joseph searched her eyes. "Is your divorce final?"

"Yes. I'm a divorced lady. The stigma I'll live with forever."

"This is all my fault, Helen. If we'd gotten married years ago, you never would have had to live through that horrible experience."

"I was the one who ignored the signs of his alcoholism and jealousy, and I married him anyway. You're not at fault. The one good thing that came from it, though, is my precious Bonnie. She's the joy of my life."

Helen looked at Bonnie sleeping peacefully under the wide-open skies and hoped her life would be peaceful and filled with love.

"I wish I could say the same about my children. In their short lives, I've barely seen them. First, I was serving overseas, and then when I got out, Lucy took off with another man. I believe he's the father of her third child, but I'm missing so much. It does my heart good to be around Bonnie, but it also reminds me my kids are calling someone else 'Daddy.'"

"We are wounded souls, Joseph. I don't know if I'll ever be whole again. Our pastor talks about searching for God's love and forgiving those who've hurt us, but I feel like I need to hold onto some pain to protect myself from being hurt again." She needed Joseph to understand why they had to remain just friends.

"I'm so sorry, Helen. I wish I could erase your pain. I hope in time you'll be able to trust me again."

She looked away. She couldn't make any promises, but the stirrings of hope filled her.

September was rushing by, and Helen was deluged with sewing. Emily's wedding dress and veil needed a few more details before she declared them finished. And her matron of honor dress had to be finished along with a frock for Bonnie.

A week before the wedding, Emily came by for the final fitting. The design Emily chose featured a bodice with a lace overlay and a sweetheart neckline. The hemline of the full satin gown swept the floor. Tiny pearl buttons fastened the dress in the back. A simple veil with a lace hairpiece and three layers of elbow-length tulle completed her outfit. Helen held her breath as Emily carefully lifted the dress over her head, and Helen fastened the buttons. Emily faced the full-length mirror in Helen's sewing parlor and gasped.

"What's wrong, Emily?"

Chapter 31

Emily's eyes glistened with emotion. "Nothing at all. It's perfect. I look like a bride."

"Yes, of course, you do. You'll be a beautiful bride."

Emily leaned toward Helen and rubbed her forehead against Helen's. "Thank you so much! This is a dream come true."

Both were choked up. "Let's not get tear stains on this satin." Helen helped her out of the gown, and they placed it in a garment bag, along with the veil.

Emily wasn't ready to go. "Let's see yours now. Try it on for me."

Helen's light blue taffeta dress was similar, but not as full and without the lace overlay. A small hairpiece completed her look.

"It's perfect, Helen. Beautiful. I can't wait for Joseph to see you in this."

"Joseph? Oh, of course, he'll be there. I nearly forgot."

Emily looked sheepish. "He's the best man. Did I forget to tell you?"

"Yes, you left out that tiny detail, but I should have guessed it. So, he'll be standing next to Jacob as we walk up the aisle. Wow! If I wasn't nervous before, I am now."

"I'm sorry, Helen. It'll be fine. You two are friends now, right?"

"Friends, yes."

The day of the wedding was windy and warmer than expected. Helen and Emily carried their veils into the church and fixed their hair together in the basement room provided for brides. As much as she loved Emily, a twang of envy washed over Helen. Why had she settled for a ten-minute wedding in a government building instead of a church wedding surrounded by friends and family? In her heart, she must have known the relationship would never last.

But today was about Emily and Jacob. The church was resplendent with candles, flowers, and pew bows. The morning sun shone through the stained-glass windows, casting sparkles of rainbows throughout the sanctuary. Guests filled the pews, and a soloist took her place. When the organist began the entrance hymn, Helen gracefully processed down the aisle. Emily wanted an uncomplicated service, so she chose no other bridesmaids or flower girls. Only Helen, followed by a radiant Emily on her father's arm. Helen breathed deeply to calm her nerves as she walked toward the altar, where Joseph was standing next to Jacob. Joseph, the best man. An ironic term.

Joseph beamed at Helen, and her shoulders relaxed. She was among friends. Beautiful music, scriptures, and a few inspirational words from the pastor filled the service. But Helen heard little of it. Her proximity to Joseph reminded her this was the wedding they dreamed of years ago.

After the service, Emily, Jacob, Helen, and Joseph formed a receiving line to accept well wishes before heading to the church basement for a casual reception. Mama laid claim to Bonnie and flaunted the adorable toddler to her friends like a prized goat at the county fair while Helen mingled with friends.

Joseph approached Helen holding two small paper plates. "Brought you some cake and mints."

"Thank you!" The significance of the day hung in the air.

"Will you throw cake at me if I tell you how beautiful you look?"

She smiled and looked him up and down.

"You cleaned up pretty well yourself!"

"I made an effort. And, Helen, Emily's dress is really something! I can't believe your talent."

"Thanks. Took a lot of time, but I think it turned out well. She looks so beautiful!"

"Yes." They ate cake for a moment, then Joseph uttered quietly. "That could have been us."

"Please don't, Joseph. It's too late."

"Okay, if you think it is, I won't push." His eyes searched hers. The usually sparkling blue eyes were dark with disappointment and concern.

"I think it's better this way."

All single women were called to the outside exit as the bridal couple was about to leave. Emily's cousins and friends jockeyed for position to see who would catch the bride's bouquet. Helen stayed in the back, feeling it was inappropriate for a divorced woman to make the catch. Emily turned her back and threw the bouquet over her head, and a frenzy ensued. A high school friend who was an exceptional volleyball player leaped in the air and snagged the bridal bouquet to the cheers of her boisterous boyfriend, and everyone laughed. Then, the crowd threw rice on Emily and Jacob as they headed off to their honeymoon in the Quad Cities.

A few days after the wedding, Joseph stopped by after work one night. He and Helen sat in rocking chairs on the porch while Grandpa watched Bonnie inside.

"I wanted to tell you I'm heading to California tomorrow. I've got some vacation time built up, and I'll spend a few days with my children. Lucy knows I'm coming, so, uh, I think it's the right thing to do."

Helen exhaled as she rocked and took in the news. "Yes, so do I. You need to see your children. Better to go now before winter sets in and the roads get icy."

"You're not worrying about me, are you?" Joseph smirked, teasing her.

"Never, just want your kids to have the chance to climb all over you."

Who was she kidding? Worry was an activity close to her heart. Helen was a world-class worrier, and there was plenty to practice now that Joseph was on the road. And the biggest worry - would he be drawn back into Lucy's claws? What if they fanned the flame into life, and he stayed with her? She stole him once; would Lucy steal him back?

Helen tried to focus on her work the first week Joseph was in California. Her temper flared more quickly when projects didn't go well, and she struggled to quell the restless stirrings in her stomach. She wished he called to say he was there safely, not eaten by snakes in the desert or fallen off a cliff. Or to say he was having fun with his children. Or to say he was no longer attracted to Lucy the floozy, as Helen referred to her. But they were just friends. He didn't have to report to her, and his life wasn't her concern. Was it?

At dinner one night, Grandpa realized something was wrong and asked Helen if she was all right.

"I guess I'm a little worried because Joseph went to California to see his kids." She tried to sound casual as she took a bite of peas.

"When do you think he'll be back?"

"Couple of weeks, I think. I'm not sure." Helen put more peas on Bonnie's highchair tray.

"He'll be back, Ole Bean. That boy's sweet on ya." Grandpa's bushy eyebrows seemed to grow into one brow across his forehead, and his eyes peered at her over the top of his bifocal glasses. "He'll be back, ya mark my words."

Helen blushed. She didn't want to admit to him she was anxious about Joseph. Grandpa would ask questions about their relationship she didn't want to answer. "Ready for pie? It's strawberry-rhubarb, your favorite."

"Oh. Where did you get rhubarb and strawberries this time of year?" He brightened up at the word "pie."

"I tucked some in the freezer last summer. Isn't the refrigerator/freezer the best invention?" Her distraction did the trick. She maneuvered the conversation to safe waters.

"Hey, Mrs. Bartlett, let's have some girl time. Want to meet at the cafe?"

Emily laughed. "I'm not used to being called 'Mrs.' yet. But yes! I'd love to see you."

Helen put a light jacket on Bonnie, a knit cap, and mittens and set her in the stroller, with a blanket on her lap. The café was a ten-minute walk—enough time to work off a bit of anxiety. Yellow oak leaves clung stubbornly to branches, creating a peek-a-boo effect with the sky. Helen and the stroller crunched their way at a quick pace, leaving dry maple leaves swirling in their wake.

She opened the heavy door and waited in the entrance for a moment for her eyes to adjust to the dimly lit café. Emily waited at a table with Saturday-casual hair pulled back into a ponytail. Seeing her friend's familiar face reassured Helen.

"How was the honeymoon?"

"Amazing! We had so much fun in the Quad Cities. There are actually five cities, not four, so we toured all of them. And we saw the new Rock Island Centennial Bridge, built to celebrate Rock Island's 100th birthday. We ate at so many restaurants, I don't think I can fit into my wedding dress again!"

"Let's hope you won't have to use it again. Cocoa for me," she told the waitress. "Don't want the caffeine to set me on edge."

"So why the nerves? What's up?" Emily could always read her.

"Joseph's in California seeing his children. He left a week after the wedding." Helen took Bonnie's cap off, removed her jacket and mittens, then asked for a high chair and some crackers to keep Bonnie happy.

"And you're worried he's taking up with Lucy again?"

"How do you always get to the point? Yes, I have to admit it. And I'm worried he may like California and decide to stay. It feels wrong saying that because it may be the best thing for his children to have him near."

"Are you two seeing each other again?"

"Yes…. And no. We're spending time together now and then, but only as friends. So why am I so worried I'll never see him again?" Helen reached into her diaper bag and got a hanky to wipe Bonnie's face.

Emily smiled and reached over to touch Helen's arm. "Helen, when are you going to admit you love him?"

"I can't. I'm terrified of getting hurt again. And I can't forgive him for running out on me. What if he does it again? I don't think I could take another rejection."

"So, you're going to live your life alone because you don't want to chance being hurt again?"

Why did Emily have to be so blunt? Helen stared into her cocoa. "Yes, I suppose that's what I'm doing. But at least I'm protecting my heart."

"By hiding it on a block of ice?"

She smiled at her friend's theatrics. "Let's talk about you. What's happening with you and Jacob?"

On a brisk November evening, Joseph called as it was getting dark outside, and Helen was in the kitchen, making supper. She snatched the phone and held it on one shoulder to reach the counter and continue chopping vegetables for soup. Her heart fluttered when he said her name.

"Helen? Joseph here."

How would she not know his voice? She heard it in her heart every night before she fell asleep. "How's California, Joseph?" She kept her voice light and smiled, thinking about how tan he must be.

"Actually, quite beautiful."

"Oh, and your kids?"

"I've only seen them twice. Of course, they don't know who I am, but I'm making some progress, and I'm hoping they'll warm to me soon if I keep making an effort."

"That's important." Helen's heart dropped as her intuition said there was more news. She set her knife on the counter, wiped her hands on an apron, and stared out the dark, cold window at trees that were mere skeletons now, stripped of their glorious fall foliage.

"I wanted to let you know I've asked for a leave of absence at work."

She held her breath, not sure what to say for fear her voice would tremble.

"I think I need to look for work here and see if I can be more of a father to my children."

"How, um, how long? I mean, how long do you think you'll stay there?" She sank into a kitchen chair.

He let out his breath. "Indefinitely."

There was a long pause as this sunk in. He was leaving – again. "You… you're leaving for good?" Her voice was nearly a whisper.

"I don't know. You've told me over and over there's no hope for us anymore. It tears me up to see you with Bonnie and to know I have children I'm not seeing. I thought you wanted me to have a place in their lives?"

She bit her lip, trying not to give in to the emotions swirling inside her. "Well, yes, isn't that what you wanted, Joseph?" She was trying to keep her voice from quivering.

"I think so. Yes, I think it's what's best for my kids. So, I'm working out visitation with Lucy."

"What else are you working out with Lucy?" *That didn't come out right.*

"Nothing, Helen. And you have no right to be jealous, even if things are better between us."

Her stomach clenched. "Better? Are you seeing her again?"

"No, for heaven's sake, Helen. Lucy and I are trying to be civil for the sake of our children. I'm trying to forget what she did to me so I can move on with my life. Something you seem unwilling to do!"

"That's not fair, Joseph." She wound the phone cord around her hand.

"Isn't it? When are you going to trust me again? As long as you hold me at the tip of your sword, our relationship is hostage to your anger. I can't go on like that, so I'm trying to build a life here – for the sake of my kids."

"I understand, so maybe it's better if we just don't speak again." Helen didn't think she could keep from weeping any longer.

"If that's what you want, Helen." His voice had a hard edge, but she couldn't take back her words.

"It is." She spoke barely above a whisper. Her heart was pulling her in one direction, but her words kept betraying her. She wound the cord so tightly it was cutting off her hand's circulation.

He exhaled on the other end of the line. "Goodbye then, Helen." He hung up.

Chapter 32

Helen put the phone back in its place on the wall, sunk down, and sat on the hardwood floor in the kitchen in a torrent of tears. She lost him – again. When he broke off their engagement years earlier, Grandma's only words of comfort were: "Men are like trolley cars. If one leaves, another one will be around the corner in a few minutes."

But that wasn't true. Men like Joseph didn't come along often. Yes, he betrayed her once, but hadn't he spent months trying to make it up to her? Why would she listen to Grandma, who never loved her? Did anyone love her? Dirk's ugly words echoed in her memory.

Why was she so stubborn and untrusting? Did she have a heart of stone, and if she did, why did it feel broken, leaving her in a puddle of pain?

She needed to talk to someone who could help her erase the ugliness playing inside her. Over the phone, she relayed what happened between sobs to Emily. He was staying in California, and their friendship – or whatever you called it - was over. She had a sinking feeling their relationship was too good to last. Now she needed to get over him forever.

Emily listened sympathetically but wasn't convinced this was the end for Helen and Joseph. Helen said for her sanity, she needed to find a way to forget him forever.

The next few weeks, Helen went through her routine in a daze. Up early to sew, then breakfast for Grandpa and Bonnie, followed by more sewing as Bonnie played with blocks and stuffed animals at Helen's feet until lunch and dishes. Bonnie still napped in the afternoons, which allowed Helen undisturbed time to tackle her most difficult alterations and see clients before preparing supper, cleaning the kitchen, bathing the baby, and working on laundry after putting Bonnie to bed. Each day was a carbon copy without Joseph to pop by and whisk them away on adventures.

She tried to block him from her thoughts but didn't have much luck since his face and voice seemed to be stamped on her heart in cement. In truth, she longed to see him but convinced herself she wasn't worthy of his or anyone's love. Time to just focus on motherhood, she told herself over and over. But his face was the first one she thought of each morning, and the last she lingered over before sleep swept her away each night into his arms, dreaming of a simpler time when he was completely hers.

Grandpa saw the dark circles under her eyes at breakfast one morning. "When's yer young fella coming back? Shouldn't he be here by now?"

"He's not my fella, and he's decided to stay in California with his kids. Probably for the best so they can get to know their father." Helen focused on serving a bowl of oatmeal for each and spooned some cooked cinnamon apples on top, blowing on a smaller dish for Bonnie to cool it. She didn't want to look at Grandpa's eyes for fear the sympathy would make her crumple into a ball of longing.

"I know it was hard for ya, Ole Bean, not getting to know yer father." Grandpa sprinkled his oatmeal and apples with brown sugar and then poured on a splash of milk.

She and Grandpa never spoke about her father.

"Once I met my Dad, he still didn't seem to want to be in my life." Helen handed him a cup of black coffee.

"Yer Dad wasn't a pleasant sort. He and yer Mama were unhappy together. When he left, he took yer sister, and it 'bout killed Cora. Life's not perfect. We do the best we can with the hand we're dealt."

Helen nodded as she ate her oatmeal. Clients would be coming soon, and she needed to finish hemming a pair of pants before noon. She washed Bonnie's face and hands, set the dishes in the sink, and got ready to face another day. Without him.

Sundays were a welcome break from the daily grind. She left Bonnie in the nursery during services now that Bonnie was a bit older so Helen could finally join the choir. Singing lifted her emotions to places she couldn't reach any other way. Songs and hymns full of Biblical verses calmed the deep hurt and fear she'd never be loved again. *It's good to belong to a group.* She felt safe with fellow worshipers.

Choir members sometimes enjoyed brunch together at one of their homes to build fellowship. Everyone would bring a coffee cake or jug of juice, and they would laugh and talk and share thoughts on the day's sermon.

Helen admired one of the senior choir members named Elizabeth, who sang with rich alto tones. They were chatting at fellowship after the service.

Elizabeth looked deep into Bonnie's eyes. "What's her name?"

"Bonnie Ann. She's 20 months."

"She has beautiful, long eyelashes and your red curls and porcelain skin. Just adorable."

"Thank you. She's the joy of my life."

"I miss my grandchildren. They moved to Florida and took my heart with them."

Helen frowned. "I thought normally the grandparents moved to Florida."

"So did I, but they left me here to endure the Iowa winters." She smiled. "Actually, it's a lovely escape in January if I get the chance to visit them."

"I lived in Texas for a few years, and I missed winter."

Elizabeth laughed. "The magic of four seasons is a wonder to behold, and when you're raised with it, it gives life rhythm and intrigue."

Winter was settling in on Greenberg. Their first snowfall dumped eight inches, then warmed enough to melt some until the temperatures dropped and turned their world into an ice skating rink. Was it only a year ago that Edwin showed up to help her shovel? They broke up months ago, and she accepted it, although he was a kind friend—a decent man but too attached to his dominating mother.

Helen had to forego her daily walks for fear of falling on the ice, and she felt more couped up than ever. Bonnie's typically even temper was also overwrought, whether from teething or being housebound, or perhaps she was picking up on her mother's angst.

Helen was grateful for another choir get-together in late November, and as they enjoyed brunch, Helen sat next to Elizabeth at the end of a long table so Bonnie could sit in a high chair next to her. She admired Elizabeth's quick laugh and light spirit. *She probably enjoyed a trouble-free life full of love.* While lively conversations sailed around them, Helen and Elizabeth found themselves sharing about their lives.

"Are you always so happy?" Helen blurted out after swallowing a bite of a lemon muffin.

Elizabeth laughed. "I try to stay joyful." She sipped her black coffee.

"What's your secret?" Helen warmed her hands on her teacup.

"There's no secret, Helen. Joy is available to all of us."

"You make it sound so easy. I rarely feel joy. Especially lately." She broke off pieces of a muffin for Bonnie and put them on her high chair tray, but Bonnie was giggling at an older child playing peek-a-boo with her.

"What about when you look at little Bonnie?" Elizabeth gazed at Bonnie.

"Yes, she's the joy of my life." She helped Bonnie take a sip of milk.

"I don't mean to pry, but where is her father? I don't see him at church with you."

Helen lowered her voice to a whisper. "I'm divorced." Helen looked away, afraid the stigma would send Elizabeth running.

"I'm so sorry. And you're so young."

"Yes, I married young and stupid. I was very impulsive."

"What happened?"

Helen kept her voice low, not wanting others to hear her. "My ex tried to kill me. He's given up all parental rights to Bonnie." She surprised herself by confiding so quickly.

"Child, I'm so sorry. Who would want to hurt such a lovely young lady like you?"

"Thank you. He, he was, is, an alcoholic. I didn't know the signs. He got ugly when he drank and sometimes even when he wasn't drinking." Helen's face contorted whenever she thought of Dirk.

"My father was also an alcoholic. When I was six, he shot and killed my mother right in front of me. They took him to prison, so I lost both parents the same day."

Helen's hand flew to her heart. "What? Oh my. I had no idea. I'm so sorry. You seem so carefree." Helen looked at Elizabeth's gently lined face, white hair, and sparkling eyes.

"It took me a long time to get over it. The trauma, the loss, then the anger. I hated my father when I was a teen, and I did a lot of stupid things out of anger."

"What changed?"

"I learned that holding onto the past hurts me more than anyone. I thought by keeping a firm grip on my hatred, I was punishing my father. But in reality, I was punishing myself."

Helen nodded. Her words rang true. "But how do I begin? I've held onto anger for so long, it's like a part of me."

"It's a poison inside of you, dear. Cancer. Sit with God in prayer. Ask God to heal your wounded heart so you can learn to trust again."

"Finding time to sit in prayer isn't easy. I'm taking care of my grandpa and my daughter and running a business." She reached over and brushed crumbs off Bonnie's face.

"Believe me, once you find time for prayer each day, the rest of your life will fall into place."

"You've given me a lot to think about. Thank you, Elizabeth."

Elizabeth's words and gentleness brought a new wave of hope.

Helen was eager for Bonnie's nap so she could dig into a shelf of her Grandma's old books to find a Bible. She opened to Mathew's Gospel and read a few passages. She tried to sit quietly and meditate on the words, but her mind danced from problems to people to work and back. Elizabeth's words sounded easy, but Helen wasn't used to sitting still.

Helen felt the need to have a long conversation with Emily, but now that she and Jacob were married, she didn't want to bother them. They needed time together, and Helen didn't want to get in the way of that. She felt frustrated and confused. With all this talk about God, how on earth was she supposed to hear him? To know his will? She hardly knew her own mind. She sat looking at the skeleton trees under the cloudy skies, and a deep gloom settled on her. What was she thinking telling Joseph it was over between them? Were her fear and stubbornness the only things keeping them apart? Without warning, she started to weep. She was tired, overwhelmed, and confused. Was this the way the rest of her life would be? She sat on the couch in the living room, her head in her hands, and allowed the tears to pour. And then Grandpa appeared and sat beside her.

"What is it, Ole Bean?"

Chapter 33

Where to begin? But now that the floodgates were open, she admitted to Grandpa what she hadn't admitted to herself. She wanted Joseph to come back.

Grandpa put an arm around her and let her cry herself out. She leaned into his rough overalls and accepted the pats of comfort. He rarely said much, but his presence was a steady drumbeat. "It'll all work itself out. Mark my words."

Between shuddering breaths, the crying stopped. "I hope you're right, Grandpa." Sometimes a good cleansing cry helped, but her head hurt from the confusion about what was best for her, Joseph, and his children. It felt like a puzzle with no answer.

Elizabeth hugged her at church the following Sunday. "How was your week?"

"I'm trying, but I don't think I'm good at praying." Helen shrugged.

"Just keep showing up. Spend time with God, and don't worry about the outcome."

"I do feel happier. But it's as if something is still holding me back." She whisked a curl out of her eyes as she took off her black hat and gloves.

"There's no healing without forgiveness, Helen. Don't let it block your heart."

Helen started to keep a journal of her thoughts during prayer. She noted what went right each day and added a gratitude list.

After church one Sunday, Mama and Warren were coming for brunch, and Helen was eager to see them after the icy roads kept them away for weeks. Mama held Bonnie during the service while Helen sang in the choir, and it warmed her heart to see her mother fawning over her granddaughter, planting kisses on her cheeks.

After brunch, Mama came upstairs to help Helen put Bonnie to bed, and the two of them crept into Helen's room for a few minutes of mother-daughter time. Helen shared her breakup with Joseph and the confusion she felt about it.

Mama reached out and tucked one of Helen's curls behind her ear. "When was the last time he called?"

"About a month ago."

"Was the split mutual?"

"Well, we both agreed he should try to have a role in his children's lives, and I don't know how he can do that from Iowa when they're in California. And he said since I'm unwilling to forgive him for breaking our engagement, he sees no future for us."

Mama was thoughtful for a moment. "Is that true, Helen? Are you still angry?"

"Not exactly angry, but I can't let go of the worry he might cheat on me again."

"That's understandable. Did he ever explain what happened?"

"Yes, in some detail." Helen went on to explain what Joseph told her of his marriage and children.

"Is he trying to repair his marriage to Lucy?"

"Heaven's no! She ran off with the father of the third child and married him. They barely speak. He's trying to establish some sort of relationship with his kids."

Mama nodded and looked away. "You were both so young when you got engaged, but you seemed so in love."

"And I think we were. And maybe we still are. We had so much fun all fall on outings as friends."

"But you can't let go of the hurt?"

"Exactly. It's like a knot inside of me."

"All tangled up with worry and doubt, right?"

"Yes! I keep thinking the best thing is just to forget him."

"But your heart won't let you?"

Helen shook her head. And they sat quietly for a moment.

"Helen, after I met Warren, I cared for him deeply, but I was terrified to make any commitment, and I kept him at a distance when I longed to be closer. I was still so angry with your father and all the pain he caused me, and I didn't think I could give anyone my heart. I realize it's not the same thing because I never loved your father, but I still think my anger bound me and may be your problem as well."

Helen nodded. "And after what happened with Dirk, I'm terrified I could be physically hurt again."

"Does Joseph drink to excess?"

"No, I've never seen evidence of that."

"Does he have a bad temper and lash out when he's angry?"

"No, in fact, he seems to hold his anger inside."

"What about jealousy? I know that was one of Dirk's triggers."

"I think Joseph was a little jealous when I was seeing Edwin but isn't that a sign he loves me?"

"As long as he didn't act on it."

262

"He didn't. So how do I get over my fear? What did you do?"

"I went to see my pastor, and he helped me forgive Frank, but it didn't happen right away."

Helen scrunched up her face. "Did you have to call Frank?"

"No, forgiveness happens in your heart. It's to help free you from anger and past hurts. I also needed to forgive my mother and even myself."

"Yourself? That seems odd. I can understand why you might be angry with your mother, but you never were to blame for what happened with Frank."

"We all make mistakes. I know I wasn't always present to you when you were growing up, and that ate at me."

"Thanks, Mama. I forgive you if it helps. I know you were often in impossible situations."

"It does help, thank you, dear. But as for you, don't expect your heart to let go of the anger all at once. Sometimes it takes many times of praying to forgive someone before you're released from it. For me, it was like a door swung open when it finally happened, and I escaped from the prison of anger." Cora smiled. "Find a bit of time each day to pray."

"You sound like Elizabeth!"

"The woman in your choir?"

"Yes, she said the same thing."

"I'm glad. Meanwhile, I hope you're patient with yourself and with God."

They hugged and went downstairs to Grandpa and Warren.

Early one December morning, Helen was in the "prayer chair" in her bedroom. The winter chill made it more challenging to get out of bed before the furnace kicked in, but she wrapped herself in a blanket and found slippers for her icy feet. Giving up a bit of sewing time before

Bonnie awoke worked best for her. She kept her Bible, journal, a pen, and a prayer book in easy reach as she started each day. Thoughts of Joseph crowded in. With all her heart, she wanted what was best for him. Whatever that meant. Was this letting go?

Christmas was only two weeks away, and she had only one wish – to forget Joseph and heal the empty place in her heart. Elizabeth had encouraged her to pray for God's will, but Helen thought that meant setting her heart free.

She was in a rush to finish preparations for Christmas - knitting hats for Grandpa and Warren, embroidering a tea towel for Emily and a bath towel for Mama, sewing a velvet dress for Bonnie, and making jam for her church choir members. She felt like a ballerina spinning on one leg, trying to finish presents, bake cookies, write a few cards, and decorate the house. She planned to join Warren and Mama at their home but wanted to do her part and longed for them to approve her efforts. Staying busy kept her from stewing over her heartache but didn't erase it.

A week before Christmas, Helen was sitting in her "prayer chair." She was having trouble concentrating because her mind kept bouncing back and forth to unfinished projects. From nowhere came the thought to call Joseph. *What would I say to him? Should I apologize for not giving him a second chance? Wait a minute. Me apologize to him? That makes no sense.*

Or did it? By holding onto her anger, was she in the wrong? Was it possible to trust him again? Throughout the day, she thought about what she'd say. She searched for and found a number for him in California. *He'll think I'm a nut.* But what did she care? If her goal was to be free of anger and fear, then she'd risk it.

She put Bonnie to bed early, and Grandpa fell asleep in his chair, reading a book. Helen went into the kitchen, where the phone was attached to the wall. Her heart pounded, and her fingers shook. *You can do this, Helen. Just get it over with. He's just a friend, right?* She dialed a string of numbers and then listened as it rang and rang. *Oh well, he's not there.* She was just about to hang up when she heard his rich baritone. "Hello."

"Joseph?"

"Helen. How are you?" His resonant voice had a musical quality.

After a few moments of small talk, Helen revved up her courage. She tangled herself in the long phone cord as she started.

"Um, well, Joseph, I ahh, I just wanted to tell you I'm sorry."

"You're sorry?"

"Yes, I held onto my anger even after you apologized, and I realize now that was wrong. I do forgive you, Joseph. I'm not angry with you, and I'm sorry it's taken me so long to tell you." She held her breath. How would he respond? *Does he think I'm a nut job?*

The long pause was eternal.

"Well…Um…Thank you, Helen. That means a lot to me."

"OK, well, Merry Christmas, Joseph. I hope you have fun with your children." She hung up quickly.

She did it! It felt great. She was so excited she got up the courage to tell him she was sorry. But he sounded so inviting, and it made her yearn to see him. She pulled on her jacket, a warm scarf, and boots and took off into the night. The cool crisp air would clear her head, wouldn't it? She needed to think.

What if I'd told him this in person while he was still here? Would he be in California?

But then, would he always wonder about being a father to his children? Isn't that the most crucial role for him? She picked up speed as she rounded the corner of Elm onto Oakwood Avenue.

Or was he back with Lucy? She didn't dare bring it up. She was driving herself mad second-guessing. She called him so that she could release her anger and get over him. But talking to him, hearing his voice in her ear did nothing to help her forget him. She longed to lay her head on his shoulder and feel the strength of his arms and the heat from his chest. To look into his warm eyes and see acceptance and…love. Why hadn't she recognized it? He showed her love for months. *What's wrong with me?* She looked down so she wouldn't slip on the ice and didn't notice a shadow coming toward her.

Chapter 34

"Helen, slow down there."

"Jacob! What are you doing here?"

"Getting some fresh air."

"Me too. Enjoying the brisk night."

After a few moments of the usual small talk about the weather, Jacob surprised her with a question.

"Have you spoken to Joseph lately? I think he's lost out there in California."

"Lost? In what way?" Helen was too embarrassed to admit she just called him. She clapped her hands on her arms to keep warm.

"He misses being here."

"But I thought he was getting lots of time with his kids." Helen was so nervous when she called him, she hadn't even asked Joseph about his visits with his kids.

"He's trying, but I'm not sure he's getting much chance to see them."

"I'm sorry, I didn't know. Lucy being difficult? Imagine that from a woman who ran out on him with three kids in tow."

Jacob nodded and blew out a ring of condensation. "So, how are you doing? Seeing anyone?"

She frowned and then looked away. "NNo. Just trying to be a good mom." *Odd question.*

They spoke for a few minutes as they walked back to her house. "Say 'hi' to Emily for me. And I'm glad the honeymoon was so much fun," she said and went inside.

What an odd night, she thought as she hung up her jacket and took off her boots. She'd be lucky to get any sleep with all of this buzzing inside her brain. It was odd she ran into Jacob. And he wasn't typically that blunt. She put on her flannel nightgown and slipped into bed and prayed "thy will be done," over and over and over until she surrendered to sleep.

She awoke with a sense of anticipation on Christmas Eve day. Mama and Warren would drive over to Greenburg for the early evening service at Helen and Grandpa's church. Helen dressed Bonnie in the midnight blue velvet dress with tiny red flowers embroidered on the bodice. *What a little doll she is.* Bonnie put out her hands to be picked up and smiled at her mother.

"Your second Christmas, little one. I can't wait for you to open your presents in the morning."

Mama made a fuss over Bonnie at church and promised to hold her through the service. Helen dashed off to join the choir. Singing was one therapy that helped her stay calm. And now that it was Christmas Eve, she let the happiness of the day wash over her. A deep peace settled within her as she marched up the aisle with her fellow choir members—a soothing balm.

After the service, Helen handed out crystal jars of strawberry-rhubarb jams she made as gifts for fellow choir members. Everyone was hugging and exchanging wishes of joy. When Helen reached Elizabeth, she whispered to her, "I called Joseph and apologized for holding onto my anger."

"Congratulations. Was it difficult?"

"My hands were shaking, but once I said the words, I felt more relaxed. After I hung up, I felt as if a weight was lifted."

"You did the right thing. Finding it in your heart to forgive someone is a huge step toward healing. Have a wonderful Christmas."

They hugged. What a blessing Elizabeth was.

Mama and Warren came back to Grandpa's house, and they enjoyed the simple meal Helen had waiting in the oven. After dinner, Helen dragged out a kettle and popped corn. They strung popcorn and cranberries onto heavy thread to make garlands for their tree. They were beautiful against the dark blue-green needles of the small blue spruce in their entryway, which Grandpa dragged in earlier. Grandpa carried Bonnie near the tree so she could smell the fresh outdoor scent.

The peace Helen felt at the Christmas Eve service stayed with her that night as she fell asleep. *Perhaps it's just because Christmas is finally here and my presents are all finished.* Whatever the reason, she clung to the comfort.

Bonnie was up earlier than usual on Christmas morning. *She couldn't possibly know about presents yet, could she?* Helen shrugged into her robe and slippers and set about boiling coffee. The day was ordinary in so many ways – making breakfast, cleaning up the kitchen. But there were a few surprises for Bonnie. Grandpa made her a tiny wooden train with wheels. Helen admired his artistry, and Bonnie was fascinated with its movement. Helen helped Bonnie unwrap the stuffed elephant she made for her. "Remember the elephants?" she asked Bonnie. Helen would cling to the memory of the circus forever.

Mama was expecting them for a midday meal, so Helen fussed over her appearance and loaded up the presents, along with the dinner rolls she baked. The phone rang, and she assumed it would be Mama reminding her to bring the rolls.

"Merry Christmas, Helen."

Her face lit up. "Merry Christmas, Joseph. What a surprise."

"A good one, I hope."

"Yes, of course. It's good to hear your voice. Are you going to see your children today?"

"No, I got to see them for a short time last night."

"So, you're spending the day alone?" She was playing with the phone cord and doodling on the message pad. She hoped that question didn't sound suspicious.

"It's giving me time to think. Your call last week meant a lot to me. Did you mean what you said about forgiving me?"

"Yes, I did."

He let out a breath. "Helen, do you think we could start over again?"

"But how? With you in California, it seems impossible." *What was he saying?*

"I don't belong here. I don't like the traffic, the heat, the long drives to get anywhere. And I'm not happy at my job."

"But what about your kids?"

"They were born while I was in the service. I couldn't help it, but I was never there. Now when I show up, they're calling another man, 'Daddy,' and frankly, my presence is confusing to them."

"So, what are you saying?" She was about to explode but wanted to be confident he was saying what she thought he was saying.

"I'm saying I want to stay connected with them, but Lucy is resisting my efforts, and right now, they see me as a stranger who is making their mother angry. That's not what I was hoping for."

"I'm sorry. I know how much you wanted to be a father to them."

"Yes, but I need to be realistic. Forcing a relationship won't make any of us happy. And, truthfully, I'm not happy without you. Plain and simple, if you give me another chance, I'll contact my old job in Greenburg and come home - to you. Helen, can we try again?"

There was no hesitation this time. "Yes, please come home, Joseph. I can't wait to see you."

"Me too. Let's hope the weather holds for the trip home. I wish I was there now. Helen, let me prove that I still love you."

Her voice was a whisper. "I'll try. And Joseph, after all these years, I love you too."

They wished each other "Merry Christmas," and he was gone.

She hung up the phone and let out a little scream. Grandpa hollered from the living room, "Everything OK in there? You didn't cut yerself, did ya, Ole Bean?"

She dashed into the living room and hugged him around the shoulders as he sat reading the newspaper.

"Joseph's coming back! Things aren't working out in California, and he's coming back to Iowa!"

"Good thing you two are just friends!" He lowered the paper and smiled up at her over the top of his glasses.

She wriggled her nose at him and smiled, but she wasn't ready to share further details. She dashed into Bonnie's room, where she was playing on the floor. She picked her up and twirled her around the room. "Joseph's coming home." Bonnie giggled from the attention.

Mama smiled back at Helen's ear-to-ear grin when she opened their front door. "You look happy."

"It's Christmas Mama, why wouldn't I be happy?" Helen handed Bonnie to her.

"Mother's intuition tells me there's something more." She took Bonnie's hat and coat off and kissed her chubby cheeks. "What do you think, Bonnie?"

Grandpa blurted out, "Joseph's coming back ta Iowa."

Mama's eyebrows shot up. "Oh, I see."

"Grandpa!" Helen scolded gently. Then turned to Mama, "He called this afternoon, and he's coming home. Things aren't working out with his children, his ex, or his job. He's miserable in California."

"And he misses you?" Mama was studying her face.

"Apparently, yes. Now let's get dinner ready." Helen's face was bright red from the scrutiny. She didn't have answers to all the questions they were about to ask, so changing the topic was a safer course. *How long will it take him to regain his job and drive back?* She prayed it wouldn't be too long. She was so excited, she felt like twirling around the living room.

A week went by without a word from Joseph. Helen was a ball of nervous energy. When would he call and tell her his plans? She tried to stay focused on being a good mother, caring for Grandpa, and running her business, but her heart was vulnerable, and she needed reassurance.

New Year's Eve, the phone rang, and Helen's heart jumped as she dashed into the kitchen to answer it.

There was a smile in Joseph's voice. "Hi, Helen! Think you can get a babysitter tonight?"

"Where are you?" Helen couldn't help squeaking a bit with excitement.

"I'm back in Greenburg. Just got in last night. I'm staying with a buddy until I can find a place of my own again. So, what do you think about the babysitter idea?

"Oh, uh yes. I think I can call Mama. What's the plan?"

"I think we should go dancing. We haven't done the Lindy or the Swing together in years. Let's see if Emily and Jacob want to come along, and we can hit the Riviera Ballroom in Des Moines."

"That sounds swell! I can't wait to see you, Joseph." Already her mind was swimming, thinking about what to wear and whether she could remember the dance step.

"Me too! Call your Mama, and I'll see you tonight."

She didn't have much time to primp, but after calling Cora, she dug through her closet and pulled out an outfit she made that fall on a week when business was slow. The royal blue blouse buttoned up the front and sported a v-neck, shoulder pads, and a peplum that flared from her tiny waist. A skirt of the same fabric was slightly flared and fell just below her knees. Black pumps with little black bows on the toes would be perfect for dancing.

While Bonnie napped, she soaked in the tub, pinned her hair with bobby pins to direct her curls and put wine-colored enamel on her nails. She still owned a pair of silk stockings from her days at the Foxy Lady, and this was the perfect occasion to wear them. Staying focused on tiny details kept her from endless worrying.

Mama and Warren came early so they could help with Bonnie while Helen finished getting ready. They oohed and ahh'd when Helen finally made her entrance. She hadn't been dancing for several years and hoped she didn't fall on her face.

The doorbell rang, and she glided into the entry, but Mama beat her to the door and opened it. Helen anticipated a long romantic embrace, but with Mama standing there, it didn't happen.

She and Joseph left quickly and scrambled down the stairs and into Joseph's car. She stifled a giggle at his erratic driving when he ran over a curb. He was nervous too, but she didn't want to point it out. He drove a few blocks to a quiet street, put the car in park, reached for her, and pulled her into a warm embrace.

"Welcome home, Joseph."

"You have no idea how happy it makes me to hear that."

They enjoyed a few playful kisses and then picked up Jacob and Emily. Like old times, she thought, only so much had happened since high school. Joseph went to war, served his country, then endured the break-up of his marriage and loss of his children. She lived through her own war married to Dirk but survived and was blessed with little Bonnie, which gave her life purpose. She felt much older now. And wiser.

Dancing with Joseph on New Year's Eve was the perfect way to end one year and begin another. The wild Lindy moves and slow waltzes were reflections of the past years' emotional ups and downs.

At midnight the band leader stopped to countdown the final seconds. Helen felt like proclaiming her love but held back. She and Joseph searched each other's eyes until Joseph reached out and pulled her into a deep kiss.

Chapter 35

The next time Helen spotted Elizabeth at church, she pulled her into a corner.

"Joseph's back! He called on Christmas and asked me if I'd give him another chance."

She raised her eyebrows. "And did you say yes?"

Her face was radiant. "Are you kidding? Of course. He got back a few days ago, and we went dancing New Year's Eve!"

Elizabeth brightened. "Love's a beautiful thing."

"We haven't talked about it all yet, but I'm hoping we will soon."

"Be patient. A lot's happened in the past few weeks."

Helen didn't have to be patient for long. When the phone rang Sunday afternoon, she dashed to the kitchen to answer it.

"Want to go for a picnic?"

Helen looked out the front room window and could barely see the street. "Don't be a wise guy, Joseph! It's nine degrees and snowing again!"

"What was I thinking leaving sunny California?"

"I don't know Buster, what were you thinking?"

"Buster, is it? You been watching too many movies again?"

"Hardly. I'm a single mother, remember?"

"Ask Bonnie if I can see her mother this afternoon."

"I'm sure she'd agree, but she's getting her beauty sleep just now. Want to pop over for a cup of cocoa?"

"I thought you'd never ask!" He hung up, and she shook her head at the phone and giggled. Then she dashed into the bathroom, brushed her hair, and spritzed herself with cologne. She pinched her cheeks and put a touch of gloss on her lips. To keep them moist in this dry weather, she told herself.

She found Grandpa in the living room. He assured her he needed his beauty sleep too. Perhaps now she and Joseph would finally get a chance to talk and share all that happened the past few months.

When she heard his car door shut, Helen opened the front door so the bell wouldn't wake Bonnie.

"Well, someone's happy to see me," Joseph teased. He shrugged out of his heavy winter coat, the knit scarf Helen made for him years ago, and gloves, and, as Helen reached for it all, he wrapped his arms around her and pulled her close. She enjoyed the nearness of him for a moment, then grinned.

"Didn't want to awaken the baby. Let's go into the living room, where it's warmer. Grandpa's resting in his room, so it's just us." She went into the kitchen, got steamy mugs of cocoa, and brought them into the living room, where they settled on the sagging couch.

Joseph let out a breath of relief. "I got my old job back. When I told them I was going to California, they said they'd hold it open for a few months, so that was a lucky break. There are so many houses going up there's a big demand for electricians." Joseph blew on his cocoa and then took a few gulps.

"Wonderful! You got great training in the service."

"A lot of the guys are going to college on the GI Bill, but I think I've had enough changes. Besides, I like working as an electrician, and as long as I stay busy, I'm happy. How's your business going?"

"Like you, I enjoy my work. I needed something that would be flexible, so I can be around Bonnie. My mother left me for three years when I was tiny to do nurses training, and I think it was hard on both of us." Helen sipped her cocoa and set it on the coffee table in front of the couch.

"Yes, and with no father around, that must have made things even more difficult for you." Joseph reached over, ran his hand across her cheek, and twirled some of her hair in his fingers.

"I think if my grandma were kinder, it would have been different, but she always resented having to care for me. And then she was jealous when Mama was home because I preferred my mother. It wasn't a good situation. But I'm working on getting over it."

He raised his eyebrows. "How are you doing that?"

This was a subject they'd never discussed. Helen felt a bit embarrassed because she wasn't sure if he'd make fun of her. But she realized it might open a meaningful discussion, so she barreled ahead. "Actually, through prayer. I'm getting up a bit earlier, reading the Bible, and spending a few minutes in prayer each day. I realized I was so angry with a laundry list of people I couldn't feel anything except the anger. A friend in my choir is encouraging me to work on it." She looked at him and wondered how he'd react.

He studied her thoughtfully. "Is that what prompted you to call me before Christmas?"

She looked down and traced the rim of her cup. "Yes, I finally had a breakthrough where I was able to release my anger toward you. And I could see how wrong I was for holding onto it. I thought I was punishing you and everyone else, but I was the one being punished." She looked up to see his reaction.

"Because you kept pushing me away?" His smile was teasing, but there was truth in his words. "Well, stop punishing yourself and come here!" He grinned, set his cocoa down, and reached for her as she scooted over closer to him. They hugged and kissed and enjoyed several chocolate-flavored kisses. "Mmm, cocoa! I always thought this religious stuff was for the weak. You know my family never went to church or talked about God or prayer."

"We went to church but never prayed during the week. It was more like a weekly habit that was just for Sundays."

Bonnie awoke and hollered from her crib. Helen changed her and brought her into the living room to see Joseph. She gave him a sleepy smile but stayed on Helen's lap, clutching her stuffed elephant.

Joseph studied the toy. "Did you make this?"

"Yes, for Christmas. A reminder of our evening at the circus."

"That was a fun day."

"The best. But, Joseph, what happened with your children when you tried to see them? I take it you didn't get to surprise them with a visit to the circus?"

"It was a mess. Lucy has sole custody of them, and I have few rights to see them. I would make a time to pick them up, and she was there with the kids only about half the time. She just didn't care. The kids are still young, and they didn't know who I was."

"Sounds painful."

"The worst part was when Lucy's husband was there. The kids all called him Daddy. I think Lucy was seeing him most of the time while I was in the service, so he's the man they know. It just burns me up to think while I was out fighting for our country, another man stepped into my life and took over my wife and children. When I think about it, I feel like punching something."

"That's horrible! I can't blame you for being angry. Did you feel like things would never get better with your kids?"

"That's sure what it looked like. I felt like a stranger trying to abduct them every time I came to take them to the park or for ice cream. The youngest, Jimmy, would cry and cling to his mother. And these were the times she was home for me to get them. Other times I would sit and knock and knock at the door. No one answered, and I felt like a chump standing there on the porch, hoping someone would answer the door. Besides, I didn't like my job, my living quarters, or the heat!"

"Was that all?" She flirted, trying to keep the mood from getting too dark.

"I admit it, I missed you like crazy, Helen, but when you said we should part ways, I thought I should try. But I just can't get over you. You're like a magnet for me."

She smiled. The words were washing over her and straight into her heart. "I tried to get over you too. I even hoped things would go well for you in California if that was what was best. But selfishly, I'm so happy you're home."

Maybe it was OK to be a bit selfish, to seek happiness. She had little to be happy about in the past. Perhaps her life was turning a corner.

When she found herself alone with Pastor Gerald one Sunday after church, Helen made an appointment to see him. She briefly poured out her life's circumstances and asked for his advice to heal her anger toward her father, grandmother, and ex-husband.

"First of all, Helen, I'm so sorry for all of this pain in your life. You are incredibly strong to have gotten this far."

"Thank you." His words touched Helen.

"You don't need someone to accept your forgiveness for you to be set free of it. Think of putting all that anger in a balloon and imagine yourself letting go of the balloon. Or imagine you bury the anger in the ground. It doesn't matter what you use, but expect you will have to forgive them over and over."

"How long do you think it will take?" Helen was eager to be free.

"It'll likely happen a little at a time."

Joseph regularly called now. Helen and Grandpa invited him for dinner a few times each week. The last Sunday in January, Joseph came over for Sunday dinner. As Helen was cleaning up the dishes afterward, Joseph was playing with Bonnie. He grabbed a storybook and sat Bonnie on his lap in the large wooden rocker in the living room. He pointed to pictures and identified the objects for her. Bonnie mimicked the words as best she could. Helen peeked around the corner and watched Joseph with Bonnie. He tenderly kissed the top of her head and patiently repeated words for Bonnie to say. *He would be such a good father. But I'm getting ahead of myself.* Bonnie leaned back on Joseph as they gently rocked and read stories. When Helen finished cleaning the kitchen, she found Bonnie asleep in Joseph's arms as he dozed in the chair. She gently lifted Bonnie and put her in her crib, then went back into the living room.

"Great job there!"

"My pleasure. And a wonderful meal. Thank you for that. I love being with Bonnie, but it's hard not to think about what I missed and am still missing."

"Are you thinking about going back to California, Joseph?"

"I'd like to visit now and then or to have the kids visit Iowa when they're older. I still want to be part of their lives."

"I think you should be – for your sake and theirs. Perhaps, you could find a time to call them each week, and you could send letters – and presents on their birthdays and at Christmas. Every year, I longed for something from my father. Just to know he thought about me would have meant so much."

Joseph stared at his hands and nodded. "You're right. I can't give up. I need to let them know I love them. And I have to get over my anger towards their mother."

One Sunday, as the choir paraded in and took their places in the choir area, Helen spotted Joseph in the church.

That afternoon as Grandpa and Bonnie napped, Helen braved the question.

"So, what drew you to church today, may I ask?"

"To hear you sing, of course!" He smiled and added, "You've spoken so highly of your pastor, I wanted to see him for myself."

"And what did you think?"

"I think you look silly in that huge choir robe!"

Helen threw a stuffed animal at him.

"OK, seriously, I liked him. He had a great message. But Helen, you know I was never baptized. Should I be attending your church?"

"Yes, of course, you're welcome. Are you interested in learning more?"

"I need time to think about it."

Joseph became a regular at Helen's church. Within a few weeks, he asked Pastor Gerald to baptize him, and Helen decided to be re-baptized with him to symbolize her desire to start over.

Mama and Warren came over to witness their baptisms, held during a Sunday service. Pastor Gerald presented them each with a new Bible.

Afterward, they all celebrated together with a casserole Helen had waiting in the oven. After lunch, Helen saw Bonnie put her arms out to Joseph, and she wanted to believe they were becoming a family, even though she wasn't totally at peace with the idea.

After Mama and Warren left, she and Joseph found quiet time alone to reflect on the day.

"I have a card for you," Joseph said.

Helen was surprised to open a Valentine's Day Card and a box of chocolates.

"I know I'm a day early, but I wanted to give you this today, after our baptisms."

She read the card. Beneath a silly poem were Joseph's words, "Helen, I've never loved anyone but you. Please be mine forever."

Helen reread the card to be sure she understood it. She looked up at Joseph. "What are you saying?"

Chapter 36

"I'm saying I love you, Helen, and I always have. Let's make this permanent."

Helen laughed, "Is this your way of proposing?"

"Yes, I guess it is. The last time I proposed, things didn't work out so well, so I thought we should decide together this time." He crooked his head to one side and took her hands in his.

"Helen, will you please marry me and let me be Bonnie's father?"

"It's because Bonnie's so adorable, right?"

"You're equally adorable, just more stubborn. But I realize I'm signing up to be more than just your husband. I also want to be Bonnie's father and help raise her."

"I've never loved anyone else but you, Joseph. I want you to know that, but I'm not sure it's right for me to marry again. I feel sullied because I'm divorced."

"Helen, no one would expect you to stay with a man who beat you and was unfaithful to you. You deserve to be loved and cherished. And I want to be the person who loves you."

"I want that too. But my heart's been broken, and I feel the need to proceed with more caution."

He thought for a moment. "Let's make an appointment with Pastor Gerald. We trust his judgment, right?"

Helen threw her arms around his neck. "That's a perfect idea."

Within days they met with Pastor Gerald and filled him in on their situations and how and why their previous marriages failed.

After an hour, he reassured them. "I think the fact you two found each other again could certainly be the work of God. You've both recommitted your lives to God and are seeking his will. Only you can make the final decision, but I don't see anything that would stand in the way of your being married. But Joseph, since you were the one who strayed, you'll have to work extra hard to rebuild Helen's trust. She may experience jealousy, and you need to be patient about it. Go out of your way to reassure her of your faithfulness if you want a successful marriage."

On the way home, Joseph drove to a deserted street and pulled over. "This is the only way we can have a bit of privacy to talk. What are you thinking now, Helen?" He took off his gloves and reached for her hand.

"I'm glad we asked for Pastor's advice. If we decide to marry, I think this time I'd like to get married in the church." Helen took off her gloves so she could feel the warmth of his hands.

"What do you mean if? Helen, what are we waiting for? Let's get married?"

"Get married? Just like that? Don't we have a lot to think about?"

"I don't. I know I love you and want to spend my life with you. I want to be Bonnie's daddy. These are the big things. After that, the rest of the details will fall into place."

"I love your confidence in us."

"I don't want to push you. Take all the time you need. As long as you say 'yes' by tomorrow!" Joseph laughed, always the clown.

"Let me think about it for a few days," she smiled back at him.

Helen let Joseph stew for a few days and then called him one evening after he was home from work.

"What's it take to get a guy to propose around here?"

"I'll be right over."

Within minutes the doorbell rang, and Joseph came in out of the cold, gave her a quick hug, rubbed his cold nose on hers, and shrugged out of his coat. "Evening, everyone!"

"Hi, Joseph! Would you like some hot cider?" Helen asked.

"In a minute, but first, I want to talk to your Grandpa. Mr. Harper, I think you know what I want to say. With your permission, I'd like to marry Helen and be a father to Bonnie."

Grandpa beamed at him and then looked at Helen. "What do you think about this, Ole Bean?"

"It's what I want more than anything."

"Well, then, I'll let you two kids be alone to work out yer plans." Grandpa went into his room and shut the door. Helen brought out two mugs of hot apple cider spiced with cinnamon and set them on the coffee table. The enticing aroma filled the air, along with romantic energy that would change the direction of their lives.

Joseph got down on one knee on the worn Oriental carpet and whipped out a small box from his pants pocket. "Helen, will you marry me and let me love you forever?" He handed her the box.

"You already got the ring? Pretty confident, weren't you?"

"I believe in us! Let's get married, Helen. What do you say?" Helen opened the little square box and marveled at the beautiful diamond.

"It's gorgeous. And yes, Joseph, of course, I'll marry you, and not just because of this beautiful ring." She pulled him to his feet, and after they embraced, he held her face in his hands, looked into her eyes, and kissed her on both cheeks before kissing her lips. Their passion made Helen feel dizzy with delight. Finally, she turned to Bonnie, who was playing on the carpet with her stuffed elephant. "Can you say Daddy?"

Bonnie looked at her uncertainly. Joseph picked her up and twirled her around. "Will you let me be your daddy?"

She squealed with delight.

"Daddy?" He said again, hopefully, but Bonnie giggled and looked away. He kept her on his lap while he and Helen settled on the warn living room couch to enjoy their cider.

"I agree that we should get married in church this time, Helen. I think we were both cheated by our first marriages, and we need God on our side."

"Agreed. The congregation is small. Shall we invite everyone?"

"Along with a few others. What do you think about asking Emily and Jacob to stand up for us?"

"I can't think of anyone else who'd be more appropriate."

The wheels of the wedding were in motion. They'd have a simple service at their church with the reception in the social hall.

Helen called Ruby and filled her sister in on the upcoming nuptials.

"I'd like you to be here with us, Ruby. Is there any chance?"

"It's difficult to travel wid children. And where'd we stayin' if'n we kin git there?"

"You could stay in Mama's extra bedrooms. Please come, Ruby. I haven't seen you in years. It'll be fun to all be together again. We're only going away for a few days, so we can have family time when we get back from our honeymoon."

Ruby said she'd talk it over with her husband but made no promises.

The second Saturday in May arrived with sunshine and the hope of a joy-filled future. After a quick breakfast with Bonnie and Grandpa, Helen fixed her hair in long waves and added a touch of coral lipstick and a wave of mascara. Her cheeks were already flaming from excitement and nerves.

She put on the cream-colored satin dress she sewed with a v-neckline, padded shoulders, a fitted bodice, and a full skirt that landed just below her knees. She cocked a felt hat to one side, then picked up her dainty bouquet of roses and baby's breath and looked at herself in the bathroom mirror. The next phase of her life was about to begin. She had always loved Joseph – had never stopped loving him. They were in love, and she prayed they'd never again have to be apart.

She hurried to put Bonnie in a rose-colored dress with a white pinafore and white lace bonnet.

She, Grandpa, and Bonnie got to the church early. Daffodils were in bloom along the walkway, next to hyacinth and iris. Helen thought of Grandma Gertrude and how she loved flowers and smiled.

She handed Bonnie to her mother before she and Grandpa waited in a side room while everyone arrived and claimed their seats.

Emily appeared looking like spring in a light blue taffeta dress. When the organist started, Emily and Helen quickly hugged before Emily swished down the short aisle. Helen took Grandpa's arm.

"Ready for this, Ole Bean?"

"Yes, Grandpa, but I'm sure glad I know everyone here. I'm so nervous."

"Don't be. Yer among friends."

When she looked out at all the people standing and turning to greet her and Grandpa, she realized he was right. She was among people who cared for her, even loved her. She was lovable, after all.

When she spotted Ruby and her four children, Helen bit her lip to keep from misting over. Ruby beamed at her and waved a little lace hanky.

Up by the alter, Joseph was waiting for her, smiling so widely his dimples emerged. His broad shoulders strained against his black suit, and his curly hair was plastered into place. But Helen was transfixed by his eyes. They radiated love as she processed toward him. When he stepped forward, Grandpa kissed Helen on the cheek and stepped away so Helen could lace her arm through Joseph's.

During the service, the choir sang several favorite numbers, and Helen and Joseph sang along. *This feels so right.* Singing put her at ease.

Pastor Gerald included Bonnie in his remarks. He noted Joseph's desire to be a good father to her and commented on the love already growing in this new family.

Joseph wanted to have his children included in the service but accepted they were too little to travel alone, and Lucy was not about to dignify his marriage by attending it. Knowing he would be a father to Bonnie helped him forget the pain of not seeing his children grow up.

After the service, members of the church served cake, mints, nuts, and punch. Helen and Joseph mingled with guests and tried to greet all who took the time to wish them well. Now and then, Helen and Joseph would catch a glimpse of each other over the crowd, and inexpressible joy filled Helen.

Toward the end of the reception, Mama carried Bonnie to Helen so she could say goodbye. Helen and Joseph were going away for a short honeymoon, and Mama would be enjoying time with her grandchild, along with Ruby and her children. Joseph came over and put out his hands to Bonnie.

"Say goodbye to Daddy." He lifted her high and then kissed her chubby cheeks, and after a moment, he surrendered her to Cora.

Bonnie waved as they walked away and said quietly, "Bye-bye, Daddy."

Joseph turned back to the tot. "Bye-bye sweet Bonnie. See you soon."

Helen looked at Joseph and said, "This is the happiest day of my life."

"Each day will be even better, Helen of Troy."

And they were off to be together forever, finally.

Afterward

The characters in *Mending Helen's Heart*, the sequel to *Mountains of Trouble*, are based on true stories. The difficulties of Cora's life spilled into Helen's, leaving her insecure and wounded from a lack of love and acceptance.

Helen, Joseph, Dirk, Cora, Ruby, Grandpa John, and Grandma Gertrude are based on actual people. However, to protect their descendants, I changed names, places, and some dates.

Helen and Joseph were not able to have more children of their own. Joseph did his best to stay in his biological children's lives, despite the long distance. And he fulfilled his promise to make Helen happy and to be a wonderful father to Bonnie. Helen said over and over that they were richly blessed.

They were married for over 60 years when Joseph died. To the end, they participated in Bible studies with other couples, and their faith remained a central part of their relationship.

Dirk never again attempted to contact Helen. Bonnie knew Joseph was not her biological father, but she never tried to find Dirk.

To read more about Helen's early years, pick up a copy of *Mountains of Trouble*, by Clare Bills, available on Amazon, Barnes and Noble, Apple Books, and other online sites.

About the Author

Clare Bills considers herself a Nearly Normal Writer and admits to a degree of eccentricity. She enjoys the challenges of writing both serious and humorous fiction and nonfiction. Her publication credits include numerous magazines, newsletters, and newspapers, as well as online sites.

After a career in radio news and public relations, she retired to the woods in Minnesota, basking in the dramatic changes of the four seasons. She is an "Equal Opportunity Host," feeding whatever wild animals or birds visit her backyard.

Clare and her husband, Ken, have been married forever. They have three amazing grown children and their wonderful spouses and seven adorable grandchildren. She and Ken also welcomed a Covid rescue creature, Bennie-the-dog, who has learned not to bark at the turkeys, opossums, and deer in the yard.

Contact Clare to be added to her newsletter list at:
clarebills@live.com
Website: www.clarebills.com
Follow Clare's Facebook page: "Nearly Normal Writer"
Instagram: clarebills2711
Although she isn't great about adding updates to social media, she loves hearing from readers.

Recipes from *Mending Helen's Heart* and *Mountains of Trouble*, as well as progress on Clare's writings, are occasionally shared on Clare's blog: Clare Bills - Nearly normal writer, author, recipe tester, and creator, in addition to her newsletter.

If you enjoyed *Mending Helen's Heart*, or *Mountains of Trouble*, **please consider leaving a review** on Amazon and/or Goodreads.

Questions to Ponder

1. Women married at an earlier age in the 1940's than they do today, but was it possible to make a confident choice at 18 years old?

2. Do you believe there are soul mates? If so, were Helen and Joseph soul mates who would only be happy together?

3. Did their strong faith play a part in the longevity of their marriage?

4. Why do you think Helen married Dirk?

5. Helen said many years later that in addition to being an alcoholic, she believed Dirk was bipolar. Do you think this is what led to his erratic behavior?

6. Why wasn't Helen able to reach out to her mother or her childhood friend, Emily, when she was married to Dirk?

7. How can we protect other women from falling into a trapped marriage as she experienced with Dirk?

8. Do you consider Helen a victim?

9. Is it more or less challenging to be a single mother today than in the 1940s?

10. Was Joseph wrong to think he had to marry Lucy because she was pregnant?

11. Was Joseph's fling with Lucy born of fear, lust, or immaturity? Why?